VOLTAIRE

Candide

A Dual-Language Book

TRANSLATED, AND WITH AN INTRODUCTION,
BY SHANE WELLER

DOVER PUBLICATIONS, INC.
New York

Published in Canada by General Publishing Company, Ltd., 30 Lesmill Road, Don Mills, Toronto, Ontario.

Published in the United Kingdom by Constable and Company, Ltd., 3 The Lanchesters, 162–164 Fulham Palace Road, London W6 9ER.

This Dover edition, first published in 1993, contains the complete and unabridged original French text of *Candide*, reprinted from a standard edition, together with a complete new English translation and new introduction by Shane Weller, both prepared specially for the present edition.

Manufactured in the United States of America
Dover Publications, Inc., 31 East 2nd Street, Mineola, N.Y. 11501

Library of Congress Cataloging-in-Publication Data

Voltaire, 1694–1778.
　　[Candide.　English & French]
　　Candide : a dual-language book / Voltaire ; English version by Shane Weller.
　　　　p.　　cm.
　　English and French.
　　ISBN 0-486-27625-2
　　I. Weller, Shane.　II. Title.
PQ2082.C3E5　1993
843'.5—dc20　　　　　　　　　　　　　　　　　　　92-37473
　　　　　　　　　　　　　　　　　　　　　　　　　　　　　　CIP

INTRODUCTION

In a literary career spanning the years of the Regency and the reign of Louis XV, François-Marie Arouet, dit Voltaire (1694–1778), produced a vast body of work ranging from the early verse tragedies and epic poetry to the later historiography and philosophy. He was elected to the Académie Française in 1746 and certainly has a claim to being the preeminent French man of letters of his generation. It is somewhat surprising, then, given his enormous literary output and standing, that today Voltaire's reputation rests almost entirely—with the notable exception of the *Lettres philosophiques* (1734) and the correspondence—on the philosophical *contes* of his final creative phase, among which *Candide ou l'optimisme* (1759) is now the most highly regarded.

Indeed, that Voltaire's reputation has not been impaired by posterity's disregard for so much of his work, that an enduring reputation could be founded on a story like *Candide*, requires some explanation. For the *conte* is a lightweight genre, one of the slightest forms of prose narrative. Without the status of the *nouvelle* or the *roman*, it resembles a short story but with the specific purpose of relating an anecdote or adventure primarily for amusement. The closest English equivalent to the *conte* would be the "tale." Moreover, *Candide* itself is a strange combination of the ideological and the personal. On the one hand, it is an impassioned and frequently scathing response to contemporary historical events (the Seven Years' War), natural catastrophes (the Lisbon earthquake of 1755), religious sectarianism and philosophical trends, all of which might seem to have little but antiquarian interest today. On the other hand, the story is a tissue of more or less disguised references to the au-

thor's own personal troubles: his financial concerns and private animosities such as the quarrels with Frederick the Great and the head of the Berlin Academy of Science, Maupertuis; the critic Elie Fréron; and a host of forgotten writers. Seemingly most damaging of all to the work's merit is the convincing argument that in satirizing the philosophical optimism of Leibniz's *Théodicée* (1710), Voltaire simplifies, even fails to grasp, the arguments against which he rails. It is now generally accepted that in *Candide* Voltaire characterizes and caricatures philosophical optimism—the belief that the universe is organized according to a preestablished harmonious plan—in a form and a vocabulary that did not belong to Leibniz at all, but to Christian Wolff, the popularizer of Leibniz, and the English writers Bolingbroke and Alexander Pope.

How, then, can the enduring popularity and importance of *Candide* be accounted for? The tale is undoubtedly a good yarn, if at the same time a parody of that form. The plot takes the reader across continents, through numerous adventures (the French word *aventure* appears time and again in the story), and contains several tales within tales. Yet, for all the trappings of a tale, *Candide* is primarily a vehicle for ideas. It is by no means a psychological drama or a mere action adventure. The education of the hero bears little resemblance to the kind of education to be found later in the Bildungsroman. The work's main theme, that this is clearly not the best of all possible worlds, is not so much developed as merely reiterated. In accordance with this thematic simplicity, the story has a simple structure. Cast from an earthly paradise (the country residence of Baron Thunder-Ten-Tronckh), the young Candide is subjected to a deliberately ridiculous concatenation of horrors in the corrupt world. He endures war, or rather sheer carnage, the Lisbon earthquake and the Inquisition. At the center of the story is the peaceful, instructive interlude in Eldorado, a kind of paradise regained, although one that cannot be permanent. Thrown back into the world, though this time by choice, Candide does not suffer any further hardships of the kind that pepper the first half of the book. Rather, he experiences the appalling tedium of life. (Voltaire is one of the first French writers to depict in fiction the distinctly modern psychological condition of boredom.) The final "paradise" of the small farm in Turkey, based in part on Voltaire's own estate at Ferney, is a place where, though things are by no means ideal, illusions about the nature of human existence have been recognized for what they are and a pragmatic and reasoned attempt is made to create a tolerable

life through cooperative labor. This final world is limited in its aspirations and expectations. It is, however, free from the kind of fanaticism, religious or secular, that prevails throughout the rest of the world that *Candide* creates.

The work is, then, a fable in which Voltaire argues for an enlightened attitude toward both religious and secular institutions, for a stripping away of all illusory forms of understanding, justification and consolation. It advocates a world view grounded in and chastened by the experience of a harsh, unaccommodating reality. The reiterated exhortation that one must travel before forming judgments is essentially a rebuttal of any philosophy that is not based upon empirical, verifiable data.

On the most general level, what accounts for the enduring success of *Candide* is that, despite the drastic simplifications, even misrepresentations, of the arguments of others, the satire addresses in the most direct and uncompromising way an issue that has remained as pertinent and as unresolved as it was in 1758: the origin and place of evil in the world, and how a world view based on reason can account for, if not neutralize, irrationality. *Candide* reveals a Voltaire deeply suspicious of the implications of the traditional Christian doctrine of the fall and the Leibnizian contention that evil is only evil when surveyed from the partial, erring human perspective. Both doctrines, according to Voltaire, result in the wholly unacceptable attitude toward life expressed most succinctly in Alexander Pope's *Essay on Man* (1733–34):

> All nature is but art, unknown to thee;
> All chance, direction which thou canst not see;
> All discord, harmony not understood;
> All partial evil, universal good;
> And, spite of pride, in erring reason's spite,
> One truth is clear, Whatever is, is right. [I, 289–294]

This is a doctrine to which Voltaire adamantly refuses his consent because it leaves no place for human progress, moral or technical.

For the most part, the reader does not require any real familiarity with Leibniz or, for that matter, with the historical and biographical material underlying the story to appreciate *Candide*'s message or enjoy its wit. Although the present edition does provide rudimentary explanations for historical and biographical allusions in the text, it should be borne in mind that the measure of Voltaire's success in

Candide is to have created a work that achieves its ends independently of the historical, philosophical and biographical material out of which it was generated. By no means presupposing a sophisticated acquaintance with specific philosophical arguments, it calls only for an awareness of the human predicament, with which the most unphilosophical mind might sympathize. The success or failure of *Candide* as a comic fable with a serious moral purpose depends finally on whether or not Voltaire's manner of holding horror up for ridicule enables one to master that horror.

Although a vehicle for serious ideas, the work has a distinctly comic-book form that goes beyond the usual demands of satirical writing. In this respect there is no kinship between Voltaire and, for example, Swift. That no real attempt is made in *Candide* to create characters with any psychological depth or to develop complex themes is suggested even by the characters' names. Nothing stands in the way of translating into English many of the proper names Voltaire assigns to his characters. Indeed, the characters might more accurately be described as ciphers for various positions that can be taken toward existence. These positions range from outright optimism (Pangloss) to thoroughgoing pessimism (Martin). The name of the eponymous hero of the *conte* translates to the English "candid," with all the connotations that word has in English. The young Candide sets out on his adventures as a naïf, unacquainted with moral evil (*mal moral*) and physical evil or hardship (*mal physique*). He is unsullied by experience, he is innocent and artless. Voltaire never quite equates this naivety with stupidity or insanity. Rather, it is the state in which the mind exists while still in an earthly paradise, sheltered from experience. And, for the most part, although Voltaire's hero passes through the most inconceivable series of calamities during his adventures, he remains unscathed by them, true to his name. He is much like a cardboard cutout that keeps popping up against all the odds. The Candide at the end of the tale is chastened, perhaps, wiser to the extent that he is more practical. He is no longer given to the superlatives (Voltaire's linguistic register for idealism) that come one on top of another throughout the text. The representative of untempered philosophical optimism, which is depicted as sheer moral blindness, is Candide's tutor, Pangloss. This name compounds the Greek *pan* (all) and *glossa* (tongue). Not only does this compound suggest, ironically, as the story shows, universal knowledge, it also clearly implies logorrhea and, in effect, an immoral proclivity for words and arguments when what is required is rational

action. Among the other translatable proper names is that of the
Venetian senator, Pococurante ("little caring," "caring for little").
He is a critic ad nauseam of all Western aesthetic culture.
Much of Voltaire's wit is directed against absurdities and unwar-
ranted pretensions reflected in language. In particular, he delights
in ridiculing the German language. In part, this is no doubt because
it was the language of Frederick the Great, from whom he was alien-
ated by 1758. But Voltaire is also playing up to a popular view of the
time that the German language was barbarous. Thus, his baron is
Thunder-Ten-Tronckh, and the only named Westphalian town is
Waldberghoff-Trarbk-Dikdorff. These are less names than garbled
masses of guttural consonants and top-heavy compounds.

On a stylistic level, *Candide* certainly demonstrates Voltaire's epi-
grammatic wit at its most acerbic and concentrated. The prose is
clear and deliberate, shifting repeatedly between the past and histori-
cal present tenses,[1] omitting connectives, moving with the rhythm
of a series of one-liners delivered with the consummate artistry of
an accomplished stand-up comedian. The overall pace of the story
is dictated by shifts between extended narrative monologue and
snappy dialogue. Vocabulary and syntactical forms are fairly limited.

The textual history of *Candide* does require brief mention. The
story was originally published in January 1759 as an anonymous
French translation from the German of a certain Doctor Ralph. The
original 1759 text was somewhat shorter than the version reprinted
here. In 1761 Voltaire interpolated an extended passage (which he
described as "the additions found in the doctor's pocket when he
died") in Chapter XXII. This interpolation was an extension of the
section describing Candide's residence in Paris and included an at-
tack on the critic Elie Fréron and the description of Candide's visit
to the theater and to the home of the Marquise de Parolignac. A few
other short interpolations by Voltaire in Chapter XXVI are generally
omitted from modern editions of *Candide* on the ground that they
give rise to inconsistencies with the 1759 text. These brief passages
have, following the common editorial practice, been omitted here.

I would like to thank Stanley Appelbaum for his valuable sugges-
tions in the preparation of this translation.

[1] The historical presents, unusual in modern English narrative, are translated
as simple pasts in the English translation used in this volume.

CANDIDE

CANDIDE
OU
L'OPTIMISME

Traduit de l'Allemand
DE MR LE DOCTEUR RALPH
Avec les additions qu'on a trouvées
dans la poche du docteur,
lorsqu'il mourut à Minden,
l'an de grâce 1759.

CHAPITRE PREMIER

COMMENT CANDIDE FUT ÉLEVÉ DANS UN BEAU CHÂTEAU, ET COMMENT IL FUT CHASSÉ D'ICELUI

Il y avait en Westphalie, dans le château de monsieur le baron de Thunder-ten-tronckh, un jeune garçon à qui la nature avait donné les mœurs les plus douces. Sa physionomie annonçait son âme. Il avait le jugement assez droit, avec l'esprit le plus simple; c'est, je crois, pour cette raison qu'on le nommait Candide. Les anciens domestiques de la maison soupçonnaient qu'il était fils de la sœur de M. le baron et d'un bon et honnête gentilhomme du voisinage, que cette demoiselle ne voulut jamais épouser parce qu'il n'avait pu prouver que soixante et onze quartiers, et que le reste de son arbre généalogique avait été perdu par l'injure du temps.

M. le baron était un des plus puissants seigneurs de la Westphalie, car son château avait une porte et des fenêtres. Sa grande salle même était ornée d'une tapisserie. Tous les chiens de ses basses-cours composaient une meute dans le besoin; ses palefreniers étaient ses piqueurs; le vicaire du village était son grand aumônier. Ils l'appelaient tous Monseigneur, et ils riaient quand il faisait des contes.

Mme la baronne, qui pesait environ trois cent cinquante livres, s'attirait par là une très grande considération, et faisait les honneurs de la maison avec une dignité qui la rendait encore plus respectable.

CANDIDE

OR

OPTIMISM

Translated from the German
OF DOCTOR RALPH
*With the additions that were found
in the doctor's pocket
when he died at Minden
in the year of our Lord 1759.*

CHAPTER I

HOW CANDIDE WAS BROUGHT UP IN A BEAUTIFUL COUNTRY RESIDENCE, AND HOW HE WAS DRIVEN FROM IT

There lived in Westphalia, in the country residence of Baron Thunder-Ten-Tronckh, a young lad whom nature had granted the sweetest of dispositions. His soul was revealed in his countenance. He had fairly sound judgment and the most artless mind; it is, I believe, for this reason that he was named Candide. The old servants of the household suspected that he was the son of the baron's sister by a good-natured and respectable gentleman of the neighborhood, whom that lady refused ever to marry because he had only been able to give proof of seventy-one heraldic quarterings, the rest of his genealogical tree having been lost through the ravages of time.

The baron was one of the most powerful noblemen in Westphalia, for his country residence had a door and windows. His great hall was even adorned with a tapestry. All the dogs from his farmyards constituted a hunting pack when necessary; his grooms served as his whippers-in; the village curate was his grand almoner. They all addressed him as "My Lord," and they laughed when he told stories.

The baroness, who weighed about three hundred and fifty pounds, acquired on that account a very high esteem, and did the honors of the household with a dignity that made her still more

Sa fille Cunégonde, âgée de dix-sept ans, était haute en couleur, fraîche, grasse, appétissante. Le fils du baron paraissait en tout digne de son père. Le précepteur Pangloss était l'oracle de la maison, et le petit Candide écoutait ses leçons avec toute la bonne foi de son âge et de son caractère.

Pangloss enseignait la métaphysico-théologo-cosmolonigologie. Il prouvait admirablement qu'il n'y a point d'effet sans cause, et que, dans ce meilleur des mondes possibles, le château de monseigneur le baron était le plus beau des châteaux et madame la meilleure des baronnes possibles.

«Il est démontré, disait-il, que les choses ne peuvent être autrement: car, tout étant fait pour une fin, tout est nécessairement pour la meilleure fin. Remarquez bien que les nez ont été faits pour porter des lunettes, aussi avons-nous des lunettes. Les jambes sont visiblement instituées pour être chaussées, et nous avons des chausses. Les pierres ont été formées pour être taillées, et pour en faire des châteaux, aussi monseigneur a un très beau château; le plus grand baron de la province doit être le mieux logé; et, les cochons étant faits pour être mangés, nous mangeons du porc toute l'année: par conséquent, ceux qui ont avancé que tout est bien ont dit une sottise; il fallait dire que tout est au mieux.»

Candide écoutait attentivement, et croyait innocemment; car il trouvait Mlle Cunégonde extrêmement belle, quoiqu'il ne prît jamais la hardiesse de le lui dire. Il concluait qu'après le bonheur d'être né baron de Thunder-ten-tronckh, le second degré de bonheur était d'être Mlle Cunégonde; le troisième, de la voir tous les jours; et le quatrième, d'entendre maître Pangloss, le plus grand philosophe de la province, et par conséquent de toute la terre.

Un jour, Cunégonde en se promenant auprès du château, dans le petit bois qu'on appelait parc, vit entre des broussailles le docteur Pangloss qui donnait une leçon de physique expérimentale à la femme de chambre de sa mère, petite brune très jolie et très docile. Comme Mlle Cunégonde avait beaucoup de disposition pour les sciences, elle observa, sans souffler, les expériences réitérées dont elle fut témoin; elle vit clairement la raison suffisante du docteur, les effets et les causes, et s'en retourna tout agitée, toute pensive, toute remplie du désir d'être savante, songeant qu'elle pourrait bien

respectable. Her daughter Cunégonde, seventeen years of age, was of a rosy complexion, hale, fleshy and desirable. The baron's son seemed in every respect worthy of his father. The tutor Pangloss was the oracle of the household, and young Candide listened to his lectures with all the good faith of his age and character. Pangloss taught metaphysico-theologo-cosmolonigology.[1] He proved admirably that there is no effect without a cause, and that, in this best of all possible worlds, the baron's country residence was the most beautiful of country residences and his wife the best of all possible baronesses.

"It is proven," he would say, "that things cannot be otherwise: for, everything having been made for a purpose, everything is necessarily made for the best purpose. Observe that noses were made to support spectacles, hence we have spectacles. Legs were obviously instituted to be clad in breeches, and we have breeches. Stones were formed to be hewn, and for country residences to be constructed from them, and so His Lordship has a very beautiful country residence; the greatest baron in the province must be the best housed; and, pigs having been created to be eaten, we eat pork all year round; consequently, those who have proposed that all is well have spoken nonsense; they should have said that all is at its best."

Candide listened attentively and believed innocently; for he found Miss Cunégonde extremely beautiful, although he never presumed to tell her so. He concluded that after the good fortune of having been born Baron Thunder-Ten-Tronckh, the second degree of good fortune was to be Miss Cunégonde; the third, to see her every day; and the fourth, to listen to Master Pangloss, the greatest philosopher in the province and, consequently, in all the world.

One day Cunégonde, while walking near the house, in the little wood that was called the "park," saw Doctor Pangloss among the thickets giving a lesson in experimental physics to her mother's chambermaid, a very pretty and very docile little brunette. As Miss Cunégonde had a considerable inclination for the sciences, she observed breathlessly the repeated experiments to which she was witness; she saw clearly the doctor's sufficient reason, the effects and their causes, and went away thoroughly agitated, deeply pensive and completely filled with the desire to be learned, musing that she might

[1] The French nonce word *cosmolonigologie* compounds *cosmologie* with *nigaud* (foolish).

être la raison suffisante du jeune Candide, qui pouvait aussi être la sienne.

Elle rencontra Candide en revenant au château, et rougit; Candide rougit aussi; elle lui dit bonjour d'une voix entrecoupée, et Candide lui parla sans savoir ce qu'il disait. Le lendemain après le dîner, comme on sortait de table, Cunégonde et Candide se trouvèrent derrière un paravent; Cunégonde laissa tomber son mouchoir, Candide le ramassa, elle lui prit innocemment la main, le jeune homme baisa innocemment la main de la jeune demoiselle avec une vivacité, une sensibilité, une grâce toute particulière; leurs bouches se rencontrèrent, leurs yeux s'enflammèrent, leurs genoux tremblèrent, leurs mains s'égarèrent. M. le baron de Thunder-ten-tronckh passa auprès du paravent, et, voyant cette cause et cet effet, chassa Candide du château à grands coups de pied dans le derrière; Cunégonde s'évanouit; elle fut souffletée par Mme la baronne dès qu'elle fut revenue à elle-même; et tout fut consterné dans le plus beau et le plus agréable des châteaux possibles.

Chapitre II

Ce que devint Candide parmi les Bulgares

Candide, chassé du paradis terrestre, marcha longtemps sans savoir où, pleurant, levant les yeux au ciel, les tournant souvent vers le plus beau des châteaux, qui renfermait la plus belle des baronnettes; il se coucha sans souper au milieu des champs entre deux sillons; la neige tombait à gros flocons. Candide, tout transi, se traîna le lendemain vers la ville voisine, qui s'appelle Valdberghoff-trarbk-dikdorff, n'ayant point d'argent, mourant de faim et de lassitude. Il s'arrêta tristement à la porte d'un cabaret. Deux hommes habillés

indeed be young Candide's sufficient reason, and that he likewise might be hers.

She came across Candide while returning to the house, and blushed; Candide blushed too; she said good morning to him in a broken voice, and Candide spoke to her without knowing what he was saying. The next day after dinner, as everyone was leaving the table, Cunégonde and Candide happened to meet behind a screen; Cunégonde dropped her handkerchief, Candide picked it up, she took him innocently by the hand, the young man innocently kissed the young lady's hand with quite uncommon vivacity, feeling and grace; their lips met, their eyes blazed, their knees trembled, their hands wandered. Baron Thunder-Ten-Tronckh passed close by the screen and, seeing that cause and that effect, drove Candide from his country residence with great kicks in the backside; Cunégonde fainted; she was slapped by the baroness as soon as she had come to; and all was consternation in the most beautiful and most agreeable of all possible country residences.

CHAPTER II

WHAT HAPPENED TO CANDIDE AMONG THE BULGARIANS[2]

Candide, driven from his earthly paradise, walked for a long time without knowing where he was going, weeping, raising his eyes to heaven and gazing back often toward the most beautiful of country residences, which contained the most beautiful of young baronesses; he lay down to sleep without having eaten any supper between two furrows out in the fields; snow was falling in large flakes. The next day Candide, chilled to the bone, trudged toward the neighboring town, which was called Waldberghoff-Trarbk-Dikdorff; he was penniless, famished and weary. He stopped gloomily at an inn door.

[2] Voltaire's Bulgarians represent the Prussians under Frederick the Great (1712–1786). The author is insinuating that Frederick was a pederast, since French *bougre* (bugger) is derived from Late Latin *Bulgarus*.

de bleu le remarquèrent: «Camarade, dit l'un, voilà un jeune homme très bien fait, et qui a la taille requise.» Ils s'avancèrent vers Candide et le prièrent à dîner très civilement. «Messieurs, leur dit Candide avec une modestie charmante, vous me faites beaucoup d'honneur, mais je n'ai pas de quoi payer mon écot.—Ah! Monsieur, lui dit un des bleus, les personnes de votre figure et de votre mérite ne paient jamais rien: n'avez-vous pas cinq pieds cinq pouces de haut?—Oui, Messieurs, c'est ma taille, dit-il en faisant la révérence.—Ah! Monsieur, mettez-vous à table; non seulement nous vous défraierons, mais nous ne souffrirons jamais qu'un homme comme vous manque d'argent; les hommes ne sont faits que pour se secourir les uns les autres.—Vous avez raison, dit Candide: c'est ce que M. Pangloss m'a toujours dit, et je vois bien que tout est au mieux.» On le prie d'accepter quelques écus, il les prend et veut faire son billet; on n'en veut point, on se met à table: «N'aimez-vous pas tendrement . . . ?—Oh! oui, répondit-il, j'aime tendrement Mlle Cunégonde.—Non, dit l'un de ces messieurs, nous vous demandons si vous n'aimez pas tendrement le roi des Bulgares.—Point du tout, dit-il, car je ne l'ai jamais vu.—Comment! c'est le plus charmant des rois, et il faut boire à sa santé.—Oh! très volontiers, Messieurs»; et il boit. «C'en est assez, lui dit-on, vous voilà l'appui, le soutien, le défenseur, le héros des Bulgares, votre fortune est faite, et votre gloire est assurée.» On lui met sur-le-champ les fers aux pieds, et on le mène au régiment. On le fait tourner à droite, à gauche, hausser la baguette, remettre la baguette, coucher en joue, tirer, doubler le pas, et on lui donne trente coups de bâton; le lendemain il fait l'exercice un peu moins mal, et il ne reçoit que vingt coups; le surlendemain on ne lui en donne que dix, et il est regardé par ses camarades comme un prodige.

Candide, tout stupéfait, ne démêlait pas encore trop bien comment il était un héros. Il s'avisa un beau jour de printemps de s'aller promener, marchant tout droit devant lui, croyant que c'était un privilège de l'espèce humaine, comme de l'espèce animale, de se servir de ses jambes à son plaisir. Il n'eut pas fait deux lieues que voilà quatre autres héros de six pieds qui l'atteignent, qui le lient, qui le mènent dans un cachot. On lui demanda juridiquement ce qu'il aimait le mieux d'être fustigé trente-six fois par tout le régiment, ou de recevoir à la fois douze balles de plomb dans la cervelle. Il eut beau dire que les volontés sont libres, et qu'il ne voulait ni l'un ni

Two men dressed in blue[3] noticed him: "Comrade," said one of them, "there's a very well-built young man who's of the required height." They went up to Candide and invited him very politely to dine with them. "Gentlemen," Candide said to them with charming modesty, "you do me a great honor, but I don't have enough money to pay my share." "Ah! sir," one of the men in blue said to him, "individuals of your build and your merit need never pay anything: aren't you five feet five inches tall?" "Yes, gentlemen, that's my height," he said, bowing. "Ah! sir, sit yourself down; not only will we pay for you, but we'll never allow a man like you to be short of money; men were created only in order to help one another." "You're right," said Candide; "that's what Dr. Pangloss always told me, and I see clearly that everything is at its best." He was asked to accept a few crowns, he took them and wished to make out a promissory note; they wouldn't hear of it; they all sat down to table. "Don't you dearly love . . . ?" "Oh! yes," he replied, "I dearly love Miss Cunégonde." "No," said one of the gentlemen, "we're asking you if you don't dearly love the King of the Bulgarians." "Not at all," he said, "for I've never seen him." "What! he's the most charming of kings, and you must drink to his health." "Oh! very gladly, gentlemen"; and he drank. "That's enough," they told him, "you're now the support, the upholder, the defender, the hero of the Bulgarians, your fortune is made and your glory is assured." Irons were immediately placed around his ankles, and he was led away to the regiment. He was compelled to make right and left turns, to raise the ramrod, to return the ramrod, to take aim, to fire, to march in double time, and he was given thirty strokes; the next day he performed the drill a little less badly and he received only twenty strokes; the day after that he was given only ten, and he was looked upon as a prodigy by his comrades.

Candide, utterly astounded, could not yet make out too clearly how he was a hero. He took it into his head one fine spring day to go for a stroll, walking straight ahead, believing that it was a privilege of mankind, as of the animals, to make use of one's legs at one's own pleasure. He had not gone two leagues when four other six-foot heroes overtook him, tied him up and conveyed him to a dungeon. He was asked juridically which he preferred: to be flogged thirty-six times by the entire regiment or to receive twelve lead bullets in his brain all at once. In vain did he say that the will is free, and that he

[3] These two men are wearing the uniforms of Prussian recruiting officers.

l'autre, il fallut faire un choix; il se détermina, en vertu du don de Dieu qu'on nomme *liberté*, à passer trente-six fois par les baguettes; il essuya deux promenades. Le régiment était composé de deux mille hommes; cela lui composa quatre mille coups de baguette, qui, depuis la nuque du cou jusqu'au cul, lui découvrirent les muscles et les nerfs. Comme on allait procéder à la troisième course, Candide, n'en pouvant plus, demanda en grâce qu'on voulût bien avoir la bonté de lui casser la tête; il obtint cette faveur; on lui bande les yeux, on le fait mettre à genoux. Le roi des Bulgares passe dans ce moment, s'informe du crime du patient; et, comme ce roi avait un grand génie, il comprit, par tout ce qu'il apprit de Candide, que c'était un jeune métaphysicien, fort ignorant des choses de ce monde, et il lui accorda sa grâce avec une clémence qui sera louée dans tous les journaux et dans tous les siècles. Un brave chirurgien guérit Candide en trois semaines avec les émollients enseignés par Dioscoride. Il avait déjà un peu de peau, et pouvait marcher, quand le roi des Bulgares livra bataille au roi des Abares.

CHAPITRE III

COMMENT CANDIDE SE SAUVA D'ENTRE LES BULGARES, ET CE QU'IL DEVINT

Rien n'était si beau, si leste, si brillant, si bien ordonné que les deux armées. Les trompettes, les fifres, les hautbois, les tambours, les canons, formaient une harmonie telle qu'il n'y en eut jamais en enfer. Les canons renversèrent d'abord à peu près six mille hommes de chaque côté; ensuite la mousqueterie ôta du meilleur des mondes environ neuf à dix mille coquins qui en infectaient la surface. La

wanted neither the one nor the other: he had to make a choice; he decided, by virtue of the gift of God called "freedom," to run the gauntlet thirty-six times; he endured two bouts. The regiment was composed of two thousand men; for him that constituted four thousand strokes of the ramrod, which laid bare the muscles and the sinews from the nape of his neck to his backside. As they were about to proceed with the third run, Candide, unable to take any more, begged that in mercy they would have the goodness to blow his brains out; he was granted this favor; he was blindfolded and made to kneel. The King of the Bulgarians passed by at this moment and inquired into the condemned man's crime; and as this king had great genius, he understood, from all he learned about Candide, that he was a young metaphysician, thoroughly unacquainted with the things of this world, and he pardoned him with a clemency that will be praised in all newspapers and in all ages. A worthy surgeon healed Candide in three weeks with the emollients prescribed by Dioscorides.[4] He already had a little skin and was able to walk when the King of the Bulgarians joined battle with the King of the Abares.[5]

Chapter III

How Candide escaped from the Bulgarians, and what became of him

Nothing was so beautiful, so elegant, so glittering or so well-ordered as the two armies. The trumpets, the fifes, the oboes, the drums and the cannons created a harmony such as was never heard in hell. First the cannons struck down nearly six thousand men on each side; then the musketry removed from the best of worlds between nine and ten thousand rogues contaminating its surface. The bayo-

[4] The Greek physician Pedanius Dioscorides (c. A.D. 40–90), whose *De materia medica* remained the foremost pharmacological work in Europe until the end of the fifteenth century.

[5] A Scythian tribe, here representing the French, who at the time *Candide* was being written were fighting the Prussians in what is now known as the Seven Years' War (1756–1763). Voltaire has the "author" of *Candide*, Doctor Ralph, die at the Battle of Minden (1759).

baïonnette fut aussi la raison suffisante de la mort de quelques milliers d'hommes. Le tout pouvait bien se monter à une trentaine de mille âmes. Candide, qui tremblait comme un philosophe, se cacha du mieux qu'il put pendant cette boucherie héroïque.

Enfin, tandis que les deux rois faisaient chanter des *Te Deum* chacun dans son camp, il prit le parti d'aller raisonner ailleurs des effets et des causes. Il passa par-dessus des tas de morts et de mourants, et gagna d'abord un village voisin; il était en cendres: c'était un village abare que les Bulgares avaient brûlé, selon les lois du droit public. Ici des vieillards criblés de coups regardaient mourir leurs femmes égorgées, qui tenaient leurs enfants à leurs mamelles sanglantes; là des filles éventrées après avoir assouvi les besoins naturels de quelques héros rendaient les derniers soupirs; d'autres, à demi brûlées, criaient qu'on achevât de leur donner la mort. Des cervelles étaient répandues sur la terre à côté de bras et de jambes coupés.

Candide s'enfuit au plus vite dans un autre village: il appartenait à des Bulgares, et les héros abares l'avaient traité de même. Candide, toujours marchant sur des membres palpitants ou à travers des ruines, arriva enfin hors du théâtre de la guerre, portant quelques petites provisions dans son bissac, et n'oubliant jamais Mlle Cunégonde. Ses provisions lui manquèrent quand il fut en Hollande; mais, ayant entendu dire que tout le monde était riche dans ce pays-là, et qu'on y était chrétien, il ne douta pas qu'on ne le traitât aussi bien qu'il l'avait été dans le château de monsieur le baron avant qu'il en eût été chassé pour les beaux yeux de Mlle Cunégonde.

Il demanda l'aumône à plusieurs graves personnages, qui lui répondirent tous que, s'il continuait à faire ce métier, on l'enfermerait dans une maison de correction pour lui apprendre à vivre.

Il s'adressa ensuite à un homme qui venait de parler tout seul une heure de suite sur la charité dans une grande assemblée. Cet orateur, le regardant de travers, lui dit: «Que venez-vous faire ici? y êtes-vous pour la bonne cause?—Il n'y a point d'effet sans cause, répondit modestement Candide, tout est enchaîné nécessairement et arrangé pour le mieux. Il a fallu que je fusse chassé d'auprès Mlle Cunégonde, que j'aie passé par les baguettes, et il faut que je demande mon pain jusqu'à ce que je puisse en gagner; tout cela ne pouvait être autrement.—Mon ami, lui dit l'orateur, croyez-vous que le pape soit l'Antéchrist?—Je ne l'avais pas encore entendu dire, répondit Candide; mais, qu'il le soit ou qu'il ne le soit pas, je manque de pain.—Tu ne mérites pas d'en manger, dit l'autre; va, coquin, va, misérable, ne m'approche de ta vie.» La femme de l'orateur, ayant

net was also the sufficient reason for the death of several thousand men. The total may well have amounted to about thirty thousand souls. Candide, who was trembling like a philosopher, hid himself as best he could during this heroic butchery.

Finally, while the two kings were having *Te Deums* sung, each in his own camp, Candide decided to go elsewhere to reason effects and causes. He passed over heaps of dead and dying men, and arrived first at a neighboring village; it was in ashes: it was an Abare village that the Bulgarians had burned in accordance with international law. Here, old men covered with wounds were watching their butchered wives dying while clasping their infants to their bleeding breasts; there, girls, disemboweled after having satisfied the natural needs of several heroes, were breathing their last; other girls, half burned, were screaming to be finished off. Brains were scattered on the ground alongside severed arms and legs.

Candide fled as fast as he could to another village; it belonged to Bulgarians, and the Abare heroes had treated it in the same manner. Candide, constantly walking over palpitating limbs or through ruins, finally arrived outside the theater of war, carrying a few small provisions in his bag, and never forgetting Miss Cunégonde. His provisions ran out by the time he was in Holland; but having heard it said that everybody was wealthy in that country, and that they were Christian there, he did not doubt that he would be treated as well as he had been in the baron's country residence before he had been driven from it for love of Miss Cunégonde.

He begged alms of several solemn personages who all replied that if he continued to ply that trade he would be locked up in a house of correction to teach him better manners.

Then he addressed himself to a man who had just spoken by himself uninterruptedly for an hour about charity to a great assembly. This orator, looking at him askance, said to him, "What are you doing here? Are you here for the good cause?" "There's no effect without a cause," replied Candide modestly, "everything is necessarily connected and arranged for the best. I had to be driven away from Miss Cunégonde, I had to run the gauntlet and I have to beg for my bread until I can earn it; all that could not have been otherwise." "My friend," the orator said to him, "do you believe that the Pope is the Antichrist?" "I've never yet heard it said," replied Candide; "but, whether he is or not, I'm in need of bread." "You don't deserve to eat any," said the other; "be off, rogue, be off, wretch, don't come near me again for as long as you live." The orator's

mis la tête à la fenêtre et avisant un homme qui doutait que le pape fût antéchrist, lui répandit sur le chef un plein . . . O Ciel! à quel excès se porte le zèle de la religion chez les dames!

Un homme qui n'avait point été baptisé, un bon anabaptiste, nommé Jacques, vit la manière cruelle et ignominieuse dont on traitait ainsi un de ses frères, un être à deux pieds sans plumes, qui avait une âme; il l'amena chez lui, le nettoya, lui donna du pain et de la bière, lui fit présent de deux florins, et voulut même lui apprendre à travailler dans ses manufactures aux étoffes de Perse qu'on fabrique en Hollande. Candide, se prosternant presque devant lui, s'écriait: «Maître Pangloss me l'avait bien dit que tout est au mieux dans ce monde, car je suis infiniment plus touché de votre extrême générosité que de la dureté de ce monsieur à manteau noir et de madame son épouse.»

Le lendemain, en se promenant, il rencontra un gueux tout couvert de pustules, les yeux morts, le bout du nez rongé, la bouche de travers, les dents noires, et parlant de la gorge, tourmenté d'une toux violente et crachant une dent à chaque effort.

Chapitre IV

Comment Candide rencontra son ancien maître de philosophie, le docteur Pangloss, et ce qui en advint

Candide, plus ému encore de compassion que d'horreur, donna à cet épouvantable gueux les deux florins qu'il avait reçus de son honnête anabaptiste Jacques. Le fantôme le regarda fixement, versa des larmes, et sauta à son cou. Candide, effrayé, recule. «Hélas! dit le misérable à l'autre misérable, ne reconnaissez-vous plus votre cher Pangloss?—Qu'entends-je? Vous, mon cher maître! vous, dans cet état horrible! Quel malheur vous est-il donc arrivé? Pourquoi n'êtes-vous plus dans le plus beau des châteaux? Qu'est devenue Mlle Cunégonde, la perle des filles, le chef-d'œuvre de la nature? —Je n'en

wife, having stuck her head out the window and espying a man who
doubted that the Pope was the Antichrist, poured on his head a full
. . . Heavens! to what excess religious zeal is carried by ladies!
A man who had not been baptized, a good Anabaptist named
Jacques, saw this cruel and ignominious treatment of one of his
fellow creatures, a featherless, two-legged being who had a soul; he
took him home, cleaned him up, gave him some bread and beer,
made him a gift of two florins and even wanted to teach him how to
work for him in his factories producing the Persian fabrics that are
made in Holland. Candide, almost prostrating himself before him,
exclaimed, "Master Pangloss had indeed told me that all is at its
best in this world, for I'm infinitely more moved by your extreme
generosity than by the hardheartedness of that gentleman in the
black cloak and his wife."

The next day, while walking, he came across a beggar covered all
over with pustules, his eyes lusterless, the tip of his nose eaten away,
his mouth twisted, his teeth black, and speaking in a hoarse voice,
racked by a violent cough and spitting out a tooth with each effort
he made to speak.

Chapter IV

How Candide came across his former philosophy master, Doctor Pangloss, and what ensued

Candide, moved even more by compassion than by horror, gave this
hideous beggar the two florins that he had received from his honest
Anabaptist, Jacques. The phantom looked at him fixedly, shed tears
and flung his arms round Candide's neck. Candide, terrified, drew
back. "Alas!" said the one wretch to the other wretch, "do you no
longer recognize your dear Pangloss?" "What do I hear? You, my
dear master! you, in this horrible condition! What misfortune has
befallen you, then? Why are you no longer in the most beautiful of
country residences? What has become of Miss Cunégonde, that
pearl among young ladies, that masterpiece of nature?" "I'm ex-

peux plus», dit Pangloss. Aussitôt Candide le mena dans l'étable de l'anabaptiste, où il lui fit manger un peu de pain; et quand Pangloss fut refait: «Eh bien, lui dit-il, Cunégonde?—Elle est morte», reprit l'autre. Candide s'évanouit à ce mot; son ami rappela ses sens avec un peu de mauvais vinaigre qui se trouva par hasard dans l'étable. Candide rouvre les yeux. «Cunégonde est morte! Ah! meilleur des mondes, où êtes-vous? Mais de quelle maladie est-elle morte? ne serait-ce point de m'avoir vu chasser du beau château de monsieur son père à grands coups de pied?—Non, dit Pangloss; elle a été éventrée par des soldats bulgares, après avoir été violée autant qu'on peut l'être; ils ont cassé la tête à M. le baron, qui voulait la défendre; Mme la baronne a été coupée en morceaux; mon pauvre pupille, traité précisément comme sa sœur; et quant au château, il n'est pas resté pierre sur pierre, pas une grange, pas un mouton, pas un canard, pas un arbre; mais nous avons été bien vengés, car les Abares en ont fait autant dans une baronnie voisine qui appartenait à un seigneur bulgare.»

A ce discours, Candide s'évanouit encore; mais, revenu à soi, et ayant dit tout ce qu'il devait dire, il s'enquit de la cause et de l'effet, et de la raison suffisante qui avait mis Pangloss dans un si piteux état. «Hélas! dit l'autre, c'est l'amour; l'amour, le consolateur du genre humain, le conservateur de l'univers, l'âme de tous les êtres sensibles, le tendre amour.—Hélas! dit Candide, je l'ai connu, cet amour, ce souverain des cœurs, cette âme de notre âme; il ne m'a jamais valu qu'un baiser et vingt coups de pied au cul. Comment cette belle cause a-t-elle pu produire en vous un effet si abominable?» Pangloss répondit en ces termes: «O mon cher Candide! vous avez connu Paquette, cette jolie suivante de notre auguste baronne; j'ai goûté dans ses bras les délices du paradis, qui ont produit ces tourments d'enfer dont vous me voyez dévoré; elle en était infectée, elle en est peut-être morte. Paquette tenait ce présent d'un cordelier très savant, qui avait remonté à la source; car il l'avait eue d'une vieille comtesse, qui l'avait reçue d'un capitaine de cavalerie, qui la devait à une marquise, qui la tenait d'un page, qui l'avait reçue d'un jésuite, qui, étant novice, l'avait eue en droite ligne d'un des compagnons de Christophe Colomb. Pour moi, je ne la donnerai à personne, car je me meurs.

—O Pangloss! s'écria Candide, voilà une étrange généalogie! n'est-ce pas le diable qui en fut la souche?—Point du tout, répliqua ce grand homme; c'était une chose indispensable dans le meilleur des

hausted," said Pangloss. Candide immediately led him to the Ana-baptist's stable, where he gave him a little bread to eat; and when Pangloss had recovered: "Well!" Candide said to him, "what of Cu-négonde?" "She's dead," rejoined the other. Candide fainted at these words; his friend restored him to his senses with a little bad vinegar that happened to be in the stable. Candide reopened his eyes. "Cu-négonde is dead! Ah! best of worlds, where are you? But what sick-ness did she die of? Wasn't it at having seen me driven away with great kicks from her father's beautiful country residence?" "No," said Pangloss; "she was disemboweled by Bulgarian soldiers, after having been raped as much as one can be; they blew the baron's brains out when he tried to defend her; the baroness was hacked to pieces; my poor pupil was treated just like his sister; and as for the country residence, not one stone was left on top of another, not one barn remained, not one sheep, not one duck, not one tree; but we were fully avenged, for the Abares did just as much in a neighboring barony belonging to a Bulgarian lord."

At this speech, Candide fainted again; but having recovered con-sciousness and having said all that was appropriate, he inquired into the cause and effect, and the sufficient reason that had reduced Pangloss to such a piteous condition. "Alas!" said the other, "it's love: love, the comforter of mankind, the preserver of the universe, the soul of all sensitive beings, tender love." "Alas!" said Candide, "I've known it, that love, the sovereign of hearts, that soul of our soul; it never brought me anything but one kiss and twenty kicks in the backside. How could that fine cause bring about such an abominable effect in you?" Pangloss replied in these terms: "O my dear Candide! you knew Paquette, our august baroness's pretty wait-ing maid; I tasted in her arms the delights of paradise, which brought about these infernal torments by which you see me consumed; she was infected with them, perhaps she has died of them. Paquette received that gift from a very learned Franciscan who had gone back to the source; for he had contracted it from an aged countess, who had received it from a cavalry captain, who owed it to a marquise, who acquired it from a page, who had received it from a Jesuit, who, when a novice, had contracted it in a direct line from one of the companions of Christopher Columbus. As for me, I shall not give it to anyone, for I'm dying."

"O Pangloss!" exclaimed Candide, "that's a strange genealogy! Wasn't the devil its origin?" "Not at all," replied that great man; "it was an indispensable thing in the best of worlds, a necessary ingredi-

mondes, un ingrédient nécessaire: car, si Colomb n'avait pas attrapé dans une île de l'Amérique cette maladie qui empoisonne la source de la génération, qui souvent même empêche la génération, et qui est évidemment l'opposé du grand but de la nature, nous n'aurions ni le chocolat ni la cochenille; il faut encore observer que jusqu'aujourd'hui, dans notre continent, cette maladie nous est particulière, comme la controverse.

Les Turcs, les Indiens, les Persans, les Chinois, les Siamois, les Japonais, ne la connaissent pas encore; mais il y a une raison suffisante pour qu'ils la connaissent à leur tour dans quelques siècles. En attendant, elle a fait un merveilleux progrès parmi nous, et surtout dans ces grandes armées composées d'honnêtes stipendiaires, bien élevés, qui décident du destin des Etats; on peut assurer que, quand trente mille hommes combattent en bataille rangée contre des troupes égales en nombre, il y a environ vingt mille vérolés de chaque côté.

—Voilà qui est admirable, dit Candide, mais il faut vous faire guérir.—Et comment le puis-je? dit Pangloss; je n'ai pas le sou, mon ami; et, dans toute l'étendue de ce globe, on ne peut ni se faire saigner ni prendre un lavement sans payer, ou sans qu'il y ait quelqu'un qui paie pour nous.»

Ce dernier discours détermina Candide; il alla se jeter aux pieds de son charitable anabaptiste Jacques, et lui fit une peinture si touchante de l'état où son ami était réduit que le bonhomme n'hésita pas à recueillir le docteur Pangloss; il le fit guérir à ses dépens. Pangloss, dans la cure, ne perdit qu'un œil et une oreille. Il écrivait bien et savait parfaitement l'arithmétique. L'anabaptiste Jacques en fit son teneur de livres. Au bout de deux mois, étant obligé d'aller à Lisbonne pour les affaires de son commerce, il mena dans son vaisseau ses deux philosophes. Pangloss lui expliqua comment tout était on ne peut mieux. Jacques n'était pas de cet avis. «Il faut bien, disait-il, que les hommes aient un peu corrompu la nature, car ils ne sont point nés loups, et ils sont devenus loups. Dieu ne leur a donné ni canons de vingt-quatre ni baïonnettes, et ils se sont fait des baïonnettes et des canons pour se détruire. Je pourrais mettre en ligne de compte les banqueroutes, et la justice qui s'empare des biens des banqueroutiers pour en frustrer les créanciers.—Tout cela était indispensable, répliquait le docteur borgne, et les malheurs particuliers font le bien général, de sorte que plus il y a de malheurs particuliers, et plus tout est bien.» Tandis qu'il raisonnait, l'air s'obscurcit, les vents soufflèrent des quatre coins du monde, et le vaisseau fut assailli de la plus horrible tempête à la vue du port de Lisbonne.

ent: for, if Columbus hadn't caught, on an American island, this disease that poisons the source of procreation, that often even prevents procreation and that is evidently contrary to the great purpose of nature, we would have neither chocolate nor cochineal; it must further be observed that so far this disease, like religious controversy, has been limited to our continent. The Turks, the Indians, the Persians, the Chinese, the Siamese and the Japanese are not yet acquainted with it; but there's a sufficient reason for them to become acquainted with it in their turn within a few centuries. In the meantime, it has made wondrous progress among us, and above all in those great armies composed of honest, well-bred mercenaries who decide the destiny of states; it can be asserted that when thirty thousand men do pitched battle against an equal number of enemy troops, there are about twenty thousand syphilitics on either side."

"That's admirable," said Candide, "but you must be cured." "And how can I be?" said Pangloss; "I'm penniless, my friend; and throughout this world you can neither be bled nor take an enema without paying for it yourself, or without someone else paying for you."

This last speech decided Candide; he went to throw himself at the feet of his charitable Anabaptist, Jacques, and painted him such a pathetic picture of the state to which his friend had been reduced that the good soul did not hesitate to take in Doctor Pangloss; he had him cured at his expense. Pangloss, in the course of the cure, lost only an eye and an ear. He could write well and had a perfect grasp of arithmetic. The Anabaptist Jacques appointed him his bookkeeper. After two months, being obliged to go to Lisbon on business matters, he took his two philosophers with him on his ship. Pangloss explained to him how everything could not be better. Jacques was not of the same opinion. "Men must have corrupted nature a little," he said, "for they were certainly not born wolves, and yet they've become wolves. God gave them neither twenty-four-pounder cannons nor bayonets, and yet they've made bayonets and cannons for themselves in order to destroy one another. I could also cite bankruptcies and the justice that seizes the goods of bankrupts to defraud the creditors." "All that was indispensable," replied the one-eyed doctor, "and individual misfortunes bring about general welfare, so that the more individual misfortunes there are, the better everything is in general." While he was reasoning, the sky darkened, the winds blew from the four corners of the earth and the ship was assailed by the most horrible tempest when in sight of the port of Lisbon.

Chapitre V

Tempête, naufrage, tremblement de terre, et ce qui advint du docteur Pangloss, de Candide, et de l'anabaptiste Jacques

La moitié des passagers, affaiblis, expirants de ces angoisses inconcevables que le roulis d'un vaisseau porte dans les nerfs et dans toutes les humeurs du corps agitées en sens contraires, n'avait pas même la force de s'inquiéter du danger. L'autre moitié jetait des cris et faisait des prières; les voiles étaient déchirées, les mâts brisés, le vaisseau entrouvert. Travaillait qui pouvait, personne ne s'entendait, personne ne commandait. L'anabaptiste aidait un peu à la manœuvre; il était sur le tillac; un matelot furieux le frappe rudement et l'étend sur les planches; mais du coup qu'il lui donna il eut lui-même une si violente secousse qu'il tomba hors du vaisseau la tête la première. Il restait suspendu et accroché à une partie de mât rompue. Le bon Jacques court à son secours, l'aide à remonter, et de l'effort qu'il fit il est précipité dans la mer à la vue du matelot, qui le laissa périr sans daigner seulement le regarder. Candide approche, voit son bienfaiteur qui reparaît un moment et qui est englouti pour jamais. Il veut se jeter après lui dans la mer; le philosophe Pangloss l'en empêche, en lui prouvant que la rade de Lisbonne avait été formée exprès pour que cet anabaptiste s'y noyât. Tandis qu'il le prouvait *a priori*, le vaisseau s'entrouvre, tout périt à la réserve de Pangloss, de Candide, et de ce brutal de matelot qui avait noyé le vertueux anabaptiste; le coquin nagea heureusement jusqu'au rivage, où Pangloss et Candide furent portés sur une planche.

Quand ils furent revenus un peu à eux, ils marchèrent vers Lisbonne; il leur restait quelque argent, avec lequel ils espéraient se sauver de la faim après avoir échappé à la tempête.

A peine ont-ils mis le pied dans la ville en pleurant la mort de leur bienfaiteur, qu'ils sentent la terre trembler sous leurs pas; la mer s'élève en bouillonnant dans le port, et brise les vaisseaux qui sont

CHAPTER V

TEMPEST, SHIPWRECK, EARTHQUAKE, AND WHAT
HAPPENED TO DOCTOR PANGLOSS, CANDIDE
AND THE ANABAPTIST JACQUES

Half of the passengers, weakened, expiring as a result of those inconceivable agonies that the rolling of a ship causes in the nerves and in all the humors of a body when they are shaken in opposing directions, did not even have the strength to worry about the danger. The other half shrieked and said prayers; the sails were torn, the masts broken, the ship split open. Those who could labored, but no one could work together, no one commanded. The Anabaptist was helping a little at the maneuvering of the ship; he was on deck; a frenzied sailor struck him roughly and laid him out on the planks; but from the blow that he delivered he himself suffered such a violent shock that he fell out of the ship headfirst. He remained suspended, hooked onto a broken section of mast. The good Jacques ran to his assistance, helped him to climb back up, and with the effort he made was flung into the sea before the eyes of the sailor, who left him to perish without deigning even to look at him. Candide approached, saw his benefactor, who bobbed up for a moment and was then engulfed forever. He wanted to throw himself into the sea after him; the philosopher Pangloss prevented him, proving to him that the Lisbon roadstead had been formed expressly so that this Anabaptist should drown there. While he was proving this *a priori*, the ship was rent asunder and everyone perished except for Pangloss, Candide and that brute of a sailor who had drowned the virtuous Anabaptist; the rogue swam safely to shore, where Pangloss and Candide were carried on a plank.

When they had revived a little, they walked toward Lisbon; they still had a little money left, with which they hoped to stave off hunger after having escaped the tempest.

Scarcely had they set foot in the city, weeping over the death of their benefactor, when they felt the earth tremble beneath their feet;[6] the sea boiled up in the harbor and smashed to pieces those

[6] The Lisbon earthquake and fire (November 1, 1755) resulted in over 30,000 deaths. Voltaire's immediate reaction to the catastrophe as the epitome of a *mal physique* is expressed in his "Poème sur le désastre de Lisbonne" [Poem on the Lisbon Disaster], written in 1755.

à l'ancre. Des tourbillons de flammes et de cendres couvrent les rues et les places publiques; les maisons s'écroulent, les toits sont renversés sur les fondements, et les fondements se dispersent; trente mille habitants de tout âge et de tout sexe sont écrasés sous des ruines. Le matelot disait en sifflant et en jurant: «Il y aura quelque chose à gagner ici.—Quelle peut être la raison suffisante de ce phénomène? disait Pangloss.—Voici le dernier jour du monde!» s'écriait Candide. Le matelot court incontinent au milieu des débris, affronte la mort pour trouver de l'argent, en trouve, s'en empare, s'enivre, et, ayant cuvé son vin, achète les faveurs de la première fille de bonne volonté qu'il rencontre sur les ruines des maisons détruites et au milieu des mourants et des morts. Pangloss le tirait cependant par la manche. «Mon ami, lui disait-il, cela n'est pas bien, vous manquez à la raison universelle, vous prenez mal votre temps. —Tête et sang! répondit l'autre, je suis matelot et né à Batavia; j'ai marché quatre fois sur le crucifix dans quatre voyages au Japon; tu as bien trouvé ton homme avec ta raison universelle!»

Quelques éclats de pierre avaient blessé Candide; il était étendu dans la rue et couvert de débris. Il disait à Pangloss: «Hélas! procure-moi un peu de vin et d'huile; je me meurs.—Ce tremblement de terre n'est pas une chose nouvelle, répondit Pangloss; la ville de Lima éprouva les mêmes secousses en Amérique l'année passée; mêmes causes, mêmes effets: il y a certainement une traînée de soufre sous terre depuis Lima jusqu'à Lisbonne.—Rien n'est plus probable, dit Candide; mais, pour Dieu, un peu d'huile et de vin.—Comment, probable? répliqua le philosophe; je soutiens que la chose est démontrée.» Candide perdit connaissance, et Pangloss lui apporta un peu d'eau d'une fontaine voisine.

Le lendemain, ayant trouvé quelques provisions de bouche en se glissant à travers des décombres, ils réparèrent un peu leurs forces. Ensuite ils travaillèrent comme les autres à soulager les habitants échappés à la mort. Quelques citoyens secourus par eux leur donnèrent un aussi bon dîner qu'on le pouvait dans un tel désastre. Il est vrai que le repas était triste; les convives arrosaient leur pain de leurs larmes; mais Pangloss les consola en les assurant que les choses ne pouvaient être autrement: «Car, dit-il, tout ceci est ce qu'il y a de mieux. Car, s'il y a un volcan à Lisbonne, il ne pouvait être ailleurs. Car il est impossible que les choses ne soient pas où elles sont. Car tout est bien.»

ships that were at anchor. Whirlwinds of flames and ashes covered the streets and public squares; houses collapsed, roofs were knocked down onto foundations and the foundations broke up; thirty thousand inhabitants of all ages and both sexes were crushed beneath the ruins. The sailor said, whistling and swearing, "There'll be something to be had here." "What can be the sufficient reason for this phenomenon?" said Pangloss. "This is the end of the world!" exclaimed Candide. The sailor ran immediately into the midst of the wreckage, braved death in search of money, found some, seized it, got drunk and, having slept it off, purchased the favors of the first willing girl he came across on the ruins of destroyed houses and in the midst of the dead and dying. Pangloss, however, pulled him by the sleeve. "My friend," he said to him, "that's not right, you're going against universal reason, you're choosing your time badly." "Bloody hell!" replied the other, "I'm a sailor, born in Batavia; I've trodden on the crucifix four times on four voyages to Japan;[7] you've found the right man to talk to about your universal reason!"

Some fragments of stone had injured Candide; he was lying in the street, covered with debris. He said to Pangloss, "Alas! get me a little wine and oil: I'm dying." "This earthquake is nothing new," replied Pangloss; "the city of Lima in America experienced identical tremors last year; same causes, same effects: there is assuredly an underground vein of sulphur from Lima to Lisbon." "Nothing is more likely," said Candide; "but, for God's sake, a little oil and wine." "What do you mean, likely?" replied the philosopher; "I maintain that the thing is proven." Candide lost consciousness, and Pangloss brought him a little water from a nearby fountain.

The next day, having found some food supplies while slipping through the ruins, they restored their strength a little. Then they labored like the others to relieve those inhabitants who had escaped death. A few citizens whom they had helped gave them as good a dinner as was possible after such a disaster. It is true that the meal was a sad one: the table companions moistened their bread with their tears; but Pangloss comforted them by assuring them that things could not be otherwise: "For," he said, "all this is the best that can be. For if there's a volcano at Lisbon, then it couldn't be elsewhere. For it's impossible that things should not be where they are. For all's well."

[7] The Japanese, suspicious of European aims in the East, had expelled the Spanish and the Portuguese by the early seventeenth century. The Dutch were permitted to continue trading but only on certain conditions.

Un petit homme noir, familier de l'Inquisition, lequel était à côté de lui, prit poliment la parole et dit: «Apparemment que monsieur ne croit pas au péché originel; car, si tout est au mieux, il n'y a donc eu ni chute ni punition.

—Je demande très humblement pardon à Votre Excellence, répondit Pangloss encore plus poliment, car la chute de l'homme et la malédiction entraient nécessairement dans le meilleur des mondes possibles.—Monsieur ne croit donc pas à la liberté? dit le familier.

—Votre Excellence m'excusera, dit Pangloss; la liberté peut subsister avec la nécessité absolue; car il était nécessaire que nous fussions libres; car enfin la volonté déterminée . . .» Pangloss était au milieu de sa phrase, quand le familier fit un signe de tête à son estafier qui lui servait à boire du vin de Porto, ou d'Oporto.

CHAPITRE VI

COMMENT ON FIT UN BEL AUTO-DA-FÉ
POUR EMPÊCHER LES TREMBLEMENTS DE TERRE,
ET COMMENT CANDIDE FUT FESSÉ

Après le tremblement de terre qui avait détruit les trois quarts de Lisbonne, les sages du pays n'avaient pas trouvé un moyen plus efficace pour prévenir une ruine totale que de donner au peuple un bel auto-da-fé; il était décidé par l'université de Coïmbre que le spectacle de quelques personnes brûlées à petit feu, en grande cérémonie, est un secret infaillible pour empêcher la terre de trembler.

On avait en conséquence saisi un Biscayen convaincu d'avoir épousé sa commère, et deux Portugais qui en mangeant un poulet en avaient arraché le lard: on vint lier après le dîner le docteur Pangloss et son disciple Candide, l'un pour avoir parlé, et l'autre pour avoir écouté avec un air d'approbation: tous deux furent menés séparément dans des appartements d'une extrême fraîcheur, dans lesquels on n'était jamais incommodé du soleil; huit jours après ils furent tous deux revêtus d'un *san-benito*, et on orna leurs têtes de

A small, swarthy man, an agent of the Inquisition, who was sitting beside him, spoke up politely, saying, "It would seem that the gentleman does not believe in original sin; for, if all's at its best, then there has been neither fall nor punishment."

"I very humbly beg Your Excellency's pardon," replied Pangloss even more politely, "for the fall of man and his curse entered necessarily into the best of all possible worlds." "Then the gentleman does not believe in freedom?" said the agent. "Your Excellency will excuse me," said Pangloss; "freedom can coexist with absolute necessity; for it was necessary that we should be free; for, after all, the determined will . . ." Pangloss was in mid-sentence when the agent nodded to his armed attendant who was filling the agent's glass with some port, or Oporto, wine.

CHAPTER VI

How a fine auto-da-fé was held to prevent earthquakes, and how Candide was flogged on the backside

After the earthquake that had destroyed three-quarters of Lisbon, the learned men of the country had not found a more efficacious means of warding off total ruin than to give the people a fine auto-da-fé;[8] it was decided by the University of Coimbra that the spectacle of a few persons being burned over a slow fire with full ceremony is an infallible formula for preventing the earth from quaking.

Consequently, they had seized a Biscayan convicted of having married his godchild's godmother, and two Portuguese who when eating a chicken dish had removed the bacon; after the dinner, men came and tied up Doctor Pangloss and his disciple Candide, the one for having spoken, and the other for having listened with an air of approval; they were taken separately to extremely chilly apartments in which one was never inconvenienced by the sun; a week later they were each clothed in a sanbenito, and their heads were adorned

[8] This auto-da-fé took place on 20 June 1756.

mitres de papier: la mitre et le san-benito de Candide étaient peints
de flammes renversées et de diables qui n'avaient ni queues ni griffes;
mais les diables de Pangloss portaient griffes et queues, et les
flammes étaient droites. Ils marchèrent en procession ainsi vêtus, et
entendirent un sermon très pathétique, suivi d'une belle musique
en faux-bourdon. Candide fut fessé en cadence, pendant qu'on
chantait; le Biscayen et les deux hommes qui n'avaient point voulu
manger de lard furent brûlés, et Pangloss fut pendu, quoique ce ne
soit pas la coutume. Le même jour la terre trembla de nouveau avec
un fracas épouvantable.

Candide, épouvanté, interdit, éperdu, tout sanglant, tout palpi-
tant, se disait à lui-même: «Si c'est ici le meilleur des mondes pos-
sibles, que sont donc les autres? Passe encore si je n'étais que fessé,
je l'ai été chez les Bulgares. Mais, ô mon cher Pangloss! le plus
grand des philosophes, faut-il vous avoir vu pendre sans que je sache
pourquoi! O mon cher anabaptiste! le meilleur des hommes, faut-il
que vous ayez été noyé dans le port! O Mlle Cunégonde! la perle
des filles, faut-il qu'on vous ait fendu le ventre!»

Il s'en retournait se soutenant à peine, prêché, fessé, absous et
béni, lorsqu'une vieille l'aborda et lui dit: «Mon fils, prenez courage,
suivez-moi.»

Chapitre VII

Comment une vieille prit soin de Candide et comment il retrouva ce qu'il aimait

Candide ne prit point courage, mais il suivit la vieille dans une ma-
sure: elle lui donna un pot de pommade pour se frotter, lui laissa à
manger et à boire; elle lui montra un petit lit assez propre; il y avait
auprès du lit un habit complet. «Mangez, buvez, dormez, lui dit-
elle, et que Notre-Dame d'Atocha, monseigneur saint Antoine de
Padoue et monseigneur saint Jacques de Compostelle prennent soin
de vous: je reviendrai demain.» Candide, toujours étonné de tout ce
qu'il avait vu, de tout ce qu'il avait souffert, et encore plus de la
charité de la vieille, voulut lui baiser la main. «Ce n'est pas ma main

with paper miters: Candide's miter and sanbenito were painted with flames pointing downward and devils who had neither tails nor claws; but Pangloss's devils bore claws and tails, and the flames were the right way up. They walked in procession thus clothed, and listened to a very moving sermon, followed by some beautiful plainsong. Candide was flogged on the backside in time to the music during the singing; the Biscayan and the two men who had refused to eat bacon were burned, and Pangloss was hanged, although this is not the custom. That same day the earth trembled once again with a frightful crash.

Candide, terrified, overwhelmed, distraught, bleeding all over, throbbing all over, said to himself, "If this is the best of all possible worlds, then what can the others be like? I might put up with it if I'd only been flogged, for I was flogged by the Bulgarians. But, O my dear Pangloss! greatest of philosophers, did I have to see you hanged without my knowing why! O my dear Anabaptist! best of men, did you have to be drowned in the harbor! O Miss Cunégonde! pearl among young ladies, did your belly have to be ripped open!"

He was walking away, barely able to remain upright, having been preached at, flogged, absolved and blessed, when an old woman approached him and said to him, "My son, take courage, follow me."

CHAPTER VII

HOW AN OLD WOMAN TOOK CARE OF CANDIDE
AND HOW HE RECOVERED WHAT HE LOVED

Candide in no way took courage, but he followed the old woman into a hovel; she gave him a jar of ointment with which to rub himself, and left him something to eat and drink; she showed him a fairly clean little bed; beside the bed was a suit of clothes. "Eat, drink and sleep," she said to him, "and may Our Lady of Atocha, Saint Anthony of Padua and Saint James of Compostela take care of you; I shall return tomorrow." Candide, still astonished by all he had seen, all he had suffered and even more by the old woman's charity, wanted to kiss her hand. "It's not my hand that you should kiss,"

qu'il faut baiser, dit la vieille; je reviendrai demain. Frottez-vous de pommade, mangez et dormez.»

Candide, malgré tant de malheurs, mangea et dormit. Le lendemain la vieille lui apporte à déjeuner, visite son dos, le frotte elle-même d'une autre pommade; elle lui apporte ensuite à dîner; elle revient sur le soir, et apporte à souper. Le surlendemain elle fit encore les mêmes cérémonies. «Qui êtes-vous? lui disait toujours Candide; qui vous a inspiré tant de bonté? quelles grâces puis-je vous rendre?» La bonne femme ne répondait jamais rien; elle revint sur le soir et n'apporta point à souper. «Venez avec moi, dit-elle, et ne dites mot.» Elle le prend sous le bras, et marche avec lui dans la campagne environ un quart de mille: ils arrivent à une maison isolée, entourée de jardins et de canaux. La vieille frappe à une porte. On ouvre; elle mène Candide, par un escalier dérobé, dans un cabinet doré, le laisse sur un canapé de brocart, referme la porte, et s'en va. Candide croyait rêver, et regardait toute sa vie comme un songe funeste, et le moment présent comme un songe agréable.

La vieille reparut bientôt; elle soutenait avec peine une femme tremblante, d'une taille majestueuse, brillante de pierreries et couverte d'un voile. «Otez ce voile», dit la vieille à Candide. Le jeune homme approche; il lève le voile d'une main timide. Quel moment! quelle surprise! il croit voir Mlle Cunégonde; il la voyait en effet, c'était elle-même. La force lui manque, il ne peut proférer une parole, il tombe à ses pieds. Cunégonde tombe sur le canapé. La vieille les accable d'eaux spiritueuses; ils reprennent leurs sens, ils se parlent: ce sont d'abord des mots entrecoupés, des demandes et des réponses, qui se croisent, des soupirs, des larmes, des cris. La vieille leur recommande de faire moins de bruit, et les laisse en liberté. «Quoi! c'est vous, lui dit Candide, vous vivez! Je vous retrouve en Portugal! On ne vous a donc pas violée? On ne vous a point fendu le ventre, comme le philosophe Pangloss me l'avait assuré?—Si fait, dit la belle Cunégonde; mais on ne meurt pas toujours de ces deux accidents.—Mais votre père et votre mère ont-ils été tués?—Il n'est que trop vrai, dit Cunégonde en pleurant.—Et votre frère?—Mon frère a été tué aussi.—Et pourquoi êtes-vous en Portugal? et comment avez-vous su que j'y étais? et par quelle étrange aventure m'avez-vous fait conduire dans cette maison?—Je vous dirai tout cela, répliqua la dame; mais il faut auparavant que vous m'appreniez

said the old woman; "I shall return tomorrow. Rub yourself with ointment, eat and sleep."

Candide, despite so many misfortunes, ate and slept. The next day the old woman brought him some breakfast, examined his back and rubbed it herself with another ointment; she then brought him some dinner; she returned in the evening, bringing him supper. The day after that she performed the same services again. "Who are you?" Candide kept asking her; "who has inspired you with such kindness? how can I thank you?" The good woman never gave any reply; she returned in the evening without bringing any supper. "Come with me," she said, "and don't say a word." She took him by the arm and walked with him into the countryside for about a quarter of a mile; they arrived at an isolated house surrounded by gardens and canals. The old woman knocked at a door. It was opened; she led Candide up a secret staircase into a small gilded room, left him on a brocaded sofa, closed the door behind her and departed. Candide thought he was dreaming and considered his entire life as a bad dream, and the present moment as a pleasant dream.

The old woman soon reappeared; she was supporting with difficulty a trembling woman of majestic stature, glittering with precious stones and wearing a veil. "Remove that veil," said the old woman to Candide. The young man approached; he lifted the veil with a timid hand. What a moment! what a surprise! he thought he saw Miss Cunégonde; he did see her, in fact; it was she herself. His strength failed him, he could not utter a word, he fell at her feet. Cunégonde fell onto the sofa. The old woman plied them with restorative spirits; they recovered their senses, they spoke to one another: at first the words were faltering, questions and answers interrupting one another, sighs, tears and cries. The old woman exhorted them to make less noise, and then left them alone. "What! it's you," Candide said to her, "you're alive! I've found you again, and in Portugal! Then you weren't raped? Your belly wasn't ripped open at all, as the philosopher Pangloss had assured me?" "It did happen," said the beautiful Cunégonde; "but one doesn't always die as a result of those two misfortunes." "But your father and mother, were they killed?" "That's only too true," said Cunégonde, weeping. "And your brother?" "My brother was also killed." "And why are you in Portugal? and how did you know that I was here? and through what strange adventure did you have me brought to this house?" "I'll tell you all that," replied the lady; "but first you must inform me of everything

tout ce qui vous est arrivé depuis le baiser innocent que vous me donnâtes et les coups de pied que vous reçûtes.» Candide lui obéit avec un profond respect, et quoiqu'il fût interdit, quoique sa voix fût faible et tremblante, quoique l'échine lui fît encore un peu mal, il lui raconta de la manière la plus naïve tout ce qu'il avait éprouvé depuis le moment de leur séparation. Cunégonde levait les yeux au ciel; elle donna des larmes à la mort du bon anabaptiste et de Pangloss; après quoi elle parla en ces termes à Candide, qui ne perdait pas une parole, et qui la dévorait des yeux.

Chapitre VIII

Histoire de Cunégonde

«J'étais dans mon lit et je dormais profondément, quand il plut au Ciel d'envoyer les Bulgares dans notre beau château de Thunder-ten-tronckh; ils égorgèrent mon père et mon frère, et coupèrent ma mère par morceaux. Un grand Bulgare, haut de six pieds, voyant qu'à ce spectacle j'avais perdu connaissance, se mit à me violer; cela me fit revenir, je repris mes sens, je criai, je me débattis, je mordis, j'égratignai, je voulais arracher les yeux à ce grand Bulgare, ne sachant pas que tout ce qui arrivait dans le château de mon père était une chose d'usage: le brutal me donna un coup de couteau dans le flanc gauche dont je porte encore la marque.—Hélas! j'espère bien la voir, dit le naïf Candide.—Vous la verrez, dit Cunégonde; mais continuons.—Continuez», dit Candide.

Elle reprit ainsi le fil de son histoire: «Un capitaine bulgare entra, il me vit toute sanglante, et le soldat ne se dérangeait pas. Le capitaine se mit en colère du peu de respect que lui témoignait ce brutal, et le tua sur mon corps. Ensuite il me fit panser, et m'emmena prisonnière de guerre dans son quartier. Je blanchissais le peu de chemises qu'il avait, je faisais sa cuisine; il me trouvait fort jolie, il faut l'avouer; et je ne nierai pas qu'il ne fût très bien fait, et qu'il n'eût la peau blanche et douce; d'ailleurs peu d'esprit, peu de philosophie, on voyait bien qu'il n'avait pas été élevé par le docteur Pan-

that's happened to you since the innocent kiss you gave me and the kicks you received." Candide obeyed her with profound respect, and although he was overwhelmed, although his voice was weak and tremulous, although his back still hurt a little, he related to her in the most artless fashion all he had experienced since the moment of their separation. Cunégonde raised her eyes to heaven; she shed tears over the death of the good Anabaptist and of Pangloss; then she spoke in these terms to Candide, who did not miss a word, and who devoured her with his eyes:

CHAPTER VIII

CUNÉGONDE'S STORY

"I was in my bed and I was fast asleep when it pleased Heaven to send the Bulgarians to our beautiful country residence of Thunder-Ten-Tronckh; they butchered my father and my brother, and hacked my mother to pieces. A big Bulgarian, six feet tall, seeing that I had lost consciousness at this sight, began to rape me; that brought me back to consciousness, I regained my senses, I cried out, I struggled, I bit, I scratched, I tried to tear out that big Bulgarian's eyes, not knowing that everything going on in my father's country residence was common practice; the brute stabbed me with a knife in the left side: I still carry the scar." "Alas! I hope to see that," said the artless Candide. "You'll see it," said Cunégonde; "but let me go on." "Go on," said Candide.

She took up the thread of her story thus: "A Bulgarian captain came in, he saw me covered with blood, but the other soldier didn't take any notice of him. The captain grew angry at the lack of respect shown him by that brute, and killed him while he was on top of me. Then he had my wounds dressed and led me away as a prisoner of war to his quarters. I washed the few shirts he possessed, I did his cooking; he found me extremely pretty, it has to be admitted; and I'll not deny that he was very well built and that he had soft white skin; on the other hand, he had little intelligence, little philosophy, it was obvious that he hadn't been brought up by Doctor Pangloss.

gloss. Au bout de trois mois, ayant perdu tout son argent et s'étant dégoûté de moi, il me vendit à un Juif nommé don Issacar, qui trafiquait en Hollande et en Portugal, et qui aimait passionnément les femmes. Ce Juif s'attacha beaucoup à ma personne, mais il ne pouvait en triompher, je lui ai mieux résisté qu'au soldat bulgare. Une personne d'honneur peut être violée une fois, mais sa vertu s'en affermit.

«Le Juif, pour m'apprivoiser, me mena dans cette maison de campagne que vous voyez. J'avais cru jusque-là qu'il n'y avait rien sur la terre de si beau que le château de Thunder-ten-tronckh; j'ai été détrompée.

«Le grand inquisiteur m'aperçut un jour à la messe; il me lorgna beaucoup, et me fit dire qu'il avait à me parler pour des affaires secrètes. Je fus conduite à son palais; je lui appris ma naissance; il me représenta combien il était au-dessous de mon rang d'appartenir à un Israélite. On proposa de sa part à don Issacar de me céder à Monseigneur. Don Issacar, qui est le banquier de la cour et homme de crédit, n'en voulut rien faire. L'inquisiteur le menaça d'un autoda-fé. Enfin mon Juif, intimidé, conclut un marché, par lequel la maison et moi leur appartiendraient à tous deux en commun; que le Juif aurait pour lui les lundis, mercredis et le jour du sabbat, et que l'inquisiteur aurait les autres jours de la semaine. Il y a six mois que cette convention subsiste. Ce n'a pas été sans querelles; car souvent il a été indécis si la nuit du samedi au dimanche appartenait à l'ancienne loi ou à la nouvelle. Pour moi, j'ai résisté jusqu'à présent à toutes les deux, et je crois que c'est pour cette raison que j'ai toujours été aimée.

«Enfin, pour détourner le fléau des tremblements de terre, et pour intimider don Issacar, il plut à monseigneur l'inquisiteur de célébrer un auto-da-fé. Il me fit l'honneur de m'y inviter. Je fus très bien placée; on servit aux dames des rafraîchissements entre la messe et l'exécution. Je fus, à la vérité, saisie d'horreur en voyant brûler ces deux Juifs et cet honnête Biscayen qui avait épousé sa commère; mais quelle fut ma surprise, mon effroi, mon trouble, quand je vis, dans un san-benito et sous une mitre, une figure qui ressemblait à celle de Pangloss! Je me frottai les yeux, je regardai attentivement, je le vis pendre; je tombai en faiblesse. A peine reprenais-je mes sens que je vous vis dépouillé tout nu: ce fut là le comble de l'horreur, de la consternation, de la douleur, du désespoir. Je vous dirai, avec vérité, que votre peau est encore plus blanche et d'un incarnat plus parfait que celle de mon capitaine des Bulgares. Cette vue redoubla

After three months, having lost all his money and become tired of me, he sold me to a Jew named Don Issachar, who traded in Holland and Portugal, and who passionately loved women. This Jew became very attached to me, but he couldn't get the better of me; I resisted him more successfully than I had the Bulgarian soldier. An honorable woman may be raped once, but her virtue only grows stronger. "The Jew, to make me more tractable, conveyed me to this country house that you see. I had believed until then that there was nothing on earth so beautiful as the country residence of Thunder-Ten-Tronckh; I was undeceived.

"The Grand Inquisitor noticed me one day at mass; he stared at me a good deal and sent word to me that he needed to speak to me about some secret matters. I was conducted to his palace; I informed him of my birth; he showed me how beneath my station it was to belong to an Israelite. On his behalf, it was proposed to Don Issachar to give me up to His Eminence. Don Issachar, who is the court banker and a man of influence, wished nothing of the kind. The inquisitor threatened him with an auto-da-fé. Finally, my Jew, intimidated, struck a bargain whereby the house and myself would belong to both of them jointly: the Jew would have for himself Mondays, Wednesdays and the day of the Sabbath, and the inquisitor would have the other days of the week. This agreement has held good for six months. It hasn't been without quarrels; for often it's been undecided whether the night from Saturday to Sunday belonged to the old law or the new. As for me, I've resisted both of them so far, and I believe it's for this reason that I've continued to be loved.

"Finally, in order to avoid the scourge of earthquakes and to intimidate Don Issachar, it pleased the inquisitor to celebrate an auto-da-fé. He did me the honor of inviting me to it. I had a very good seat; the ladies were served refreshments between the mass and the execution. I was, to tell the truth, seized with horror on seeing those two Jews burned along with that honest Biscayan who had married his godchild's godmother; but what was my surprise, my terror, my confusion, when I saw, dressed in a sanbenito and a miter, a figure resembling that of Pangloss! I rubbed my eyes, I gazed attentively, I saw him hanged; I swooned. Scarcely had I regained consciousness when I saw you stripped naked: it was then that I felt the utmost horror, consternation, suffering and despair. I'll tell you truly that your skin is even whiter and of a more perfect rose-red than my Bulgarian captain's. That sight redoubled all those feelings that were

tous les sentiments qui m'accablaient, qui me dévoraient. Je m'écriai, je voulus dire: «Arrêtez, barbares!» mais la voix me manqua, et mes cris auraient été inutiles. Quand vous eûtes été bien fessé: «Comment se peut-il faire, disais-je, que l'aimable Candide et «le sage Pangloss se trouvent à Lisbonne, l'un pour recevoir cent «coups de fouet, et l'autre pour être pendu par l'ordre de monsei-«gneur l'inquisiteur dont je suis la bien-aimée? Pangloss m'a donc «bien cruellement trompée quand il me disait que tout va le mieux «du monde.»

«Agitée, éperdue, tantôt hors de moi-même, et tantôt prête de mourir de faiblesse, j'avais la tête remplie du massacre de mon père, de ma mère, de mon frère, de l'insolence de mon vilain soldat bulgare, du coup de couteau qu'il me donna, de ma servitude, de mon métier de cuisinière, de mon capitaine bulgare, de mon vilain don Issacar, de mon abominable inquisiteur, de la pendaison du docteur Pangloss, de ce grand *miserere* en faux-bourdon pendant lequel on vous fessait, et surtout du baiser que je vous ai donné derrière un paravent, le jour que je vous avais vu pour la dernière fois. Je louai Dieu qui vous ramenait à moi par tant d'épreuves. Je recommandai à ma vieille d'avoir soin de vous, et de vous amener ici dès qu'elle le pourrait. Elle a très bien exécuté ma commission; j'ai goûté le plaisir inexprimable de vous revoir, de vous entendre, de vous parler. Vous devez avoir une faim dévorante; j'ai grand appétit; commençons par souper.»

Les voilà qui se mettent tous deux à table; et, après le souper, ils se replacent sur ce beau canapé dont on a déjà parlé; ils y étaient quand le signor don Issacar, l'un des maîtres de la maison, arriva. C'était le jour du sabbat. Il venait jouir de ses droits, et expliquer son tendre amour.

CHAPITRE IX

CE QUI ADVINT DE CUNÉGONDE, DE CANDIDE, DU GRAND INQUISITEUR ET D'UN JUIF

Cet Issacar était le plus colérique Hébreu qu'on eût vu dans Israël depuis la captivité en Babylone. «Quoi! dit-il, chienne de Galiléenne, ce n'est pas assez de M. l'inquisiteur? Il faut que ce coquin partage aussi avec moi?» En disant cela il tira un long poignard dont il était toujours pourvu, et, ne croyant pas que son adverse partie eût des armes, il se jette sur Candide; mais notre bon Westphalien

overwhelming me, consuming me. I cried out, I wanted to say, 'Stop, barbarians!' but my voice failed me, and my cries would have been useless. When you'd been well flogged, I said, 'How can it be that lovely Candide and wise Pangloss are in Lisbon, the one to receive a hundred lashes, and the other to be hanged by order of the inquisitor whose beloved I am? Pangloss cruelly deceived me, then, when he told me that everything happens in the very best way.'

"Agitated, distraught, now beside myself, now ready to die of faintness, my head was filled with the thought of the slaughter of my father, my mother and my brother, the insolence of my vile Bulgarian soldier, the knife wound he gave me, my servitude, my work as a cook, my Bulgarian captain, my vile Don Issachar, my loathsome inquisitor, the hanging of Doctor Pangloss, that great plainsong *miserere* during which you were flogged and, above all, the kiss I gave you behind a screen on the day I had seen you for the last time. I praised God for having led you back to me through so many trials. I exhorted my old female servant to take care of you and to bring you here as soon as she could. She has carried out my commission very well; I've enjoyed the inexpressible pleasure of seeing you again, of hearing you, of talking to you. You must be famished; I'm very hungry myself; let's begin by having supper."

And so the two of them sat down to table; and after supper they returned to the beautiful sofa that has already been described; they were there when Señor Don Issachar, one of the masters of the house, arrived. It was the day of the Sabbath. He was coming to enjoy his rights and to express his tender love.

CHAPTER IX

What happened to Cunégonde, Candide, the Grand Inquisitor and a Jew

This Issachar was the most irascible Hebrew to have been seen in Israel since the Babylonian captivity. "What!" he said, "Galilean bitch, is the inquisitor not enough? Must this rogue share you with me too?" Saying that, he drew a long dagger with which he was always armed, and, thinking that his opponent had no weapons, he threw himself on Candide; but our good Westphalian had received

avait reçu une belle épée de la vieille avec l'habit complet. Il tire son épée, quoiqu'il eût les mœurs fort douces, et vous étend l'Israélite roide mort sur le carreau, aux pieds de la belle Cunégonde. «Sainte Vierge! s'écria-t-elle, qu'allons-nous devenir? Un homme tué chez moi! si la justice vient, nous sommes perdus.—Si Pangloss n'avait pas été pendu, dit Candide, il nous donnerait un bon conseil dans cette extrémité, car c'était un grand philosophe. A son défaut consultons la vieille.» Elle était fort prudente, et commençait à dire son avis, quand une autre petite porte s'ouvrit. Il était une heure après minuit, c'était le commencement du dimanche. Ce jour appartenait à monsieur l'inquisiteur. Il entre et voit le fessé Candide l'épée à la main, un mort étendu par terre, Cunégonde effarée, et la vieille donnant des conseils.

Voici dans ce moment ce qui se passa dans l'âme de Candide, et comment il raisonna: «Si ce saint homme appelle du secours, il me fera infailliblement brûler; il pourra en faire autant de Cunégonde; il m'a fait fouetter impitoyablement; il est mon rival; je suis en train de tuer, il n'y a pas à balancer.» Ce raisonnement fut net et rapide; et, sans donner le temps à l'inquisiteur de revenir de sa surprise, il le perce d'outre en outre, et le jette à côté du Juif. «En voici bien d'une autre, dit Cunégonde; il n'y a plus de rémission; nous sommes excommuniés, notre dernière heure est venue. Comment avez-vous fait, vous qui êtes né si doux, pour tuer en deux minutes un Juif et un prélat?—Ma belle demoiselle, répondit Candide, quand on est amoureux, jaloux et fouetté par l'Inquisition, on ne se connaît plus.»

La vieille prit alors la parole et dit: «Il y a trois chevaux andalous dans l'écurie, avec leurs selles et leurs brides: que le brave Candide les prépare; madame a des moyadors et des diamants: montons vite à cheval, quoique je ne puisse me tenir que sur une fesse, et allons à Cadix; il fait le plus beau temps du monde, et c'est un grand plaisir de voyager pendant la fraîcheur de la nuit.»

Aussitôt Candide selle les trois chevaux. Cunégonde, la vieille et lui font trente milles d'une traite. Pendant qu'ils s'éloignaient, la Sainte-Hermandad arrive dans la maison; on enterre monseigneur

a fine sword along with the suit of clothes from the old woman. He drew his sword, although he had the sweetest of dispositions, and laid the Israelite out stone dead on the tiled flooring at the feet of the beautiful Cunégonde. "Holy Virgin!" she exclaimed, "what will become of us? A man murdered in my house! if the law comes, we're lost." "If Pangloss hadn't been hanged," said Candide, "he'd give us good advice in this extremity, for he was a great philosopher. For lack of him, let's consult the old woman." She was extremely prudent and was beginning to give her opinion when another little door opened. It was one hour after midnight, it was Sunday morning. That day belonged to the inquisitor. He came in and saw the flogged Candide sword in hand, a dead man stretched out on the floor, Cunégonde bewildered and the old woman giving advice.

Here is what passed through Candide's mind at that moment, and how he reasoned: "If this holy man calls for help, he will certainly have me burned; he might do as much to Cunégonde; he had me flogged pitilessly; he's my rival; I'm in the act of murder, there can be no hesitation." This reasoning was distinct and rapid; and, without giving the inquisitor time to recover from his surprise, he ran him through and cast him down beside the Jew. "Here's a predicament!" said Cunégonde; "there can be no forgiveness; we'll be excommunicated, our last hour has come. How could you, you who were so gentle by birth, murder in the space of two minutes a Jew and a prelate?" "My beautiful young lady," replied Candide, "when one is in love, is jealous and has been flogged by the Inquisition, one is no longer oneself."

The old woman spoke up then, saying, "There are three Andalusian horses in the stable, with their saddles and bridles; let the brave Candide prepare them; Madam has some moidores and some diamonds; let's mount up quickly, although I can only sit on one buttock, and go to Cadiz; the weather's perfect, and it's a great pleasure to travel in the coolness of the night."

Candide immediately saddled the three horses. Cunégonde, the old woman and he covered thirty miles at a stretch. While they were riding off, the Santa Hermandad[9] entered the house; His Eminence

[9] "Holy Brotherhood," an agency with police powers created in the late fifteenth century by Ferdinand and Isabella of Spain. With its main headquarters in Toledo, the Brotherhood had regional headquarters throughout Spain that consisted of alcaldes (magistrates) and a mounted militia. The Brotherhood was notorious for the severe penalties it imposed.

dans une belle église, et on jette Issacar à la voirie.

Candide, Cunégonde et la vieille étaient déjà dans la petite ville d'Avacéna, au milieu des montagnes de la Sierra-Morena; et ils parlaient ainsi dans un cabaret.

CHAPITRE X

DANS QUELLE DÉTRESSE CANDIDE, CUNÉGONDE ET LA VIEILLE ARRIVENT À CADIX, ET DE LEUR EMBARQUEMENT

«Qui a donc pu me voler mes pistoles et mes diamants? disait en pleurant Cunégonde; de quoi vivrons-nous? comment ferons-nous? où trouver des inquisiteurs et des Juifs qui m'en donnent d'autres?—Hélas! dit la vieille, je soupçonne fort un révérend père cordelier qui coucha hier dans la même auberge que nous à Badajoz; Dieu me garde de faire un jugement téméraire! mais il entra deux fois dans notre chambre, et il partit longtemps avant nous.—Hélas! dit Candide, le bon Pangloss m'avait souvent prouvé que les biens de la terre sont communs à tous les hommes, que chacun y a un droit égal. Ce cordelier devait bien, suivant ces principes, nous laisser de quoi achever notre voyage. Il ne vous reste donc rien du tout, ma belle Cunégonde?—Pas un maravédis, dit-elle.—Quel parti prendre? dit Candide.—Vendons un des chevaux, dit la vieille; je monterai en croupe derrière mademoiselle, quoique je ne puisse me tenir que sur une fesse, et nous arriverons à Cadix».

Il y avait dans la même hôtellerie un prieur de bénédictins; il acheta le cheval bon marché. Candide, Cunégonde et la vieille passèrent par Lucena, par Chillas, par Lebrixa, et arrivèrent enfin à Cadix. On y équipait une flotte, et on y assemblait des troupes pour mettre à la raison les révérends pères jésuites du Paraguay, qu'on accusait d'avoir fait révolter une de leurs hordes contre les rois d'Espagne et du Portugal, auprès de la ville du Saint-Sacrement. Candide, ayant servi chez les Bulgares, fit l'exercice bulgarien devant le général de la petite armée avec tant de grâce, de célérité, d'adresse,

was buried in a beautiful church, and Issachar was thrown onto the refuse dump.

Candide, Cunégonde and the old woman were already in the small town of Avacena, in the middle of the Sierra Morena mountains; and they were talking as follows at an inn:

CHAPTER X

IN WHAT DISTRESS CANDIDE, CUNÉGONDE AND THE OLD WOMAN ARRIVED AT CADIZ, AND OF THEIR EMBARKATION

"Who, then, could have stolen my pistoles and my diamonds?" Cunégonde was saying, weeping; "what shall we live on? what shall we do? where shall I find inquisitors and Jews to give me others?" "Alas!" said the old woman, "I strongly suspect a reverend Franciscan father who slept yesterday at the same inn as us at Badajoz; God keep me from making a rash judgment! but he entered our room twice, and he left the inn long before us." "Alas!" said Candide, "the good Pangloss often proved to me that the goods of this world are common property to all men and that each person has an equal right to them. This Franciscan should really, following those principles, have left us enough to complete our journey. Have you nothing left at all, then, my beautiful Cunégonde?" "Not a maravedi," she said. "What's to be done?" said Candide. "Let's sell one of the horses," said the old woman; "I'll ride behind Madam, although I can only sit on one buttock, and that way we'll reach Cadiz."

There was at the same inn a Benedictine prior; he bought the horse cheaply. Candide, Cunégonde and the old woman passed through Lucena, Chillas and Lebrija and finally reached Cadiz. A fleet was being fitted out there, and troops were being assembled to bring back to their senses the Jesuit reverend fathers in Paraguay who were accused of having incited one of their tribes near the town of San Sacramento to revolt against the kings of Spain and Portugal. Candide, having served with the Bulgarians, performed the Bulgarian drill in front of the general of the small army with such graceful-

de fierté, d'agilité, qu'on lui donna une compagnie d'infanterie à commander. Le voilà capitaine; il s'embarque avec Mlle Cunégonde, la vieille, deux valets, et les deux chevaux andalous qui avaient appartenu à M. le grand inquisiteur de Portugal. Pendant toute la traversée ils raisonnèrent beaucoup sur la philosophie du pauvre Pangloss. «Nous allons dans un autre univers, disait Candide; c'est dans celui-là sans doute que tout est bien. Car il faut avouer qu'on pourrait gémir un peu de ce qui se passe dans le nôtre en physique et en morale.—Je vous aime de tout mon cœur, disait Cunégonde; mais j'ai encore l'âme tout effarouchée de ce que j'ai vu, de ce que j'ai éprouvé.—Tout ira bien, répliquait Candide; la mer de ce nouveau monde vaut déjà mieux que les mers de notre Europe; elle est plus calme, les vents plus constants. C'est certainement le nouveau monde qui est le meilleur des univers possibles.—Dieu le veuille! disait Cunégonde; mais j'ai été si horriblement malheureuse dans le mien que mon cœur est presque fermé à l'espérance.—Vous vous plaignez, leur dit la vieille; hélas! vous n'avez pas éprouvé des infortunes telles que les miennes.» Cunégonde se mit presque à rire, et trouva cette bonne femme fort plaisante de prétendre être plus malheureuse qu'elle. «Hélas! lui dit-elle, ma bonne, à moins que vous n'ayez été violée par deux Bulgares, que vous n'ayez reçu deux coups de couteau dans le ventre, qu'on n'ait démoli deux de vos châteaux, qu'on n'ait égorgé à vos yeux deux mères et deux pères, et que vous n'ayez vu deux de vos amants fouettés dans un auto-da-fé, je ne vois pas que vous puissiez l'emporter sur moi; ajoutez que je suis née baronne avec soixante et douze quartiers, et que j'ai été cuisinière.—Mademoiselle, répondit la vieille, vous ne savez pas quelle est ma naissance; et, si je vous montrais mon derrière, vous ne parleriez pas comme vous faites, et vous suspendriez votre jugement.» Ce discours fit naître une extrême curiosité dans l'esprit de Cunégonde et de Candide. La vieille leur parla en ces termes.

ness, celerity, skill, pride and agility that he was put in command of an infantry company. And so he was a captain; he embarked with Miss Cunégonde, the old woman, two valets and the two Andalusian horses that had belonged to the Grand Inquisitor of Portugal. During the entire crossing they reasoned a great deal on poor Pangloss's philosophy. "We're going to another world," said Candide; "undoubtedly it's there that all's well. For it must be acknowledged that one could complain a little about what occurs physically and morally in our world." "I love you with all my heart," said Cunégonde; "but my mind is still thoroughly amazed by what I've seen and what I've gone through." "Everything will be all right," replied Candide; "the sea in this new world is already better than our European seas; it's calmer, the winds are more constant. Certainly it's the New World that is the best of all possible worlds." "May it please God that it is so!" said Cunégonde; "but I've been so horribly unfortunate in my world that my heart is almost closed to hope." "You complain," the old woman said to them; "alas! you haven't suffered misfortunes such as mine." Cunégonde almost began to laugh, and found this good woman extremely funny in claiming to be more unfortunate than she. "Alas! my good woman," she said to her, "unless you've been raped by two Bulgarians, received two knife wounds in the belly, had two of your country residences demolished, had two mothers and two fathers butchered before your eyes and seen two of your lovers flogged at an auto-da-fé, I don't see how you can be worse off than me; add to this that I was born a baroness with seventy-two heraldic quarterings, and that I've been a cook." "Miss," replied the old woman, "you know nothing of my birth; and, were I to show you my backside, you wouldn't talk as you do, and you'd suspend your judgment." This speech aroused an extreme curiosity in the minds of Cunégonde and Candide. The old woman spoke to them in these terms:

Chapitre XI

Histoire de la vieille

«Je n'ai pas eu toujours les yeux éraillés et bordés d'écarlate; mon nez n'a pas toujours touché à mon menton et je n'ai pas toujours été servante. Je suis la fille du pape Urbain X, et de la princesse de Palestrine.* On m'éleva jusqu'à quatorze ans dans un palais auquel tous les châteaux de vos barons allemands n'auraient pas servi d'écurie; et une de mes robes valait mieux que toutes les magnificences de la Westphalie. Je croissais en beauté, en grâces, en talents, au milieu des plaisirs, des respects et des espérances. J'inspirai déjà de l'amour, ma gorge se formait; et quelle gorge! blanche, ferme, taillée comme celle de la Vénus de Médicis; et quels yeux! quelles paupières! quels sourcils noirs! quelles flammes brûlaient dans mes deux prunelles, et effaçaient la scintillation des étoiles, comme me disaient les poètes du quartier. Les femmes qui m'habillaient et qui me déshabillaient tombaient en extase en me regardant par-devant et par-derrière, et tous les hommes auraient voulu être à leur place.

«Je fus fiancée à un prince souverain de Massa-Carrara. Quel prince! aussi beau que moi, pétri de douceur et d'agréments, brillant d'esprit et brûlant d'amour. Je l'aimais comme on aime pour la première fois, avec idolâtrie, avec emportement. Les noces furent préparées. C'était une pompe, une magnificence inouïe; c'étaient des fêtes, des carrousels, des opera-buffa continuels; et toute l'Italie fit pour moi des sonnets dont il n'y eut pas un seul de passable. Je touchais au moment de mon bonheur, quand une vieille marquise qui avait été maîtresse de mon prince l'invita à prendre du chocolat chez elle. Il mourut en moins de deux heures avec des convulsions épouvantables. Mais ce n'est qu'une bagatelle. Ma mère, au désespoir, et bien moins affligée que moi, voulut s'arracher pour quelque temps à un séjour si funeste. Elle avait une très belle terre auprès de Gaète. Nous nous embarquâmes sur une galère du pays, dorée comme l'autel de Saint-Pierre de Rome. Voilà qu'un corsaire de Salé fond sur nous et nous aborde. Nos soldats se défendirent comme

* Voyez l'extrême discrétion de l'auteur; il n'y eut jusqu'à présent aucun pape nommé Urbain X; il craint de donner une bâtarde à un pape connu. Quelle circonspection! quelle délicatesse de conscience!

Chapter XI

The old woman's story

"I didn't always have bloodshot eyes rimmed with scarlet; my nose didn't always touch my chin and I wasn't always a servant. I am the daughter of Pope Urban X and the Princess of Palestrina.[10] I was brought up until the age of fourteen in a palace to which all the country residences of your German barons would not have served as stables; and a single one of my gowns was worth more than all the splendors of Westphalia. I grew in beauty, charms and talents amid pleasures, respect and expectations. I already inspired love, my bosom was forming; and what a bosom! white, firm and shaped like that of the Venus de' Medici; and what eyes! what eyelids! what dark eyebrows! what fires burned in my two pupils, surpassing the twinkling of the stars, as the local poets would tell me. The women who dressed and undressed me fell into raptures when gazing at me from in front and behind, and all men would have wished to be in their place.

"I was betrothed to a sovereign prince of Massa-Carrara. What a prince! as handsome as I, endowed with gentleness and charm, brilliantly witty and burning with love. I loved him as one loves for the first time: with idolatry, with passion. The wedding preparations were made. There was unheard of pomp and splendor; there were continual festivities, tournaments and opera buffas; and all Italy wrote sonnets for me, not one of which was passable. The moment of my happiness was at hand when an aged marquise who had been my prince's mistress invited him to come for chocolate at her home. He died less than two hours later in appalling convulsions. But that's a mere trifle. My mother, in despair, though considerably less grieved than I, wished to get away for a short while from such a baneful place. She had a very fine estate near Gaeta. We embarked on a local galley gilded like the altar of St. Peter's in Rome. Suddenly a corsair from Salé bore down on us and boarded us. Our soldiers defended themselves like papal soldiers: they all fell to their knees,

[10] Observe the author's extreme discretion; hitherto there has been no pope named Urban X; he fears attributing a bastard daughter to a known pope. What circumspection! what delicacy of conscience! [Voltaire's note, first published in 1829]

des soldats du pape: ils se mirent tous à genoux en jetant leurs armes, et en demandant au corsaire une absolution *in articulo mortis.*

«Aussitôt on les dépouilla nus comme des singes, et ma mère aussi, nos filles d'honneur aussi, et moi aussi. C'est une chose admirable que la diligence avec laquelle ces messieurs déshabillent le monde. Mais ce qui me surprit davantage, c'est qu'ils nous mirent à tous le doigt dans un endroit où nous autres femmes nous ne nous laissons mettre d'ordinaire que des canules. Cette cérémonie me paraissait bien étrange: voilà comme on juge de tout quand on n'est pas sorti de son pays. J'appris bientôt que c'était pour voir si nous n'avions pas caché là quelques diamants: c'est un usage établi de temps immémorial parmi les nations policées qui courent sur mer. J'ai su que messieurs les religieux chevaliers de Malte n'y manquent jamais quand ils prennent des Turcs et des Turques; c'est une loi du droit des gens à laquelle on n'a jamais dérogé.

«Je ne vous dirai point combien il est dur pour une jeune princesse d'être menée esclave à Maroc avec sa mère. Vous concevez assez tout ce que nous eûmes à souffrir dans le vaisseau corsaire. Ma mère était encore très belle; nos filles d'honneur, nos simples femmes de chambre, avaient plus de charmes qu'on n'en peut trouver dans toute l'Afrique. Pour moi, j'étais ravissante, j'étais la beauté, la grâce même et j'étais pucelle; je ne le fus pas longtemps: cette fleur qui avait été réservée pour le beau prince de Massa-Carrara me fut ravie par le capitaine corsaire; c'était un nègre abominable, qui croyait encore me faire beaucoup d'honneur. Certes il fallait que Mme la princesse de Palestrine et moi fussions bien fortes pour résister à tout ce que nous éprouvâmes jusqu'à notre arrivée à Maroc. Mais passons! ce sont des choses si communes qu'elles ne valent pas la peine qu'on en parle.

«Maroc nageait dans le sang quand nous arrivâmes. Cinquante fils de l'empereur Muley-Ismaël avaient chacun leur parti: ce qui produisait en effet cinquante guerres civiles, de noirs contre noirs, de noirs contre basanés, de basanés contre basanés, de mulâtres contre mulâtres. C'était un carnage continuel dans toute l'étendue de l'empire.

«A peine fûmes-nous débarqués que des noirs d'une faction ennemie de celle de mon corsaire se présentèrent pour lui enlever son butin. Nous étions, après les diamants et l'or, ce qu'il avait de plus précieux. Je fus témoin d'un combat tel que vous n'en voyez jamais dans vos climats d'Europe. Les peuples septentrionaux n'ont pas le sang assez ardent. Ils n'ont pas la rage des femmes au point où elle est commune en Afrique. Il semble que vos Européens aient du lait dans les veines; c'est du vitriol, c'est du feu qui coule dans celles des habitants du mont Atlas et des pays voisins. On combattit avec la

throwing down their weapons and begging the corsair for absolution *in articulo mortis.*

"Immediately they were stripped as naked as monkeys, my mother too, our maids of honor and I. It's a remarkable thing, the diligence with which those gentlemen undress people. But what surprised me more was that with all of us they stuck their fingers in a place where we women usually allow only cannulas to be put. This ceremony seemed very strange to me: that's how one judges everything when one hasn't traveled abroad. I soon learned that it was in order to see whether we hadn't hidden some diamonds up there: it's a custom established since time immemorial among civilized seafaring nations. I learned that those religious Knights of Malta never fail to do it when they capture Turkish men and women; it's an international law that's never been departed from.

"I'll tell you nothing of how distressful it is for a young princess to be taken as a slave with her mother to Morocco. You can imagine well enough all we had to suffer on the pirate ship. My mother was still very beautiful; our maids of honor, our mere chambermaids had more charms than can be found in all Africa. As for me, I was exquisite, I was beauty, I was grace itself, and I was a virgin; I did not remain so for long: that flower that had been reserved for the handsome Prince of Massa-Carrara was ravished from me by the pirate captain; he was a loathsome Negro who even believed he was doing me a great honor. Certainly the Princess of Palestrina and I had to be very strong to bear all we went through until our arrival in Morocco. But let's pass over that! those are such common things that they're not worth the trouble of being spoken of.

"Morocco was swimming in blood when we arrived. Fifty sons of the Emperor Muley Ismael each had their own faction, which in effect produced fifty civil wars: blacks against blacks, blacks against browns, browns against browns, mulattoes against mullatoes. There was uninterrupted carnage throughout the empire.

"Scarcely had we disembarked when some blacks of a faction opposed to that of my corsair appeared, intent upon carrying off his booty. We were, after the diamonds and gold, his most precious possessions. I was witness to a fight such as you never see in your European climes. Northern peoples aren't hot-blooded enough. They don't have a mania for women to the degree that is common in Africa. It seems that your Europeans have milk in their veins; it's vitriol, it's fire that flows in the veins of the inhabitants of Mount Atlas and the surrounding regions. They fought with the fury of the

fureur des lions, des tigres et des serpents de la contrée, pour savoir à qui nous aurait. Un Maure saisit ma mère par le bras droit, le lieutenant de mon capitaine la retint par le bras gauche; un soldat maure la prit par une jambe, un de nos pirates la tenait par l'autre. Nos filles se trouvèrent presque toutes en ce moment tirées ainsi à quatre soldats. Mon capitaine me tenait cachée derrière lui. Il avait le cimeterre au poing, et tuait tout ce qui s'opposait à sa rage. Enfin, je vis toutes nos Italiennes et ma mère déchirées, coupées, massacrées par les monstres qui se les disputaient. Les captifs mes compagnons, ceux qui les avaient pris, soldats, matelots, noirs, basanés, blancs, mulâtres, et enfin mon capitaine, tout fut tué, et je demeurai mourante sur un tas de morts. Des scènes pareilles se passaient comme on sait, dans l'étendue de plus de trois cents lieues, sans qu'on manquât aux cinq prières par jour ordonnées par Mahomet.

«Je me débarrassai avec beaucoup de peine de la foule de tant de cadavres sanglants entassés, et je me traînai sous un grand oranger au bord d'un ruisseau voisin; j'y tombai d'effroi, de lassitude, d'horreur, de désespoir et de faim. Bientôt après, mes sens accablés se livrèrent à un sommeil qui tenait plus de l'évanouissement que du repos. J'étais dans cet état de faiblesse et d'insensibilité, entre la mort et la vie, quand je me sentis pressée de quelque chose qui s'agitait sur mon corps. J'ouvris les yeux, je vis un homme blanc et de bonne mine qui soupirait, et qui disait entre ses dents: O che sciagura d'essere senza coglioni!

CHAPITRE XII

SUITE DES MALHEURS DE LA VIEILLE

«Etonnée et ravie d'entendre la langue de ma patrie, et non moins surprise des paroles que proférait cet homme, je lui répondis qu'il y avait de plus grands malheurs que celui dont il se plaignait. Je l'instruisis en peu de mots des horreurs que j'avais essuyées, et je

native lions, tigers and snakes to determine who would have us. A Moor seized my mother by the right arm, my captain's lieutenant held her back by the left arm; a Moorish soldier took hold of her by one leg, one of our pirates held her by the other. Almost all our servant girls were in that instant tugged at in the same way by four soldiers. My captain kept me hidden behind him. He had his scimitar clasped in his hand, and was killing all those who opposed his rage. Finally I saw my mother and all our Italian women torn asunder, cut up, slaughtered by the monsters who were disputing over them. My fellow captives, those who had taken them, soldiers, sailors, blacks, browns, whites, mulattoes and finally my captain, all were killed, and I remained dying on a heap of dead bodies. As everyone knows, such scenes occurred for more than three hundred leagues round about without anyone neglecting the five daily prayers ordained by Muhammad.

"I freed myself with a great deal of difficulty from the mass of so many heaped-up bloodstained corpses, and I dragged myself beneath a large orange tree on the bank of a nearby stream; I collapsed there in fear, weariness, horror, despair and hunger. Soon afterward, my overwhelmed senses surrendered to a slumber that was more like a fainting fit than sleep. I was in that state of weakness and insensibility between life and death when I felt myself pressed upon by something moving on my body. I opened my eyes, I saw a white man of good appearance who was sighing, and who was saying between his teeth, '*O che sciagura d'essere senza coglioni!*'[11]

CHAPTER XII

CONTINUATION OF THE OLD WOMAN'S MISFORTUNES

"Amazed and delighted to hear the language of my native land, and no less surprised at the words this man was uttering, I replied that there were greater misfortunes than the one of which he was complaining. I informed him in few words of the horrors I had endured,

[11] "Oh what a calamity to have no balls!"

retombai en faiblesse. Il m'emporta dans une maison voisine, me fit mettre au lit, me fit donner à manger, me servit, me consola, me flatta, me dit qu'il n'avait rien vu de si beau que moi, et que jamais il n'avait tant regretté ce que personne ne pouvait lui rendre. «Je «suis né à Naples, me dit-il; on y chaponne deux ou trois mille en-«fants tous les ans; les uns en meurent, les autres acquièrent une «voix plus belle que celle des femmes, les autres vont gouverner des «Etats. On me fit cette opération avec un très grand succès, et j'ai «été musicien de la chapelle de Mme la princesse de Palestrine.—De «ma mère! m'écriai-je.—De votre mère! s'écria-t-il en pleurant. «Quoi! vous seriez cette jeune princesse que j'ai élevée jusqu'à l'âge «de six ans, et qui promettait déjà d'être aussi belle que vous «êtes?—C'est moi-même; ma mère est à quatre cents pas d'ici, cou-«pée en quartiers sous un tas de morts . . .»

«Je lui contai tout ce qui m'était arrivé; il me conta aussi ses aventures, et m'apprit comment il avait été envoyé chez le roi de Maroc par une puissance chrétienne, pour conclure avec ce monarque un traité, par lequel on lui fournirait de la poudre, des canons et des vaisseaux, pour l'aider à exterminer le commerce des autres chrétiens. «Ma mission est faite, dit cet honnête eunuque; je vais m'em-«barquer à Ceuta, et je vous ramènerai en Italie. *Ma che sciagura* «*d'essere senza coglioni!*»

«Je le remerciai avec des larmes d'attendrissement; et, au lieu de me mener en Italie, il me conduisit à Alger et me vendit au dey de cette province. A peine fus-je vendue que cette peste qui a fait le tour de l'Afrique, de l'Asie et de l'Europe, se déclara dans Alger avec fureur. Vous avez vu des tremblements de terre; mais, Mademoiselle, avez-vous jamais eu la peste?—Jamais, répondit la baronne.

—Si vous l'aviez eue, reprit la vieille, vous avoueriez qu'elle est bien au-dessus d'un tremblement de terre. Elle est fort commune en Afrique; j'en fus attaquée. Figurez-vous quelle situation pour la fille d'un pape, âgée de quinze ans, qui en trois mois de temps avait éprouvé la pauvreté, l'esclavage, avait été violée presque tous les jours, avait vu couper sa mère en quatre, avait essuyé la faim et la guerre, et mourait pestiférée dans Alger. Je n'en mourus pourtant pas. Mais mon eunuque et le dey, et presque tout le sérail d'Alger, périrent.

«Quand les premiers ravages de cette épouvantable peste furent passés, on vendit les esclaves du dey. Un marchand m'acheta et me mena à Tunis; il me vendit à un autre marchand, qui me revendit à Tripoli; de Tripoli je fus revendue à Alexandrie, d'Alexandrie reven-

and then I fainted again. He carried me off to a nearby house, had me put to bed and given some food, waited on me, comforted me, flattered me and told me that he'd never seen anything so beautiful as I, and that never had he regretted so much that which no one could restore to him. 'I was born in Naples,' he told me; 'two or three thousand children are caponized there every year; some of them die as a result; others acquire a voice more beautiful than that of a woman; others go on to govern states. This operation was performed on me with very great success and I became a musician in the chapel of the Princess of Palestrina.' 'Of my mother!' I exclaimed. 'Of your mother!' he exclaimed, weeping. 'What! could you be that young princess I brought up until she was six years old, and who already promised to become as beautiful as you are?' 'It is I; my mother is four hundred paces from here, cut into quarters beneath a heap of corpses . . .'

"I told him everything that had happened to me; he too related to me his adventures, informing me how he had been sent to the King of Morocco by a Christian power to conclude a treaty with that monarch whereby he would be supplied with gunpowder, cannons and ships to assist in stamping out the commerce of the other Christian powers. 'My mission is accomplished,' said this honest eunuch; 'I'm going to embark at Ceuta, and I'll take you back to Italy. *Ma che sciagura d'essere senza coglioni!*'

"I thanked him with tears of gratitude; and, instead of taking me back to Italy, he took me to Algiers and sold me to the dey of that province. Scarcely had I been sold when the plague that has swept through Africa, Asia and Europe broke out with a fury in Algiers. You've seen earthquakes; but, Miss, have you ever had the plague?"

"Never," replied the baroness.

"If you'd had it," the old woman continued, "you would admit that it's far worse than an earthquake. It's very common in Africa; I contracted it. Imagine what a predicament that was for a pope's daughter, fifteen years old, who in three months had experienced poverty and slavery, had been raped almost every day, had seen her mother quartered, had endured hunger and war, and was dying plague-stricken in Algiers. However, I didn't die of it. But my eunuch and the dey, and almost the entire seraglio in Algiers, perished.

"When the first ravages of that terrible plague were over, the dey's slaves were sold. A merchant bought me and took me to Tunis; he sold me to another merchant who resold me at Tripoli; from Tripoli I was resold to Alexandria, from Alexandria I was resold to Smyrna,

due à Smyrne, de Smyrne à Constantinople. J'appartins enfin à un aga des janissaires, qui fut bientôt commandé pour aller défendre Azof contre les Russes qui l'assiégeaient.

«L'aga, qui était un très galant homme, mena avec lui tout son sérail, et nous logea dans un petit fort sur les Palus-Méotides, gardé par deux eunuques noirs et vingt soldats. On tua prodigieusement de Russes, mais ils nous le rendirent bien. Azof fut mis à feu et à sang, et on ne pardonna ni au sexe ni à l'âge; il ne resta que notre petit fort; les ennemis voulurent nous prendre par famine. Les vingt janissaires avaient juré de ne se jamais rendre. Les extrémités de la faim où ils furent réduits les contraignirent à manger nos deux eunuques, de peur de violer leur serment. Au bout de quelques jours, ils résolurent de manger les femmes.

«Nous avions un iman très pieux et très compatissant, qui leur fit un beau sermon par lequel il leur persuada de ne pas nous tuer tout à fait. «Coupez, dit-il, seulement une fesse à chacune de ces dames, «vous ferez très bonne chère; s'il faut y revenir, vous en aurez en-«core autant dans quelques jours; le Ciel vous saura gré d'une action «si charitable, et vous serez secourus.»

«Il avait beaucoup d'éloquence; il les persuada. On nous fit cette horrible opération. L'iman nous appliqua le même baume qu'on met aux enfants qu'on vient de circoncire. Nous étions toutes à la mort.

«A peine les janissaires eurent-ils fait le repas que nous leur avions fourni que les Russes arrivent sur des bateaux plats; il ne réchappa pas un janissaire. Les Russes ne firent aucune attention à l'état où nous étions. Il y a partout des chirurgiens français: un d'eux, qui était fort adroit, prit soin de nous; il nous guérit, et je me souviendrai toute ma vie que, quand mes plaies furent bien fermées, il me fit des propositions. Au reste, il nous dit à toutes de nous consoler; il nous assura que dans plusieurs sièges pareille chose était arrivée, et que c'était la loi de la guerre.

«Dès que mes compagnes purent marcher, on les fit aller à Moscou. J'échus en partage à un boyard qui me fit sa jardinière, et qui me donnait vingt coups de fouet par jour. Mais ce seigneur ayant été roué au bout de deux ans avec une trentaine de boyards pour quelque tracasserie de cour, je profitai de cette aventure; je m'enfuis; je traversai toute la Russie; je fus longtemps servante de cabaret à

from Smyrna to Constantinople. I belonged finally to an aga of the Janissaries, who was soon ordered to go to defend Azov against the Russians who were besieging it.

"The aga, who was a very gallant man, took with him his entire seraglio, and lodged us in a small fort on the Maeotian Marsh, guarded by two black eunuchs and twenty soldiers. The Russians were killed in large numbers, but they paid us back well. Azov was put to fire and sword, and there was no pardon either for age or sex; only our small fort remained; the enemy tried to starve us out. The twenty Janissaries had sworn never to surrender. The extremities of hunger to which they were reduced compelled them to eat our two eunuchs, for fear of breaking their oath. A few days later, they resolved to eat the women.

"We had a very pious and very compassionate imam who preached them a fine sermon in which he sought to persuade them not to kill us outright. 'Cut,' he said, 'only one buttock from each of these ladies, you'll have plenty to eat; if you need more, you can have just as much again in a few days; Heaven will be grateful to you for such a charitable action, and you'll be relieved.'

"He had considerable eloquence; he persuaded them. This horrible operation was performed on us. The imam applied to us the same balm that is used on children who have just been circumcised. We were all at death's door.

"Scarcely had the Janissaries finished the meal we had supplied them when the Russians arrived on flatboats; not one Janissary escaped. The Russians paid no attention to the condition we were in. There are French surgeons everywhere: one of them, who was very skillful, took care of us; he healed us, and I shall remember for the rest of my life that when my wounds were healed over he made propositions to me. Furthermore, he told us all to console ourselves; he assured us that in several sieges a similar thing had happened, and that it was the law of warfare.

"As soon as my companions were able to walk, they were sent to Moscow. I fell to the lot of a Boyar who made me his gardener and who gave me twenty lashes each day. But this lord having been broken upon the wheel two years later along with about thirty other Boyars for some court intrigue,[12] I availed myself of this piece of luck: I fled; I crossed all of Russia; for a long time I was a barmaid

[12] A revolt in 1698 against Peter the Great (1672–1725) by the Moscow Streltzi (a military corps with special privileges). It resulted in extreme reprisals.

Riga, puis à Rostock, à Vismar, à Leipsick, à Cassel, à Utrecht, à Leyde, à La Haye, à Rotterdam: j'ai vieilli dans la misère et dans l'opprobre, n'ayant que la moitié d'un derrière, me souvenant toujours que j'étais fille d'un pape; je voulus cent fois me tuer, mais j'aimais encore la vie. Cette faiblesse ridicule est peut-être un de nos penchants les plus funestes: car y a-t-il rien de plus sot que de vouloir porter continuellement un fardeau qu'on peut toujours jeter par terre? d'avoir son être en horreur, et de tenir à son être? enfin de caresser le serpent qui nous dévore, jusqu'à ce qu'il nous ait mangé le cœur?

«J'ai vu dans les pays que le sort m'a fait parcourir, et dans les cabarets où j'ai servi, un nombre prodigieux de personnes qui avaient leur existence en exécration; mais je n'en ai vu que douze qui aient mis volontairement fin à leur misère: trois nègres, quatre Anglais, quatre Genevois et un professeur allemand nommé Robeck. J'ai fini par être servante chez le Juif don Issacar; il me mit auprès de vous, ma belle demoiselle; je me suis attachée à votre destinée, et j'ai été plus occupée de vos aventures que des miennes. Je ne vous aurais même jamais parlé de mes malheurs, si vous ne m'aviez pas un peu piquée, et s'il n'était d'usage dans un vaisseau de conter des histoires pour se désennuyer. Enfin, Mademoiselle, j'ai de l'expérience, je connais le monde; donnez-vous un plaisir, engagez chaque passager à vous conter son histoire; et s'il s'en trouve un seul qui n'ait souvent maudit sa vie, qui ne se soit souvent dit à lui-même qu'il était le plus malheureux des hommes, jetez-moi dans la mer la tête la première.»

in Riga, then in Rostock, Wismar, Leipzig, Kassel, Utrecht, Leiden, The Hague and Rotterdam; I have grown old in poverty and opprobrium, having only half a backside, constantly remembering that I was a pope's daughter; a hundred times I wanted to kill myself, but I still loved life. That ridiculous weakness is perhaps one of our most baneful inclinations: for is there anything more foolish than to wish to carry continually a burden that one can always throw down? to abhor one's existence, and yet to cling to that existence? in short, to cherish the serpent that devours us, until it has eaten our heart?

"I've seen in the countries that fate caused me to travel through, and in the taverns in which I served, a prodigious number of people who abhorred their own existence; but I've seen only twelve who voluntarily put an end to their misery: three Negroes, four Englishmen, four Genevans and a German professor named Robeck.[13] I ended up as a servant in the house of the Jew Don Issachar; he appointed me to you, my beautiful young lady; I attached myself to your destiny, and I was more occupied with your adventures than with my own. I would never have even spoken to you of my misfortunes if you hadn't nettled me a little, and if it weren't customary on a ship to tell stories to relieve the boredom. In short, Miss, I have experience, I know the world; amuse yourself, induce each passenger to tell you his story; and if there's a single one who hasn't often cursed his own life, who hasn't often said to himself that he's the most unfortunate of men, then throw me headfirst into the ocean."

[13] Johann Robeck (1672–1739), author of a treatise advocating suicide who took his own life by drowning at the age of 67.

Chapitre XIII

Comment Candide fut obligé de se séparer de la belle Cunégonde et de la vieille

La belle Cunégonde, ayant entendu l'histoire de la vieille, lui fit toutes les politesses qu'on devait à une personne de son rang et de son mérite. Elle accepta la proposition; elle engagea tous les passagers l'un après l'autre à lui conter leurs aventures. Candide et elle avouèrent que la vieille avait raison. «C'est bien dommage, disait Candide, que le sage Pangloss ait été pendu contre la coutume dans un auto-da-fé; il nous dirait des choses admirables sur le mal physique et sur le mal moral qui couvrent la terre et la mer, et je me sentirais assez de force pour oser lui faire respectueusement quelques objections.»

A mesure que chacun racontait son histoire, le vaisseau avançait. On aborda dans Buenos Aires. Cunégonde, le capitaine Candide et la vieille allèrent chez le gouverneur Don Fernando d'Ibaraa, y Figueora, y Mascarenes, y Lampourdos, y Souza. Ce seigneur avait une fierté convenable à un homme qui portait tant de noms. Il parlait aux hommes avec le dédain le plus noble, portant le nez si haut, élevant si impitoyablement la voix, prenant un ton si imposant, affectant une démarche si altière, que tous ceux qui le saluaient étaient tentés de le battre. Il aimait les femmes à la fureur. Cunégonde lui parut ce qu'il avait jamais vu de plus beau. La première chose qu'il fit fut de demander si elle n'était point la femme du capitaine. L'air dont il fit cette question alarma Candide: il n'osa pas dire qu'elle était sa femme, parce qu'en effet elle ne l'était point; il n'osait pas dire que c'était sa sœur, parce qu'elle ne l'était pas non plus; et quoique ce mensonge officieux eût été autrefois très à la mode chez les anciens, et qu'il pût être utile aux modernes, son âme était trop pure pour trahir la vérité. «Mlle Cunégonde, dit-il, doit me faire l'honneur de m'épouser, et nous supplions Votre Excellence de daigner faire notre noce.»

Don Fernando d'Ibaraa, y Figueora, y Mascarenes, y Lampourdos, y Souza, relevant sa moustache, sourit amèrement, et ordonna au capitaine Candide d'aller faire la revue de sa compagnie. Candide obéit; le gouverneur demeura avec Mlle Cunégonde. Il lui déclara sa passion, lui protesta que le lendemain il l'épouserait à la face de

CHAPTER XIII

HOW CANDIDE WAS OBLIGED TO PART COMPANY WITH THE BEAUTIFUL CUNÉGONDE AND THE OLD WOMAN

The beautiful Cunégonde, having heard the old woman's story, showed her all the respect befitting a person of her rank and worth. She accepted the old woman's proposal; she induced all the passengers one after another to tell her of their adventures. She and Candide admitted that the old woman was right. "It's really a shame," said Candide, "that the wise Pangloss was hanged, contrary to custom, at an auto-da-fé; he'd have wonderful things to say to us on the physical evil and the moral evil that cover land and sea, and I'd feel confident enough to venture to make, respectfully, a few objections."

As each passenger told his story, the ship sailed on. They landed at Buenos Aires. Cunégonde, Captain Candide and the old woman went to call on the governor, Don Fernando de Ibaraa y Figueora y Mascarenes y Lampourdos y Souza. This lord had a pride befitting a man bearing so many names. He spoke to other men with the noblest disdain, turning his nose up so high, raising his voice so pitilessly, adopting such a commanding tone of voice and affecting such a haughty bearing that all those who greeted him were tempted to strike him. He loved women with a passion. Cunégonde seemed to him the most beautiful creature he had ever seen. The first thing he did was to ask whether she was not the captain's wife. The manner in which he put this question alarmed Candide; he did not dare to say that she was his wife because in fact she was not; he did not dare to say that she was his sister because she was not that either; and although that diplomatic lie was formerly very much in fashion with the ancients, and although it might prove useful to the moderns, his soul was too pure to misrepresent the truth. "Miss Cunégonde," he said, "is to do me the honor of marrying me, and we beseech Your Excellency to deign to preside over our wedding."

Don Fernando de Ibaraa y Figueora y Mascarenes y Lampourdos y Souza, twirling his mustache, smiled sardonically and ordered Captain Candide to go and inspect his company. Candide obeyed; the governor remained with Miss Cunégonde. He declared his passion for her, protested that he would marry her on the following day

l'Eglise, ou autrement, ainsi qu'il plairait à ses charmes. Cunégonde lui demanda un quart d'heure pour se recueillir, pour consulter la vieille et pour se déterminer.

La vieille dit à Cunégonde: «Mademoiselle, vous avez soixante et douze quartiers, et pas une obole; il ne tient qu'à vous d'être la femme du plus grand seigneur de l'Amérique méridionale, qui a une très belle moustache; est-ce à vous de vous piquer d'une fidélité à toute épreuve? Vous avez été violée par les Bulgares; un Juif et un inquisiteur ont eu vos bonnes grâces: les malheurs donnent des droits. J'avoue que, si j'étais à votre place, je ne ferais aucun scrupule d'épouser M. le gouverneur et de faire la fortune de M. le capitaine Candide.» Tandis que la vieille parlait avec toute la prudence que l'âge et l'expérience donnent, on vit entrer dans le port un petit vaisseau; il portait un alcade et des alguazils, et voici ce qui était arrivé.

La vieille avait très bien deviné que ce fut un cordelier à la grande manche qui vola l'argent et les bijoux de Cunégonde dans la ville de Badajoz, lorsqu'elle fuyait en hâte avec Candide. Ce moine voulut vendre quelques-unes des pierreries à un joaillier. Le marchand les reconnut pour celles du grand inquisiteur. Le cordelier, avant d'être pendu, avoua qu'il les avait volées; il indiqua les personnes et la route qu'elles prenaient. La fuite de Cunégonde et de Candide était déjà connue. On les suivit à Cadix; on envoya sans perdre de temps un vaisseau à leur poursuite. Le vaisseau était déjà dans le port de Buenos Aires. Le bruit se répandit qu'un alcade allait débarquer, et qu'on poursuivait les meurtriers de monseigneur le grand inquisiteur. La prudente vieille vit dans l'instant tout ce qui était à faire. «Vous ne pouvez fuir, dit-elle à Cunégonde, et vous n'avez rien à craindre; ce n'est pas vous qui avez tué monseigneur; et d'ailleurs le gouverneur, qui vous aime, ne souffrira pas qu'on vous maltraite; demeurez.» Elle court sur-le-champ à Candide: «Fuyez, dit-elle, ou dans une heure vous allez être brûlé.» Il n'y a pas un moment à perdre; mais comment se séparer de Cunégonde, et où se réfugier?

as prescribed by the church, or after another fashion, as it would please her charms. Cunégonde asked him for a quarter of an hour in which to collect her thoughts, consult the old woman and make up her mind.

The old woman said to Cunégonde, "Miss, you have seventy-two heraldic quarterings, but you're not worth a groat; it rests entirely with you to become the wife of the greatest lord in South America; he has a very handsome mustache; are you in a position to pride yourself on an unflinching fidelity? You were raped by the Bulgarians; a Jew and an inquisitor received your kind favors: misfortunes give certain rights. I admit that, were I in your position, I wouldn't scruple to marry the governor and thereby make Captain Candide's fortune." While the old woman was speaking with all the prudence granted by age and experience, a small ship was seen entering the harbor; it carried an alcalde and some alguazils, and here is what had happened:

The old woman had guessed correctly that it was a long-sleeved Franciscan who had stolen Cunégonde's money and jewelry in the town of Badajoz, when she was fleeing in such haste with Candide. This monk tried to sell some of the precious stones to a jeweler. The merchant recognized them as those belonging to the Grand Inquisitor. The Franciscan, before being hanged, confessed that he had stolen them; he indicated the persons and the road they were taking. The flight of Cunégonde and Candide was already known. They were followed to Cadiz; without delay a ship was sent in pursuit of them. This ship was already in the harbor of Buenos Aires. The rumor spread that an alcalde was about to disembark and that the Grand Inquisitor's murderers were being pursued. The prudent old woman saw in an instant all that had to be done. "You can't flee," she said to Cunégonde, "and you have nothing to fear; it isn't you who killed His Eminence; and, moreover, the governor, who loves you, won't permit you to be mistreated; stay." She ran at once to Candide: "Flee," she said, "or within the hour you'll be burned." There was not a moment to lose; but how could he part company with Cunégonde, and where could he seek refuge?

Chapitre **XIV**

Comment Candide et Cacambo furent reçus
chez les jésuites du Paraguay

Candide avait amené de Cadix un valet tel qu'on en trouve beaucoup sur les côtes d'Espagne et dans les colonies. C'était un quart d'Espagnol, né d'un métis dans le Tucuman; il avait été enfant de chœur, sacristain, matelot, moine, facteur, soldat, laquais. Il s'appelait Cacambo, et aimait fort son maître, parce que son maître était un fort bon homme. Il sella au plus vite les deux chevaux andalous. «Allons, mon maître, suivons le conseil de la vieille; partons, et courons sans regarder derrière nous.» Candide versa des larmes: «O ma chère Cunégonde! faut-il vous abandonner dans le temps que M. le gouverneur va faire vos noces! Cunégonde amenée de si loin, que deviendrez-vous?—Elle deviendra ce qu'elle pourra, dit Cacambo; les femmes ne sont jamais embarrassées d'elles; Dieu y pourvoit; courons.—Où me mènes-tu? où allons-nous? que ferons-nous sans Cunégonde? disait Candide.—Par saint Jacques de Compostelle, dit Cacambo, vous alliez faire la guerre aux jésuites; allons la faire pour eux: je sais assez les chemins, je vous mènerai dans leur royaume, ils seront charmés d'avoir un capitaine qui fasse l'exercice à la bulgare; vous ferez une fortune prodigieuse; quand on n'a pas son compte dans un monde, on le trouve dans un autre. C'est un très grand plaisir de voir et de faire des choses nouvelles.

—Tu as donc été déjà dans le Paraguay? dit Candide.

—Eh vraiment, oui! dit Cacambo; j'ai été cuistre dans le collège de l'Assomption, et je connais le gouvernement de Los Padres comme je connais les rues de Cadix. C'est une chose admirable que ce gouvernement. Le royaume a déjà plus de trois cents lieues de diamètre; il est divisé en trente provinces. Los Padres y ont tout, et les peuples rien. C'est le chef-d'œuvre de la raison et de la justice. Pour moi, je ne vois rien de si divin que Los Padres, qui font ici la guerre au roi d'Espagne et au roi de Portugal, et qui en Europe confessent ces rois; qui tuent ici des Espagnols, et qui à Madrid les envoient au ciel: cela me ravit; avançons; vous allez être le plus

CHAPTER XIV

HOW CANDIDE AND CACAMBO WERE RECEIVED
BY THE JESUITS OF PARAGUAY

Candide had brought from Cadiz a valet of a kind found in large numbers on the coasts of Spain and in the colonies. He was a quarter Spanish, born of a half-breed in Tucumán; he had been a choirboy, sexton, sailor, monk, commission agent, soldier and lackey. His name was Cacambo, and he loved his master dearly because his master was a very good man. He saddled the two Andalusian horses as quickly as possible. "Come on, master, let's follow the old woman's advice; let's leave in all haste without looking behind us." Candide shed tears. "O my beloved Cunégonde! must I forsake you just when the governor is about to preside over your wedding! Cunégonde, brought from so far away, what will become of you?" "She'll become what she can," said Cacambo; "women are never at a loss; God provides for them; let's hurry." "Where are you taking me? where are we going? what will we do without Cunégonde?" Candide kept saying. "By Saint James of Compostela," said Cacambo, "you were going to make war on the Jesuits; let's go and make war for them: I know the roads fairly well, I'll take you into their kingdom, they'll be charmed to have a captain who drills troops in the Bulgarian manner; you'll make a vast fortune; when a man doesn't receive his due in one world, he finds it in another. It's a very great pleasure to see and do new things."

"Then you've already been in Paraguay?" said Candide.

"Yes, indeed!" said Cacambo; "I was a serving man in the College of the Assumption, and I know the government of Los Padres[14] as well as I know the streets of Cadiz. It's a wonderful thing, that government. The kingdom is already more than three hundred leagues in diameter; it's divided into thirty provinces. Los Padres have everything there, and the people nothing. It's a masterpiece of reason and justice. As for me, I can imagine nothing so divine as Los Padres, who make war here on the King of Spain and the King of Portugal, and who in Europe are those kings' confessors; who kill the Spaniards here, and who in Madrid send them to heaven; that delights me; come on; you'll be the happiest of all men. How pleased

[14] "The Fathers," i.e., the Jesuits, who were in Paraguay from 1607 to 1767.

heureux de tous les hommes. Quel plaisir auront Los Padres quand ils sauront qu'il leur vient un capitaine qui sait l'exercice bulgare!» Dès qu'ils furent arrivés à la première barrière, Cacambo dit à la garde avancée qu'un capitaine demandait à parler à monseigneur le commandant. On alla avertir la grande garde. Un officier paraguain courut aux pieds du commandant lui donner part de la nouvelle. Candide et Cacambo furent d'abord désarmés; on se saisit de leurs deux chevaux andalous. Les deux étrangers sont introduits au milieu de deux files de soldats; le commandant était au bout, le bonnet à trois cornes en tête, la robe retroussée, l'épée au côté, l'esponton à la main. Il fit un signe; aussitôt vingt-quatre soldats entourent les deux nouveaux venus. Un sergent leur dit qu'il faut attendre, que le commandant ne peut leur parler, que le révérend père provincial ne permet pas qu'aucun Espagnol ouvre la bouche qu'en sa présence, et demeure plus de trois heures dans le pays. «Et où est le révérend père provincial? dit Cacambo.—Il est à la parade après avoir dit sa messe, répondit le sergent; et vous ne pourrez baiser ses éperons que dans trois heures.—Mais, dit Cacambo, M. le capitaine, qui meurt de faim comme moi, n'est point Espagnol, il est Allemand; ne pourrions-nous point déjeuner en attendant Sa Révérence?»

Le sergent alla sur-le-champ rendre compte de ce discours au commandant. «Dieu soit béni! dit ce seigneur; puisqu'il est Allemand, je peux lui parler; qu'on le mène dans ma feuillée.» Aussitôt on conduit Candide dans un cabinet de verdure orné d'une très jolie colonnade de marbre vert et or, et de treillages qui renfermaient des perroquets, des colibris, des oiseaux-mouches, des pintades, et tous les oiseaux les plus rares. Un excellent déjeuner était préparé dans des vases d'or; et tandis que les Paraguains mangèrent du maïs dans des écuelles de bois, en plein champ, à l'ardeur du soleil, le révérend père commandant entra dans la feuillée.

C'était un très beau jeune homme, le visage plein, assez blanc, haut en couleur, le sourcil relevé, l'œil vif, l'oreille rouge, les lèvres vermeilles, l'air fier, mais d'une fierté qui n'était ni celle d'un Espagnol, ni celle d'un jésuite. On rendit à Candide et à Cacambo leurs armes, qu'on leur avait saisies, ainsi que les deux chevaux andalous;

Los Padres will be when they find out that a captain is coming to them who knows the Bulgarian drill!"

As soon as they had arrived at the first border post, Cacambo told the border guard that a captain requested to speak to the commandant. They went to inform the main guard. A Paraguayan officer raced to the feet of the commandant to report the news to him. First, Candide and Cacambo were disarmed; their two Andalusian horses were seized. The two strangers were ushered between two ranks of soldiers; the commandant was at the end, a three-cornered hat on his head, his robe tucked up, a sword at his side and a spontoon in his hand. He made a sign; immediately twenty-four soldiers surrounded the two newcomers. A sergeant told them that they would have to wait, that the commandant could not speak to them, that the reverend father provincial allowed no Spaniard to open his mouth except in his presence, or to remain more than three hours in the country. "And where is the reverend father provincial?" said Cacambo. "He's reviewing his troops after having said mass," replied the sergeant; "and you'll only be able to kiss his spurs in three hours." "But," said Cacambo, "the captain, who's starving like me, isn't a Spaniard at all, he's a German; couldn't we have lunch while waiting for His Reverence?"

The sergeant went at once to report this speech to the commandant. "God be praised!" said this lord; "since he's a German, I can speak to him; have him brought to my bower." Candide was immediately conducted into a leafy bower adorned with a very pretty colonnade of green and gold marble, and trelliswork that caged in parrots, colibris, hummingbirds,[15] guinea fowl and all the rarest species of birds. An excellent luncheon had been prepared in gold vessels; and while the Paraguayans were eating corn from wooden bowls in the open fields in the intense heat of the sun, the reverend father commandant entered the bower.

He was a very handsome young man, full in the face, with a fairish complexion, rosy cheeks, arched eyebrows, bright eyes, pink ears, ruby lips and a haughty manner, but a haughtiness that was neither that of a Spaniard nor that of a Jesuit. The weapons that had been seized and the two Andalusian horses were returned to Candide and

[15] On the authority of the French naturalist Georges, Comte de Buffon (1707–1788), Voltaire makes here and elsewhere in *Candide* a fallacious distinction between *colibris* and *oiseaux-mouches*, both of which are hummingbirds.

Cacambo leur fit manger l'avoine auprès de la feuillée, ayant toujours l'œil sur eux, crainte de surprise. Candide baisa d'abord le bas de la robe du commandant, ensuite ils se mirent à table. «Vous êtes donc Allemand? lui dit le jésuite en cette langue.—Oui, mon révérend père», dit Candide. L'un et l'autre, en prononçant ces paroles, se regardaient avec une extrême surprise et une émotion dont ils n'étaient pas les maîtres. «Et de quel pays d'Allemagne êtes-vous? dit le jésuite.—De la sale province de Westphalie, dit Candide: je suis né dans le château de Thunderten-tronckh.—O Ciel! est-il possible? s'écria le commandant.—Quel miracle! s'écria Candide.—Serait-ce vous? dit le commandant. —Cela n'est pas possible», dit Candide. Ils se laissent tomber tous deux à la renverse, ils s'embrassent, ils versent des ruisseaux de larmes. «Quoi! serait-ce vous, mon révérend père? vous, le frère de la belle Cunégonde! vous, qui fûtes tué par les Bulgares! vous, le fils de M. le baron! vous, jésuite au Paraguay! Il faut avouer que ce monde est une étrange chose. O Pangloss! Pangloss! que vous seriez aise si vous n'aviez pas été pendu!»

Le commandant fit retirer les esclaves nègres et les Paraguains qui servaient à boire dans des gobelets de cristal de roche. Il remercia Dieu et saint Ignace mille fois; il serrait Candide entre ses bras; leurs visages étaient baignés de pleurs. «Vous seriez bien plus étonné, plus attendri, plus hors de vous-même, dit Candide, si je vous disais que Mlle Cunégonde votre sœur, que vous avez crue éventrée, est pleine de santé.—Où?—Dans votre voisinage, chez M. le gouverneur de Buenos Aires; et je venais pour vous faire la guerre.» Chaque mot qu'ils prononcèrent dans cette longue conversation accumulait prodige sur prodige. Leur âme tout entière volait sur leur langue, était attentive dans leurs oreilles et étincelante dans leurs yeux. Comme ils étaient Allemands, ils tinrent table longtemps, en attendant le révérend père provincial; et le commandant parla ainsi à son cher Candide.

Cacambo; Cacambo had them fed oats near the bower, keeping his eye on them, for fear of a surprise attack. First, Candide kissed the hem of the commandant's robe, then they sat down to table. "So you're a German?" said the Jesuit to him in that tongue. "Yes, Reverend Father," said Candide. Both of them, uttering these words, gazed at one another with extreme surprise and an emotion they were unable to master. "And from which region in Germany do you come?" said the Jesuit. "From the foul province of Westphalia," said Candide: "I was born in the country residence of Thunder-Ten-Tronckh." "Heavens! is it possible?" exclaimed the commandant. "What a miracle!" exclaimed Candide. "Could it be you?" said the commandant. "It's not possible," said Candide. They both fell backward in surprise, they embraced one another, they shed floods of tears. "What! could it be you, Reverend Father? you, beautiful Cunégonde's brother! you who were killed by the Bulgarians! you, the baron's son! you, a Jesuit in Paraguay! I must confess that this world is a strange place. O Pangloss! Pangloss! how glad you would be if you hadn't been hanged!"

The commandant ordered the Negro slaves and the Paraguayans who were serving them drinks in rock-crystal goblets to withdraw. He thanked God and Saint Ignatius a thousand times; he clasped Candide in his arms; their faces were bathed in tears. "You would be even more amazed, more affected, more beside yourself," said Candide, "were I to tell you that your sister, Miss Cunégonde, whom you believed to have been disemboweled, is in the best of health." "Where?" "In your vicinity, with the Governor of Buenos Aires; and I was coming to make war on you." Each word that they uttered during this long conversation heaped wonder upon wonder. Their entire souls danced on their tongues, listened in their ears and sparkled in their eyes. As they were Germans, they remained at table for a long time, awaiting the reverend father provincial; and the commandant spoke thus to his dear Candide:

Chapitre XV

Comment Candide tua le frère de sa chère Cunégonde

«J'aurai toute ma vie présent à la mémoire le jour horrible où je vis tuer mon père et ma mère, et violer ma sœur. Quand les Bulgares furent retirés, on ne trouva point cette sœur adorable, et on mit dans une charrette ma mère, mon père et moi, deux servantes et trois petits garçons égorgés, pour nous aller enterrer dans une chapelle de jésuites, à deux lieues du château de mes pères. Un jésuite nous jeta de l'eau bénite; elle était horriblement salée; il en entra quelques gouttes dans mes yeux; le père s'aperçut que ma paupière faisait un petit mouvement: il mit la main sur mon cœur et le sentit palpiter; je fus secouru, et, au bout de trois semaines, il n'y paraissait pas. Vous savez, mon cher Candide, que j'étais fort joli, je le devins encore davantage; aussi le révérend père Croust, supérieur de la maison, prit pour moi la plus tendre amitié; il me donna l'habit de novice; quelque temps après je fus envoyé à Rome. Le père général avait besoin d'une recrue de jeunes jésuites allemands. Les souverains du Paraguay reçoivent le moins qu'ils peuvent de jésuites espagnols; ils aiment mieux les étrangers, dont ils se croient plus maîtres. Je fus jugé propre par le révérend père général pour aller travailler dans cette vigne. Nous partîmes, un Polonais, un Tyrolien et moi. Je fus honoré, en arrivant, du sous-diaconat et d'une lieutenance; je suis aujourd'hui colonel et prêtre. Nous recevons vigoureusement les troupes du roi d'Espagne; je vous réponds qu'elles seront excommuniées et battues. La Providence vous envoie ici pour nous seconder. Mais est-il bien vrai que ma chère sœur Cunégonde soit dans le voisinage, chez le gouverneur de Buenos Aires?» Candide l'assura par serment que rien n'était plus vrai. Leurs larmes recommencèrent à couler.

Le baron ne pouvait se lasser d'embrasser Candide; il l'appelait son frère, son sauveur. «Ah! peut-être, lui dit-il, nous pourrons ensemble, mon cher Candide, entrer en vainqueurs dans la ville, et reprendre ma sœur Cunégonde.—C'est ce que je souhaite, dit Candide; car je comptais l'épouser, et je l'espère encore.—Vous, inso-

Chapter XV

How Candide killed his beloved Cunégonde's brother

"For the rest of my life I shall have present in my memory the horrible day on which I saw my father and mother killed, and my sister raped. When the Bulgarians had withdrawn, that adorable sister of mine was nowhere to be found; and my mother, my father and I, two maidservants and three little boys who'd been butchered were placed in a cart, to take us for burial in a Jesuit chapel two leagues from the country residence of my forefathers. A Jesuit sprinkled some holy water on us; it was horribly salty; a few drops of it got in my eyes; the Jesuit father noticed that my eyelids fluttered: he placed his hand over my heart and felt it beating; I was cared for, and after three weeks there were no signs left of my injuries. You know, my dear Candide, that I was very handsome; I became still more so; thus, Reverend Father Croust,[16] the superior of the house, conceived the most tender friendship for me; he gave me a novice's habit; a short while afterward I was sent to Rome. The father general needed some young German Jesuit recruits. The sovereigns of Paraguay accept as few Spanish Jesuits as they can; they prefer foreigners, over whom they believe themselves to be more fully masters. I was judged suitable by the reverend father general to go to labor in that vineyard. We set out, a Pole, a Tirolean and I. I was honored on arrival with a subdeaconship and a lieutenancy; today I'm a colonel and a priest. We shall give a vigorous reception to the King of Spain's troops; I guarantee you that they'll be excommunicated and defeated. Providence has sent you here to assist us. But is it really true that my dear sister Cunégonde is in the vicinity, at the home of the Governor of Buenos Aires?" Candide swore to him that nothing could be truer. Their tears began to flow once again.

The baron could not tire of embracing Candide; he called him his brother, his savior. "Ah! perhaps, my dear Candide," he said to him, "we shall enter the city together as conquerors and recover my sister Cunégonde." "That's what I desire," said Candide; "for I was intent upon marrying her, and I still hope to do so." "You insolent fellow!"

[16] Antoine Croust, a German Jesuit rector at Colmar with whom Voltaire argued in 1754.

lent! répondit le baron, vous auriez l'impudence d'épouser ma sœur qui a soixante et douze quartiers! Je vous trouve bien effronté d'oser me parler d'un dessein si téméraire!» Candide, pétrifié d'un tel discours, lui répondit: «Mon révérend père, tous les quartiers du monde n'y font rien; j'ai tiré votre sœur des bras d'un Juif et d'un inquisiteur; elle m'a assez d'obligations, elle veut m'épouser. Maître Pangloss m'a toujours dit que les hommes sont égaux, et assurément je l'épouserai.—C'est ce que nous verrons, coquin!» dit le jésuite baron de Thunder-ten-tronckh, et en même temps il lui donna un grand coup du plat de son épée sur le visage. Candide dans l'instant tire la sienne et l'enfonce jusqu'à la garde dans le ventre du baron jésuite; mais, en la retirant toute fumante, il se mit à pleurer: «Hélas! mon Dieu, dit-il, j'ai tué mon ancien maître, mon ami, mon beau-frère; je suis le meilleur homme du monde, et voilà déjà trois hommes que je tue; et dans ces trois il y a deux prêtres.»

Cacambo, qui faisait sentinelle à la porte de la feuillée, accourut. «Il ne nous reste qu'à vendre cher notre vie, lui dit son maître: on va sans doute entrer dans la feuillée, il faut mourir les armes à la main.» Cacambo, qui en avait vu bien d'autres, ne perdit point la tête; il prit la robe de jésuite que portait le baron, la mit sur le corps de Candide, lui donna le bonnet carré du mort, et le fit monter à cheval. Tout cela se fit en un clin d'œil. «Galopons, mon maître; tout le monde vous prendra pour un jésuite qui va donner des ordres; et nous aurons passé les frontières avant qu'on puisse courir après nous.» Il volait déjà en prononçant ces paroles, et en criant en espagnol: «Place, place pour le révérend père colonel.»

replied the baron, "you'd have the impudence to marry my sister who has seventy-two heraldic quarterings! I find it shameless that you dare to speak to me of such a foolhardy scheme!" Candide, stupefied by such a speech, answered him, "Reverend Father, all the quarterings in the world are irrelevant; I saved your sister from the clutches of a Jew and an inquisitor; she's under obligation to me on several counts, she wants to marry me. Master Pangloss always told me that all men are equal, and assuredly I shall marry her." "We'll see about that, rogue!" said the Jesuit Baron Thunder-Ten-Tronckh, at the same time striking him violently on the face with the flat of his sword. In an instant Candide drew his own sword and thrust it up to the hilt in the Jesuit baron's belly; but, withdrawing the smoking blade, he began to weep. "Alas! My God," he said, "I've murdered my former master, my friend, my brother-in-law; I'm the kindest man in the world, and already I've murdered three men; and of these three two were priests."

Cacambo, who was standing watch at the bower door, came running. "There's nothing left for us but to sell our lives dearly," his master said to him: "doubtless they'll come into the bower; we must die weapons in hand." Cacambo, who had seen many similar situations, did not lose his head; he grabbed the Jesuit's robe worn by the baron, put it on Candide, gave him the dead man's square hat, and made him mount his horse. All this happened in the twinkling of an eye. "Let's gallop away, master; everyone will take you for a Jesuit who's going to deliver orders; and we'll have crossed the border before they can chase after us." While pronouncing these words he was already in full flight, crying out in Spanish, "Make way, make way for the reverend father colonel."

Chapitre XVI

Ce qui advint aux deux voyageurs avec deux filles, deux singes et les sauvages nommés Oreillons

Candide et son valet furent au-delà des barrières, et personne ne savait encore dans le camp la mort du jésuite allemand. Le vigilant Cacambo avait eu soin de remplir sa valise de pain, de chocolat, de jambon, de fruits, et de quelques mesures de vin. Ils s'enfoncèrent avec leurs chevaux andalous dans un pays inconnu, où ils ne découvrirent aucune route. Enfin une belle prairie entrecoupée de ruisseaux se présenta devant eux. Nos deux voyageurs font repaître leurs montures. Cacambo propose à son maître de manger, et lui en donne l'exemple. «Comment veux-tu, disait Candide, que je mange du jambon, quand j'ai tué le fils de M. le baron, et que je me vois condamné à ne revoir la belle Cunégonde de ma vie? à quoi me servira de prolonger mes misérables jours, puisque je dois les traîner loin d'elle, dans les remords et dans le désespoir? et que dira le journal de Trévoux?»

En parlant ainsi, il ne laissa pas de manger. Le soleil se couchait. Les deux égarés entendirent quelques petits cris qui paraissaient poussés par des femmes. Ils ne savaient si ces cris étaient de douleur ou de joie; mais ils se levèrent précipitamment avec cette inquiétude et cette alarme que tout inspire dans un pays inconnu. Ces clameurs partaient de deux filles toutes nues qui couraient légèrement au bord de la prairie, tandis que deux singes les suivaient en leur mordant les fesses. Candide fut touché de pitié; il avait appris à tirer chez les Bulgares, et il aurait abattu une noisette dans un buisson sans toucher aux feuilles. Il prend son fusil espagnol à deux coups, tire, et tue les deux singes. «Dieu soit loué, mon cher Cacambo! j'ai délivré d'un grand péril ces deux pauvres créatures; si j'ai commis un péché en tuant un inquisiteur et un jésuite, je l'ai bien réparé en

CHAPTER XVI

WHAT HAPPENED TO THE TWO TRAVELERS WITH TWO GIRLS, TWO MONKEYS AND THE SAVAGES CALLED THE OREILLONS[17]

Candide and his valet were beyond the border posts, and still no one in the camp knew about the death of the German Jesuit. The vigilant Cacambo had taken care to fill his traveling bag with bread, chocolate, ham, fruit and several bottles of wine. On their Andalusian horses they penetrated deep into an unknown country where they could find no road. At last, a beautiful meadow crisscrossed by streams opened up before them. Our two travelers stopped to feed their mounts. Cacambo proposed to his master that they eat, and set him an example. "How can you expect me to eat ham," said Candide, "when I've murdered the baron's son, and find myself doomed never to see the lovely Cunégonde again for the rest of my life? why should I prolong my wretched days, since I must drag them out far from her in remorse and despair? and what will the *Journal de Trévoux*[18] say?"

While speaking thus, he did not neglect to eat. The sun was setting. The two lost travelers heard several little cries that seemed to have been uttered by women. They did not know whether these were cries of pain or joy; but they got up quickly with that disquiet and alarm inspired by all things in an unknown land. Those cries came from two completely naked girls who were running nimbly along the edge of the meadow while two monkeys were following them and biting them on the buttocks. Candide was moved by pity; he had learned to shoot when among the Bulgarians, and he could have hit a hazelnut in a bush without touching the leaves. He picked up his double-barreled Spanish gun, fired and killed the two monkeys. "God be praised, my dear Cacambo! I've delivered those two poor creatures from a great danger; if I committed a sin by killing an inquisitor and a Jesuit, I've thoroughly made amends for it by saving

[17] Voltaire derives this word from Spanish *Orejones* (suggesting large or pierced ears) as used by Garcilaso de la Vega (1539–1616) in his writings on Peru.

[18] A Jesuit publication founded in 1701 and hostile to Voltaire. Its principal editor was Guillaume-Hyacinthe Berthier (1704–1782), lampooned by Voltaire in his *Relation de la mort du jésuite Berthier* [Narrative of the Death of the Jesuit Berthier], written in 1759.

sauvant la vie à deux filles. Ce sont peut-être deux demoiselles de condition, et cette aventure peut nous procurer de très grands avantages dans le pays.»

Il allait continuer, mais sa langue devint percluse quand il vit ces deux filles embrasser tendrement les deux singes, fondre en larmes sur leurs corps et remplir l'air des cris les plus douloureux. «Je ne m'attendais pas à tant de bonté d'âme», dit-il enfin à Cacambo; lequel lui répliqua: «Vous avez fait là un beau chef-d'œuvre, mon maître; vous avez tué les deux amants de ces demoiselles.—Leurs amants! serait-il possible? vous vous moquez de moi, Cacambo; le moyen de vous croire?—Mon cher maître, reprit Cacambo, vous êtes toujours étonné de tout; pourquoi trouvez-vous si étrange que dans quelques pays il y ait des singes qui obtiennent les bonnes grâces des dames? Ils sont des quarts d'hommes, comme je suis un quart d'Espagnol.—Hélas! reprit Candide, je me souviens d'avoir entendu dire à maître Pangloss qu'autrefois pareils accidents étaient arrivés, et que ces mélanges avaient produit des égipans, des faunes, des satyres; que plusieurs grands personnages de l'Antiquité en avaient vu; mais je prenais cela pour des fables.—Vous devez être convaincu à présent, dit Cacambo, que c'est une vérité, et vous voyez comment en usent les personnes qui n'ont pas reçu une certaine éducation; tout ce que je crains, c'est que ces dames ne nous fassent quelque méchante affaire.»

Ces réflexions solides engagèrent Candide à quitter la prairie et à s'enfoncer dans un bois. Il y soupa avec Cacambo; et tous deux, après avoir maudit l'inquisiteur de Portugal, le gouverneur de Buenos Aires et le baron, s'endormirent sur de la mousse. A leur réveil, ils sentirent qu'ils ne pouvaient remuer; la raison en était que pendant la nuit les Oreillons, habitants du pays, à qui les deux dames les avaient dénoncés, les avaient garrottés avec des cordes d'écorce d'arbre. Ils étaient entourés d'une cinquantaine d'Oreillons tout nus, armés de flèches, de massues et de haches de caillou: les uns faisaient bouillir une grande chaudière; les autres préparaient des broches, et tous criaient: «C'est un jésuite, c'est un jésuite! nous serons vengés, et nous ferons bonne chère; mangeons du jésuite, mangeons du jésuite!»

«Je vous l'avais bien dit, mon cher maître, s'écria tristement Cacambo, que ces deux filles nous joueraient un mauvais tour.» Candide, apercevant la chaudière et les broches, s'écria: «Nous allons certainement être rôtis ou bouillis. Ah! que dirait maître Pangloss, s'il voyait comme la pure nature est faite? Toute est bien; soit, mais j'avoue qu'il est bien cruel d'avoir perdu Mlle Cunégonde et d'être mis à la broche par des Oreillons.» Cacambo ne perdait jamais la

the life of two girls. They are perhaps two young ladies of some social standing, and this incident could procure very great advantages for us in this country."

He was about to continue, but his tongue was paralyzed when he saw those two girls embrace the two monkeys tenderly, burst into tears over their bodies and fill the air with the most sorrowful cries. "I wasn't expecting such kindheartedness," he said at last to Cacambo, who answered him, "That's a fine piece of work you've done there, master; you've killed those young ladies' two lovers." "Their lovers! could it be possible? you're making fun of me, Cacambo; how can I believe you?" "My dear master," rejoined Cacambo, "you're always amazed by everything; why do you find it so strange that in some countries monkeys obtain ladies' favors? They're a quarter human, just as I'm a quarter Spanish." "Alas!" rejoined Candide, "I remember having heard Master Pangloss say that in the past similar mishaps had occurred and that these mixtures had produced Aegipans, fauns and satyrs; and that several great personages of antiquity had seen them; but I took all that for fables." "You must now be convinced that it's the truth," said Cacambo, "and you can see how people who haven't had a certain kind of upbringing behave; all I'm afraid of is that those ladies will cause us some trouble."

These sound reflections persuaded Candide to leave the meadow and make his way deep into a wood. He had supper there with Cacambo; and both of them, after having cursed the Inquisitor of Portugal, the Governor of Buenos Aires and the baron, went to sleep on the moss. On waking, they perceived that they were unable to move; the reason for this was that during the night the inhabitants of that land, the Oreillons, to whom the two ladies had denounced them, had tied them down with ropes made of tree bark. They were surrounded by about fifty stark-naked Oreillons, armed with arrows, clubs and stone axes; some were boiling a large cauldron; others were preparing spits, and all were shouting, "It's a Jesuit, it's a Jesuit! we'll be avenged, and we'll have a good meal; let's eat Jesuit, let's eat Jesuit!"

"I told you, my dear master," exclaimed Cacambo gloomily, "that those two girls would do us some mischief." Candide, noticing the cauldron and the spits, exclaimed, "We'll be roasted or boiled for certain. Oh! what would Master Pangloss say, were he to see what the pure state of nature is like? All's well; agreed; but I confess that it's most cruel to have lost Miss Cunégonde and to be cooked on a spit by the Oreillons." At no time did Cacambo lose his head. "Don't

tête. «Ne désespérez de rien, dit-il au désolé Candide; j'entends un peu le jargon de ces peuples, je vais leur parler.—Ne manquez pas, dit Candide, de leur représenter quelle est l'inhumanité affreuse de faire cuire des hommes, et combien cela est peu chrétien.»

«Messieurs, dit Cacambo, vous comptez donc manger aujourd'hui un jésuite: c'est très bien fait; rien n'est plus juste que de traiter ainsi ses ennemis. En effet le droit naturel nous enseigne à tuer notre prochain, et c'est ainsi qu'on en agit dans toute la terre. Si nous n'usons pas du droit de le manger, c'est que nous avons d'ailleurs de quoi faire bonne chère; mais vous n'avez pas les mêmes ressources que nous; certainement il vaut mieux manger ses ennemis que d'abandonner aux corbeaux et aux corneilles le fruit de sa victoire. Mais, Messieurs, vous ne voudriez pas manger vos amis. Vous croyez aller mettre un jésuite en broche, et c'est votre défenseur, c'est l'ennemi de vos ennemis que vous allez rôtir. Pour moi, je suis né dans votre pays; monsieur que vous voyez est mon maître, et, bien loin d'être jésuite, il vient de tuer un jésuite, il en porte les dépouilles: voilà le sujet de votre méprise. Pour vérifier ce que je vous dis, prenez sa robe, portez-la à la première barrière du royaume de Los Padres; informez-vous si mon maître n'a pas tué un officier jésuite. Il vous faudra peu de temps; vous pourrez toujours nous manger si vous trouvez que je vous ai menti. Mais, si je vous ai dit la vérité, vous connaissez trop les principes du droit public, les mœurs et les lois, pour ne nous pas faire grâce.»

Les Oreillons trouvèrent ce discours très raisonnable; ils députèrent deux notables pour aller en diligence s'informer de la vérité; les deux députés s'acquittèrent de leur commission en gens d'esprit, et revinrent bientôt apporter de bonnes nouvelles. Les Oreillons délièrent leurs deux prisonniers, leur firent toutes sortes de civilités, leur offrirent des filles, leur donnèrent des rafraîchissements, et les reconduisirent jusqu'aux confins de leurs Etats, en criant avec allégresse: «Il n'est point jésuite, il n'est point jésuite!»

Candide ne se lassait point d'admirer le sujet de sa délivrance. «Quel peuple! disait-il, quels hommes! quelles mœurs! Si je n'avais pas eu le bonheur de donner un grand coup d'épée au travers du corps du frère de Mlle Cunégonde, j'étais mangé sans rémission. Mais, après tout, la pure nature est bonne, puisque ces gens-ci, au lieu de me manger, m'ont fait mille honnêtetés dès qu'ils ont su que je n'étais pas jésuite.»

despair," he said to the disconsolate Candide; "I understand a little of these people's lingo, I'll speak to them." "Don't neglect," said Candide, "to make plain to them the frightful inhumanity of cooking human beings, and how unchristian it is."

"So, gentlemen," said Cacambo, "you reckon upon eating a Jesuit today: that's fine; nothing is more just than to treat one's enemies that way. Indeed, natural law teaches us to kill our neighbor, and that's how people act all over the world. If we don't exercise the right to eat him, it's only because we have enough other food to make a good meal; but you don't have the same resources as us; certainly it's better to eat one's enemies than to abandon the fruit of victory to the ravens and crows. But, gentlemen, you wouldn't want to eat your friends. You think you're going to put a Jesuit on the spit, and yet it's your defender, it's the enemy of your enemies that you're about to roast. As for me, I was born in your country; the gentleman you see is my master, and, far from being a Jesuit, he's just killed a Jesuit, he's wearing his spoils: that's the cause of your mistake. To verify what I'm telling you, take his robe, carry it to the nearest border post of the kingdom of Los Padres; inquire whether my master hasn't killed a Jesuit officer. It won't take you much time; you can still eat us if you find out that I've lied to you. But if I've told you the truth, you know only too well the principles of public justice, good breeding and laws, not to spare us."

The Oreillons found this speech very reasonable; they delegated two notables to go off in all haste to inquire into the truth; the two delegates performed their errand like intelligent men and soon returned bringing good news. The Oreillons untied their two prisoners, treated them with the utmost civility, offered them some girls, gave them refreshments, and took them back to the confines of their territory, shouting for joy, "He's not a Jesuit, he's not a Jesuit!"

Candide did not tire of marveling at the reason for his deliverance. "What a people!" he said, "what men! what customs! If I hadn't had the good fortune to have run through Miss Cunégonde's brother with my sword, I'd have been eaten with no hope of remission. But, after all, the pure state of nature is good, since these people, instead of eating me, showed me a thousand civilities as soon as they learned that I wasn't a Jesuit."

Chapitre XVII

Arrivée de Candide et de son valet au pays d'Eldorado, et ce qu'ils y virent

Quand ils furent aux frontières des Oreillons: «Vous voyez, dit Cacambo à Candide, que cet hémisphère-ci ne vaut pas mieux que l'autre: croyez-moi, retournons en Europe par le plus court.—Comment y retourner? dit Candide, et où aller? Si je vais dans mon pays, les Bulgares et les Abares y égorgent tout; si je retourne en Portugal, j'y suis brûlé; si nous restons dans ce pays-ci, nous risquons à tout moment d'être mis en broche. Mais comment se résoudre à quitter la partie du monde que Mlle Cunégonde habite?

—Tournons vers la Cayenne, dit Cacambo: nous y trouverons des Français, qui vont par tout le monde; ils pourront nous aider. Dieu aura peut-être pitié de nous.»

Il n'était pas facile d'aller à la Cayenne: ils savaient bien à peu près de quel côté il fallait marcher; mais des montagnes, des fleuves, des précipices, des brigands, des sauvages, étaient partout de terribles obstacles. Leurs chevaux moururent de fatigue; leurs provisions furent consumées; ils se nourrirent un mois entier de fruits sauvages, et se trouvèrent enfin auprès d'une petite rivière bordée de cocotiers, qui soutinrent leur vie et leurs espérances.

Cacambo, qui donnait toujours d'aussi bons conseils que la vieille, dit à Candide: «Nous n'en pouvons plus, nous avons assez marché; j'aperçois un canot vide sur le rivage; emplissons-le de cocos, jetons-nous dans cette petite barque, laissons-nous aller au courant; une rivière mène toujours à quelque endroit habité. Si nous ne trouvons pas des choses agréables, nous trouverons du moins des choses nouvelles.—Allons, dit Candide, recommandons-nous à la Providence.»

Ils voguèrent quelques lieues entre des bords tantôt fleuris, tantôt arides, tantôt unis, tantôt escarpés. La rivière s'élargissait toujours; enfin elle se perdait sous une voûte de rochers épouvantables qui s'élevaient jusqu'au ciel. Les deux voyageurs eurent la hardiesse de s'abandonner aux flots sous cette voûte. Le fleuve, resserré en cet endroit, les porta avec une rapidité et un bruit horrible. Au bout de vingt-quatre heures ils revirent le jour; mais leur canot se fracassa

ARRIVAL OF CANDIDE AND HIS VALET IN THE LAND OF
ELDORADO, AND WHAT THEY SAW THERE

When they were at the Oreillon border, Cacambo said to Candide, "You see, this hemisphere is no better than the other; believe me, we should return to Europe by the shortest route." "How can we return there?" said Candide, "and where can we go? If I return to my own country, the Bulgarians and the Abares will be slaughtering everyone; if I return to Portugal, I'll be burned; if we remain in this country we run the risk of being put on a spit at every moment. But how could I resolve to leave that part of the world in which Miss Cunégonde is living?"

"Let's head toward Cayenne," said Cacambo; "we'll find Frenchmen there, they go everywhere; they'll be able to help us. Perhaps God will take pity on us."

It was not easy to go to Cayenne: they knew roughly in which direction they had to travel; but mountains, rivers, precipices, brigands and savages constituted terrible obstacles everywhere. Their horses died of fatigue; their provisions were consumed; they fed themselves for an entire month on wild fruit, and found themselves at last on the bank of a small river bordered with coconut trees that sustained their lives and their hopes.

Cacambo, who always gave as good advice as the old woman, said to Candide, "We can't go on like this, we've walked far enough; I can see an empty canoe on the bank; let's fill it with coconuts, throw ourselves into that little boat and let ourselves be carried by the current; a river always leads to some inhabited place. If we don't find anything pleasant, at least we'll find something new." "Come on," said Candide, "let's commend ourselves to Providence."

They floated for several leagues between riverbanks that were sometimes covered with flowers, sometimes arid, sometimes flat and sometimes steep. The river grew ever wider; at last it disappeared beneath a vault of frightful rocks that rose high up into the sky. The two travelers had the daring to abandon themselves to the torrent that flowed beneath this vault. The river, which narrowed at this point, carried them along with dreadful rapidity and noise. After twenty-four hours they saw daylight once again; but their canoe was

contre les écueils; il fallut se traîner de rocher en rocher pendant une lieue entière; enfin ils découvrirent un horizon immense, bordé de montagnes inaccessibles. Le pays était cultivé pour le plaisir comme pour le besoin; partout l'utile était agréable. Les chemins étaient couverts ou plutôt ornés de voitures d'une forme et d'une matière brillante, portant des hommes et des femmes d'une beauté singulière, traînés rapidement par de gros moutons rouges qui surpassaient en vitesse les plus beaux chevaux d'Andalousie, de Tétuan et de Méquinez.

«Voilà pourtant, dit Candide, un pays qui vaut mieux que la Westphalie.» Il mit pied à terre avec Cacambo auprès du premier village qu'il rencontra. Quelques enfants du village, couverts de brocarts d'or tout déchirés, jouaient au palet à l'entrée du bourg; nos deux hommes de l'autre monde s'amusèrent à les regarder: leurs palets étaient d'assez larges pièces rondes, jaunes, rouges, vertes, qui jetaient un éclat singulier. Il prit envie aux voyageurs d'en ramasser quelques-uns; c'était de l'or, c'étaient des émeraudes, des rubis, dont le moindre aurait été le plus grand ornement du trône du Mogol. «Sans doute, dit Cacambo, ces enfants sont les fils du roi du pays qui jouent au petit palet.» Le magister du village parut dans ce moment pour les faire rentrer à l'école. «Voilà, dit Candide, le précepteur de la famille royale.»

Les petits gueux quittèrent aussitôt le jeu, en laissant à terre leurs palets et tout ce qui avait servi à leurs divertissements. Candide les ramasse, court au précepteur, et les lui présente humblement, lui faisant entendre par signes que Leurs Altesses Royales avaient oublié leur or et leurs pierreries. Le magister du village, en souriant, les jeta par terre, regarda un moment la figure de Candide avec beaucoup de surprise, et continua son chemin.

Les voyageurs ne manquèrent pas de ramasser l'or, les rubis et les émeraudes. «Où sommes-nous? s'écria Candide; il faut que les enfants des rois de ce pays soient bien élevés, puisqu'on leur apprend à mépriser l'or et les pierreries.» Cacambo était aussi surpris que Candide. Ils approchèrent enfin de la première maison du village; elle était bâtie comme un palais d'Europe. Une foule de monde s'empressait à la porte, et encore plus dans le logis. Une musique

smashed against some rocks; they had to drag themselves from rock to rock for an entire league; at last they discovered a vast horizon bordered by impassable mountains. The land was cultivated both for pleasure and to supply needs; everywhere the useful was at the same time agreeable. The roads were covered, or rather adorned, with splendidly formed carriages made of a glittering material, carrying men and women of singular beauty, and drawn swiftly by large red sheep[19] that surpassed in speed the finest horses of Andalusia, Tétouan and Meknes.

"Now here's a finer land than Westphalia," said Candide. He stopped with Cacambo near the first village he came to. A few children from the village, clothed in ragged gold brocade, were playing at quoits[20] at the entrance to the village; our two men from the other world amused themselves by watching them: the discs they were tossing were rather big and round, yellow, red or green, and sparkled in a singular manner. The travelers felt inclined to pick up a few of them; some were gold, others were emeralds or rubies, the smallest of which would have been the greatest ornament of the Mogul's throne. "Doubtless," said Cacambo, "these children playing at quoits are the sons of the king of this country." The village schoolmaster appeared at that moment to call the children back to school. "There," said Candide, "is the royal family's tutor."

The little ragamuffins immediately abandoned their game, leaving on the ground their quoits and all the other objects that had served for their amusements. Candide picked them up, ran up to the tutor and humbly presented them to him, making him understand by signs that Their Royal Highnesses had forgotten their gold and precious stones. The village schoolmaster, smiling, threw them on the ground, looked at Candide for a moment with considerable surprise and continued on his way.

The travelers did not fail to pick up the gold, rubies and emeralds. "Where are we?" exclaimed Candide; "the children of the kings of this country must be well brought up, since they're taught to scorn gold and precious stones." Cacambo was as surprised as Candide. At last they drew near to the first house in the village; it was built like a European palace. A crowd of people were bustling about at the door, and there were even more inside the dwelling. They could

[19] Now known as llamas or alpacas.
[20] Quoits, narrowly defined, is played with rings. The children here are playing a variation on the game.

très agréable se faisait entendre, et une odeur délicieuse de cuisine se faisait sentir.

Cacambo s'approcha de la porte, et entendit qu'on parlait péruvien; c'était sa langue maternelle: car tout le monde sait que Cacambo était né au Tucuman, dans un village où l'on ne connaissait que cette langue. «Je vous servirai d'interprète, dit-il à Candide; entrons, c'est ici un cabaret.»

Aussitôt deux garçons et deux filles de l'hôtellerie, vêtus de drap d'or, et les cheveux noués avec des rubans, les invitent à se mettre à la table de l'hôte. On servit quatre potages garnis chacun de deux perroquets, un contour bouilli qui pesait deux cents livres, deux singes rôtis d'un goût excellent, trois cents colibris dans un plat, et six cents oiseaux-mouches dans un autre; des ragoûts exquis, des pâtisseries délicieuses; le tout dans des plats d'une espèce de cristal de roche. Les garçons et les filles de l'hôtellerie versaient plusieurs liqueurs faites de canne de sucre.

Les convives étaient pour la plupart des marchands et des voituriers, tous d'une politesse extrême, qui firent quelques questions à Cacambo avec la discrétion la plus circonspecte, et qui répondirent aux siennes d'une manière à le satisfaire.

Quand le repas fut fini, Cacambo crut, ainsi que Candide, bien payer son écot en jetant sur la table de l'hôte deux de ces larges pièces d'or qu'il avait ramassées; l'hôte et l'hôtesse éclatèrent de rire, et se tinrent longtemps les côtés. Enfin ils se remirent: «Messieurs, dit l'hôte, nous voyons bien que vous êtes des étrangers; nous ne sommes pas accoutumés à en voir. Pardonnez-nous si nous nous sommes mis à rire quand vous nous avez offert en paiement les cailloux de nos grands chemins. Vous n'avez pas sans doute de la monnaie du pays, mais il n'est pas nécessaire d'en avoir pour dîner ici. Toutes les hôtelleries établies pour la commodité du commerce sont payées par le gouvernement. Vous avez fait mauvaise chère ici, parce que c'est un pauvre village; mais partout ailleurs vous serez reçus comme vous méritez de l'être.» Cacambo expliquait à Candide tous les discours de l'hôte, et Candide les écoutait avec la même admiration et le même égarement que son ami Cacambo les rendait. «Quel est donc ce pays, disaient-ils l'un et l'autre, inconnu à tout le reste de la terre, et où toute la nature est d'une espèce si différente de la nôtre? C'est probablement le pays où tout va bien; car il faut absolument qu'il y en ait de cette espèce. Et quoi qu'en dît maître Pangloss, je me suis souvent aperçu que tout allait mal en Westphalie.»

hear very pleasant music, and they could smell a delicious aroma of cooking. Cacambo approached the door and heard Peruvian being spoken; that was his mother tongue: for everyone knows that Cacambo was born in Tucumán, in a village where only that language was known. "I'll serve as your interpreter," he said to Candide; "let's go inside, this is an inn."

Immediately two waiters and two waitresses of the inn, dressed in gold cloth, their hair tied with ribbons, invited them to sit down at the host's table. They were served four kinds of soup, each garnished with two parrots, a boiled condor that weighed two hundred pounds, two deliciously tasty roast monkeys, three hundred colibris in one dish and six hundred hummingbirds in another, some exquisite stews and some delicious pastries; everything was served in dishes made from a kind of rock crystal. The waiters and waitresses of the inn poured out several kinds of drink made from sugarcane.

Their table companions were for the most part merchants and carters, all extremely polite, who asked Cacambo a few questions with the most circumspect discretion, and who answered his questions in a most satisfactory manner.

When the meal was over, Cacambo thought, like Candide, that he had fully paid his bill by throwing down on the host's table two of those large pieces of gold he had picked up; the host and the hostess burst out laughing and held their sides for a long while. At last they regained their composure: "Gentlemen," said the host, "it's obvious that you're foreigners; we're not accustomed to seeing any. Excuse us if we began to laugh when you offered us in payment some pebbles from our highways. No doubt you don't have any of our currency, but you don't need any to dine here. All those inns established for the convenience of commerce are paid for by the government. You haven't had a very good meal here, since this is a poor village; but everywhere else you'll be received as you deserve to be." Cacambo explained the host's entire speech to Candide, and Candide listened to it with the same wonder and the same bewilderment with which Cacambo translated it. "What country is this, then," they said to one another, "unknown to the rest of the world, and where all of nature is of a kind so different from our own? It's probably the country where all goes well; for there absolutely must be such a country somewhere. And whatever Master Pangloss said, I often perceived that everything went badly in Westphalia."

Chapitre XVIII

Ce qu'ils virent dans le pays d'Eldorado

Cacambo témoigna à son hôte toute sa curiosité; l'hôte lui dit: «Je suis fort ignorant, et je m'en trouve bien; mais nous avons ici un vieillard retiré de la cour, qui est le plus savant homme du royaume, et le plus communicatif.» Aussitôt il mène Cacambo chez le vieillard. Candide ne jouait plus que le second personnage, et accompagnait son valet. Ils entrèrent dans une maison fort simple, car la porte n'était que d'argent, et les lambris des appartements n'étaient que d'or, mais travaillés avec tant de goût que les plus riches lambris ne l'effaçaient pas. L'antichambre n'était à la vérité incrustée que de rubis et d'émeraudes; mais l'ordre dans lequel tout était arrangé réparait bien cette extrême simplicité.

Le vieillard reçut les deux étrangers sur un sofa matelassé de plumes de colibri, et leur fit présenter des liqueurs dans des vases de diamants; après quoi il satisfit à leur curiosité en ces termes:

« Je suis âgé de cent soixante et douze ans, et j'ai appris de feu mon père, écuyer du roi, les étonnantes révolutions du Pérou dont il avait été témoin. Le royaume où nous sommes est l'ancienne patrie des Incas, qui en sortirent très imprudemment pour aller subjuguer une partie du monde, et qui furent enfin détruits par les Espagnols.

«Les princes de leur famille qui restèrent dans leur pays natal furent plus sages; ils ordonnèrent, du consentement de la nation, qu'aucun habitant ne sortirait jamais de notre petit royaume; et c'est ce qui nous a conservé notre innocence et notre félicité. Les Espagnols ont eu une connaissance confuse de ce pays, ils l'ont appelé El Dorado, et un Anglais, nommé le chevalier Raleigh, en a même approché il y a environ cent années; mais, comme nous sommes entourés de rochers inabordables et de précipices, nous avons toujours été jusqu'à présent à l'abri de la rapacité des nations de l'Europe, qui ont une fureur inconcevable pour les cailloux et pour la fange de notre terre, et qui, pour en avoir, nous tueraient tous jusqu'au dernier.»

La conversation fut longue; elle roula sur la forme du gouvernement, sur les mœurs, sur les femmes, sur les spectacles publics, sur les arts. Enfin Candide, qui avait toujours du goût pour la métaphysique, fit demander par Cacambo si dans le pays il y avait une religion.

Chapter XVIII

What they saw in the land of Eldorado

Cacambo expressed all his curiosity to his host; the host said to him, "I'm extremely ignorant, and I'm happy that way; but we have here an old man retired from the court who is the most learned man in the kingdom, and the most communicative." Immediately he took Cacambo to the old man's house. Candide was merely playing second fiddle now, and accompanied his valet. They entered a very simple house, for the door was only made of silver, and the paneling in the rooms was only gold, although wrought with such good taste that the richest paneling did not surpass it. The antechamber was, to tell the truth, inlaid only with rubies and emeralds; but the order in which everything was arranged made up fully for this extreme simplicity.

The old man received the two foreigners on a sofa stuffed with colibri feathers, and he had them served drinks in diamond vessels; then he satisfied their curiosity in these terms:

"I am one hundred and seventy-two years old, and I learned from my late father, the king's equerry, about the astonishing Peruvian revolutions he had witnessed. This kingdom in which we live is the former home of the Incas, who very imprudently left it to go and subjugate another part of the world, and who were finally wiped out by the Spaniards.

"The princes of their race who remained in their native land were wiser; they ordered, with the consent of the people, that no inhabitant should ever leave our little kingdom; and that has preserved our innocence and our happiness. The Spaniards had a confused knowledge of this land, they named it El Dorado; and an English knight by the name of Raleigh even came near to it about a hundred years ago; but as we're surrounded by impassable crags and cliffs, so far we've always been sheltered from the rapacity of the European nations, who have an inconceivable passion for the pebbles and the mud of our land, and who, to possess them, would kill us to the last man."

The conversation was a long one; it turned on the form of government, the customs, the women, the public spectacles and the arts. Finally Candide, who always had a taste for metaphysics, had Cacambo ask whether there was a religion in that country.

Le vieillard rougit un peu. «Comment donc, dit-il, en pouvez-vous douter? Est-ce que vous nous prenez pour des ingrats?» Cacambo demanda humblement quelle était la religion d'Eldorado. Le vieillard rougit encore. «Est-ce qu'il peut y avoir deux religions? dit-il; nous avons, je crois, la religion de tout le monde: nous adorons Dieu du soir jusqu'au matin.—N'adorez-vous qu'un seul Dieu? dit Cacambo, qui servait toujours d'interprète aux doutes de Candide.—Apparemment, dit le vieillard, qu'il n'y en a ni deux, ni trois, ni quatre. Je vous avoue que les gens de votre monde font des questions bien singulières.» Candide ne se lassait pas de faire interroger ce bon vieillard; il voulut savoir comment on priait Dieu dans l'Eldorado. «Nous ne le prions point, dit le bon et respectable sage; nous n'avons rien à lui demander; il nous a donné tout ce qu'il nous faut; nous le remercions sans cesse.» Candide eut la curiosité de voir des prêtres; il fit demander où ils étaient. Le bon vieillard sourit. «Mes amis, dit-il, nous sommes tous prêtres; le roi et tous les chefs de famille chantent des cantiques d'actions de grâces solennellement tous les matins; et cinq ou six mille musiciens les accompagnent.—Quoi! vous n'avez point de moines qui enseignent, qui disputent, qui gouvernent, qui cabalent, et qui font brûler les gens qui ne sont point de leur avis?—Il faudrait que nous fussions fous, dit le vieillard; nous sommes tous ici du même avis, et nous n'entendons pas ce que vous voulez dire avec vos moines.» Candide à tous ces discours demeurait en extase, et disait en lui-même: «Ceci est bien différent de la Westphalie et du château de monsieur le baron: si notre ami Pangloss avait vu Eldorado, il n'aurait plus dit que le château de Thunder-ten-tronckh était ce qu'il y avait de mieux sur la terre; il est certain qu'il faut voyager.»

Après cette longue conversation, le bon vieillard fit atteler un carrosse à six moutons, et donna douze de ses domestiques aux deux voyageurs pour les conduire à la cour: «Excusez-moi, leur dit-il, si mon âge me prive de l'honneur de vous accompagner. Le roi vous recevra d'une manière dont vous ne serez pas mécontents, et vous pardonnerez sans doute aux usages du pays s'il y en a quelques-uns qui vous déplaisent.»

Candide et Cacambo montent en carrosse; les six moutons volaient, et en moins de quatre heures on arriva au palais du roi, situé à un bout de la capitale. Le portail était de deux cent vingt pieds de haut et de cent de large; il est impossible d'exprimer quelle en était

The old man flushed slightly. "What!" he said, "can you doubt that? Do you take us for ingrates?" Cacambo asked humbly what the religion of Eldorado was. The old man flushed again. "Can there be two religions?" he said; "we have, I believe, the same religion as everybody else: we worship God from dusk to dawn."[21] "Do you worship only one God?" said Cacambo, who continued to serve as the interpreter of Candide's doubts. "Evidently," said the old man, "since there aren't two, or three, or four. I have to admit to you that people from your world ask very peculiar questions." Candide did not tire of having this good old man interrogated; he wanted to know how they prayed to God in Eldorado. "We don't pray to him at all," said the good and respectable sage; "we have nothing to ask of him; he has granted us all we need; we thank him constantly." Candide was curious to see some priests; he had Cacambo ask where they were. The good old man smiled. "My friends," he said, "we're all priests; the king and all the heads of households solemnly sing hymns of thanksgiving every morning; and five or six thousand musicians accompany them." "What! you have no monks who teach, argue, govern, intrigue and have those people burned who aren't of their opinion?" "We'd have to be mad," said the old man; "we're all of the same opinion here, and we don't understand what you mean by monks." Candide was in raptures at all these remarks, and said to himself, "This is very different from Westphalia and the baron's country residence; if our friend Pangloss had seen Eldorado, he would no longer have said that the country residence of Thunder-Ten-Tronckh was the best place on earth; one certainly ought to travel."

After this long conversation, the good old man had a carriage harnessed with six sheep, and assigned twelve of his domestic servants to conduct the two travelers to the court. "Forgive me," he said to them, "if my age deprives me of the honor of accompanying you. The king will receive you in a manner that will not leave you dissatisfied, and no doubt you'll forgive us if there are a few native customs that displease you."

Candide and Cacambo climbed into the carriage; the six sheep sped off, and in less than four hours they arrived at the king's palace, located at one end of the capital. The portal was two hundred and twenty feet high and one hundred feet wide; it is impossible to de-

[21] A deliberate inversion of the expression *du matin jusqu'au soir* (from dawn to dusk).

la matière. On voit assez quelle supériorité prodigieuse elle devait avoir sur ces cailloux et sur ce sable que nous nommons *or* et *pierreries*.

Vingt belles filles de la garde reçurent Candide et Cacambo à la descente du carrosse, les conduisirent aux bains, les vêtirent de robes d'un tissu de duvet de colibri; après quoi les grands officiers et les grandes officières de la couronne les menèrent à l'appartement de Sa Majesté, au milieu de deux files chacune de mille musiciens, selon l'usage ordinaire. Quand ils approchèrent de la salle du trône, Cacambo demanda à un grand officier comment il fallait s'y prendre pour saluer Sa Majesté; si on se jetait à genoux ou ventre à terre; si on mettait les mains sur la tête ou sur le derrière; si on léchait la poussière de la salle; en un mot, quelle était la cérémonie. «L'usage, dit le grand officier, est d'embrasser le roi et de le baiser des deux côtés.» Candide et Cacambo sautèrent au cou de Sa Majesté, qui les reçut avec toute la grâce imaginable, et qui les pria poliment à souper.

En attendant, on leur fit voir la ville, les édifices publics élevés jusqu'aux nues, les marchés ornés de mille colonnes, les fontaines d'eau pure, les fontaines d'eau rose, celles de liqueurs de canne de sucre, qui coulaient continuellement dans de grandes places, pavées d'une espèce de pierreries qui répandaient une odeur semblable à celle du girofle et de la cannelle. Candide demanda à voir la cour de justice, le parlement; on lui dit qu'il n'y en avait point, et qu'on ne plaidait jamais. Il s'informa s'il y avait des prisons, et on lui dit que non. Ce qui le surprit davantage, et qui lui fit le plus de plaisir, ce fut le palais des sciences, dans lequel il vit une galerie de deux mille pas, toute pleine d'instruments de mathématique et de physique.

Après avoir parcouru, toute l'après-dînée, à peu près la millième partie de la ville, on les remena chez le roi. Candide se mit à table entre Sa Majesté, son valet Cacambo et plusieurs dames. Jamais on ne fit meilleure chère, et jamais on n'eut plus d'esprit à souper qu'en eut Sa Majesté. Cacambo expliquait les bons mots du roi à Candide, et, quoique traduits, ils paraissaient toujours des bons mots. De tout ce qui étonnait Candide, ce n'était pas ce qui l'étonna le moins.

Ils passèrent un mois dans cet hospice. Candide ne cessait de dire à Cacambo: «Il est vrai, mon ami, encore une fois, que le château

scribe the material from which it was fashioned. It is easy enough to see what tremendous superiority it must have had over those pebbles and sand we call "gold" and "precious stones."

Twenty beautiful girls of the guard received Candide and Cacambo as they alighted from the carriage, escorted them to the baths and clothed them in robes of a fabric made from colibri down; then the chief male and female officers of the crown led them to His Majesty's suite, taking them, according to custom, between two ranks of a thousand musicians each. As they approached the throne room, Cacambo asked one of the chief officers how they should behave when greeting His Majesty: whether they should throw themselves to their knees or flat on their faces; whether they should put their hands on their heads or on their backsides; whether they should lick the dust on the floor; in short, what the proper ceremony was. "The custom," said the chief officer, "is to embrace the king and to kiss him on both cheeks." Candide and Cacambo flung their arms round the neck of His Majesty, who received them with all imaginable grace and who politely invited them to have supper with him.

In the meantime, they were shown the city: public buildings that touched the clouds, marketplaces adorned with a thousand columns, fountains of pure water, fountains of rose water or of sugar-cane liquors that flowed continuously in the large public squares paved with a kind of precious stone that gave off a scent like that of clove and cinnamon. Candide asked to see the law court, the high judicial court; he was told that there was none, and that no one ever brought a lawsuit. He inquired whether there were any prisons, and was told there were not. What surprised him more, and gave him the most pleasure, was the Palace of Science, in which he saw a gallery two thousand paces long, entirely filled with mathematical and physical instruments.

After having surveyed during the entire afternoon only about a thousandth part of the city, they were brought back to the king's palace. Candide sat down to table with His Majesty, his valet Cacambo and several ladies. Never was finer food eaten and never did anyone have wittier supper conversation than His Majesty. Cacambo explained the king's witty remarks to Candide, and even when translated they always seemed witty. Of all the things that astonished Candide, that did not astonish him the least.

They spent a month in this refuge. Candide did not stop saying to Cacambo, "It's proven true again, my friend, the country residence

où je suis né ne vaut pas le pays où nous sommes; mais enfin Mlle Cunégonde n'y est pas, et vous avez sans doute quelque maîtresse en Europe. Si nous restons ici, nous n'y serons que comme les autres; au lieu que si nous retournons dans notre monde seulement avec douze moutons chargés de cailloux d'Eldorado, nous serons plus riches que tous les rois ensemble, nous n'aurons plus d'inquisiteurs à craindre, et nous pourrons aisément reprendre Mlle Cunégonde.»

Ce discours plut à Cacambo: on aime tant à courir, à se faire valoir chez les siens, à faire parade de ce qu'on a vu dans ses voyages, que les deux heureux résolurent de ne plus l'être et de demander leur congé à Sa Majesté.

«Vous faites une sottise, leur dit le roi; je sais bien que mon pays est peu de chose; mais, quand on est passablement quelque part, il faut y rester; je n'ai pas assurément le droit de retenir des étrangers; c'est une tyrannie qui n'est ni dans nos mœurs, ni dans nos lois: tous les hommes sont libres; partez quand vous voudrez, mais la sortie est bien difficile. Il est impossible de remonter la rivière rapide sur laquelle vous êtes arrivés par miracle, et qui court sous des voûtes de rochers. Les montagnes qui entourent tout mon royaume ont dix mille pieds de hauteur, et sont droites comme des murailles; elles occupent chacune en largeur un espace de plus de dix lieues; on ne peut en descendre que par des précipices. Cependant, puisque vous voulez absolument partir, je vais donner ordre aux intendants des machines d'en faire une qui puisse vous transporter commodément. Quand on vous aura conduits au revers des montagnes, personne ne pourra vous accompagner; car mes sujets ont fait vœu de ne jamais sortir de leur enceinte, et ils sont trop sages pour rompre leur vœu. Demandez-moi d'ailleurs tout ce qu'il vous plaira.—Nous ne demandons à Votre Majesté, dit Cacambo, que quelques moutons chargés de vivres, de cailloux, et de la boue du pays.» Le roi rit. «Je ne conçois pas, dit-il, quel goût vos gens d'Europe ont pour notre boue jaune; mais emportez-en tant que vous voudrez, et grand bien vous fasse.»

Il donna l'ordre sur-le-champ à ses ingénieurs de faire une machine pour guinder ces deux hommes extraordinaires hors du royaume. Trois mille bons physiciens y travaillèrent; elle fut prête au bout de quinze jours, et ne coûta pas plus de vingt millions de livres sterling, monnaie du pays. On mit sur la machine Candide et Cacambo; il y avait deux grands moutons rouges sellés et bridés pour leur servir de monture quand ils auraient franchi les montagnes, vingt moutons de bât chargés de vivres, trente qui portaient des présents de ce que le pays a de plus curieux, et cinquante chargés

where I was born cannot compare with this country; but, after all, Miss Cunégonde isn't here, and no doubt you have some mistress in Europe. If we remain here, we'll only be like everyone else; whereas if we return to our world with only twelve sheep laden with pebbles from Eldorado, we'll be wealthier than all the kings together, we'll have no more inquisitors to fear, and we'll easily be able to recover Miss Cunégonde."

This speech pleased Cacambo: a man likes so much to travel, then to show off among his own people, to brag about what he has seen on his travels; and so the two fortunates made up their minds to be fortunate no longer and to ask His Majesty for permission to leave.

"You're doing a foolish thing," the king said to them; "I know my country isn't much to speak of; but when one is tolerably well off somewhere, one should stay there; I certainly don't have the right to make foreigners stay: that is an act of tyranny that is neither part of our customs nor our laws; all men are free; leave when you wish, but the way out is very difficult. It's impossible to go back up the fast-flowing river on which, by a miracle, you arrived, and which flows beneath vaults of rock. The mountains that surround my entire kingdom are ten thousand feet high and are as sheer as walls; they're each over ten leagues wide; the descent is possible only down cliffs. However, since you absolutely insist upon leaving, I'll give orders to the engineers to construct a machine that will be able to transport you in comfort. When you've been conducted to the other side of the mountains, no one will be able to accompany you any further; for my subjects have vowed never to go beyond that perimeter, and they're too wise to break their vow. However, ask of me anything else you please." "We ask nothing of Your Majesty," said Cacambo, "except a few sheep laden with some provisions and some pebbles and mud from your country." The king laughed. "I can't understand," he said, "what liking you Europeans have for our yellow mud; but take as much of it as you want, and much good may it do you!"

He gave the order at once to his engineers to construct a machine to hoist those two extraordinary men out of the kingdom. Three thousand fine physicists worked at it; it was ready in two weeks, and cost no more than twenty million pounds sterling in the currency of that country. Candide and Cacambo were placed on the machine; there were two large red sheep, saddled and bridled, to serve as their mounts when they had crossed the mountains, twenty pack sheep laden with provisions, thirty carrying gifts of the most unusual things

d'or, de pierreries et de diamants. Le roi embrassa tendrement les deux vagabonds.

Ce fut un beau spectacle que leur départ, et la manière ingénieuse dont ils furent hissés, eux et leurs moutons, au haut des montagnes. Les physiciens prirent congé d'eux après les avoir mis en sûreté, et Candide n'eut plus d'autre désir et d'autre objet que d'aller présenter ses moutons à Mlle Cunégonde. «Nous avons, dit-il, de quoi payer le gouverneur de Buenos Aires, si Mlle Cunégonde peut être mise à prix. Marchons vers la Cayenne, embarquons-nous, et nous verrons ensuite quel royaume nous pourrons acheter.»

Chapitre XIX

Ce qui leur arriva à Surinam, et comment Candide fit connaissance avec Martin

La première journée de nos deux voyageurs fut assez agréable. Ils étaient encouragés par l'idée de se voir possesseurs de plus de trésors que l'Asie, l'Europe et l'Afrique n'en pouvaient rassembler. Candide, transporté, écrivit le nom de Cunégonde sur les arbres. A la seconde journée deux de leurs moutons s'enfoncèrent dans des marais, et y furent abîmés avec leurs charges; deux autres moutons moururent de fatigue quelques jours après; sept ou huit périrent ensuite de faim dans un désert; d'autres tombèrent au bout de quelques jours dans des précipices. Enfin, après cent jours de marche, il ne leur resta que deux moutons. Candide dit à Cacambo: «Mon ami, vous voyez comme les richesses de ce monde sont périssables; il n'y a rien de solide que la vertu et le bonheur de revoir Mlle Cunégonde.—Je l'avoue, dit Cacambo; mais il nous reste encore deux moutons avec plus de trésors que n'en aura jamais le roi d'Espagne, et je vois de loin une ville que je soupçonne être Surinam, appartenant aux Hollandais. Nous sommes au bout de nos peines et au commencement de notre félicité.»

En approchant de la ville, ils rencontrèrent un nègre étendu par terre, n'ayant plus que la moitié de son habit, c'est-à-dire d'un caleçon de toile bleue; il manquait à ce pauvre homme la jambe gauche

to be found in that country, and fifty laden with gold, precious stones and diamonds. The king affectionately embraced the two rovers.

Their departure was a fine sight, as was the ingenious manner in which both they and their sheep were hoisted to the top of the mountains. The physicists took leave of them after having got them out of harm's way, and Candide had no other desire and no other objective than to go and present his sheep to Miss Cunégonde. "We have enough," he said, "to pay the Governor of Buenos Aires, if a price can be set on Miss Cunégonde. Let's travel toward Cayenne, embark there and then we'll see which kingdom we can buy."

Chapter XIX

What happened to them at Surinam, and how Candide made the acquaintance of Martin

The first day was fairly pleasant for our two travelers. They were encouraged by the thought of seeing themselves the possessors of more treasure than could be amassed by all Asia, Europe and Africa. Candide, in raptures, wrote Cunégonde's name on the trees. On the second day, two of their sheep got stuck in a swamp and were swallowed up there with their loads; two more sheep died of exhaustion a few days later; then seven or eight perished from hunger in a desert; some others fell down some precipices after a few more days. Finally, after a hundred days of travel, they had only two sheep left. Candide said to Cacambo, "My friend, you see how perishable are the riches of this world; there's nothing permanent except virtue and the happiness of seeing Miss Cunégonde again." "I admit that," said Cacambo; "but we still have two sheep left with more treasure than the King of Spain will ever possess, and I see in the distance a town that I surmise to be Surinam, which belongs to the Dutch. We're at the end of our troubles and the beginning of our happiness."

Approaching the town, they came across a Negro stretched out on the ground with only half his outfit left on him, that is to say, the remnants of a pair of blue cloth shorts; this poor man was missing

et la main droite. «Eh, mon Dieu! lui dit Candide en hollandais, que fais-tu là, mon ami, dans l'état horrible où je te vois?—J'attends mon maître, monsieur Vanderdendur, le fameux négociant, répondit le nègre.—Est-ce M. Vanderdendur, dit Candide, qui t'a traité ainsi?—Oui, Monsieur, dit le nègre, c'est l'usage. On nous donne un caleçon de toile pour tout vêtement deux fois l'année. Quand nous travaillons aux sucreries, et que la meule nous attrape le doigt, on nous coupe la main; quand nous voulons nous enfuir, on nous coupe la jambe: je me suis trouvé dans les deux cas. C'est à ce prix que vous mangez du sucre en Europe. Cependant, lorsque ma mère me vendit dix écus patagons sur la côte de Guinée, elle me disait: «Mon cher enfant, bénis nos fétiches, adore-les toujours, ils te «feront vivre heureux; tu as l'honneur d'être esclave de nos seigneurs «les blancs, et tu fais par là la fortune de ton père et de ta mère.» Hélas! je ne sais pas si j'ai fait leur fortune, mais ils n'ont pas fait la mienne. Les chiens, les singes et les perroquets sont mille fois moins malheureux que nous. Les fétiches hollandais qui m'ont converti me disent tous les dimanches que nous sommes tous enfants d'Adam, blancs et noirs. Je ne suis pas généalogiste; mais, si ces prêcheurs disent vrai, nous sommes tous cousins issus de germains. Or vous m'avouerez qu'on ne peut pas en user avec ses parents d'une manière plus horrible.

—O Pangloss! s'écria Candide, tu n'avais pas deviné cette abomination; c'en est fait, il faudra qu'à la fin je renonce à ton optimisme.—Qu'est-ce qu'optimisme? disait Cacambo.—Hélas! dit Candide, c'est la rage de soutenir que tout est bien quand on est mal.» Et il versait des larmes en regardant son nègre, et, en pleurant, il entra dans Surinam.

La première chose dont ils s'informent, c'est s'il n'y a point au port quelque vaisseau qu'on pût envoyer à Buenos Aires. Celui à qui ils s'adressèrent était justement un patron espagnol, qui s'offrit à faire avec eux un marché honnête. Il leur donna rendez-vous dans un cabaret. Candide et le fidèle Cacambo allèrent l'y attendre avec leurs deux moutons.

Candide, qui avait le cœur sur les lèvres, conta à l'Espagnol toutes ses aventures, et lui avoua qu'il voulait enlever Mlle Cunégonde. «Je me garderai bien de vous passer à Buenos Aires, dit le patron: je serais pendu et vous aussi. La belle Cunégonde est la maîtresse favo-

his left leg and his right hand. "My God!" Candide said to him in Dutch, "what are you doing there, my friend, in such a terrible state?" "I'm waiting for my master, Mr. Vanderdendur,[22] the famous merchant," replied the Negro. "Was it Mr. Vanderdendur who treated you in this way?" said Candide. "Yes, sir," said the Negro, "it's the custom. We're given a pair of cloth shorts twice a year as all our clothing. If, when we're working at the sugar mills, we get one of our fingers caught in the grindstone, our hand is cut off; if we try to run away, one of our legs is cut off: I've been in both predicaments. That's the price for your eating sugar in Europe. However, when my mother sold me for ten Patagonian crowns on the coast of Guinea, she said to me, 'My dear child, praise our fetishes, worship them always, they'll bring you a happy life; you have the honor to be a slave of our lords, the whites, and thereby you're making your mother and father's fortune.' Alas! I don't know if I've made their fortune, but they didn't make mine. Dogs, monkeys and parrots are a thousand times less unfortunate than we are. The Dutch fetishes who converted me tell me every Sunday that we're all children of Adam, both blacks and whites. I'm no genealogist; but if those preachers speak the truth, we're all first cousins once removed. Now, you'll admit to me that one couldn't treat one's relatives more horribly."

"O Pangloss!" exclaimed Candide, "you hadn't guessed at this abomination; it's decided, I'll have to renounce your optimism at last." "What is optimism?" said Cacambo. "Alas!" said Candide, "it's the mania for affirming that all's well when you're in a bad way." And he shed tears as he looked at the Negro, and he was still weeping when he entered Surinam.

The first thing they inquired into was whether there was any ship in the harbor that could be sent to Buenos Aires. The very man they spoke to proved to be a Spanish captain, who offered to make an honest bargain with them. He arranged to meet with them at an inn. Candide and the faithful Cacambo went there with their two sheep to wait for him.

Candide, who always spoke from the heart, related all his adventures to the Spaniard and admitted to him that he wanted to carry off Miss Cunégonde. "I certainly won't take you to Buenos Aires," said the captain; "I'd be hanged, and so would you. The beautiful

[22] An allusion to a Dutch bookseller named Van Duren with whom Voltaire had argued on financial matters.

rite de monseigneur.» Ce fut un coup de foudre pour Candide; il pleura longtemps; enfin il tira à part Cacambo: «Voici, mon cher ami, lui dit-il, ce qu'il faut que tu fasses. Nous avons chacun dans nos poches pour cinq ou six millions de diamants; tu es plus habile que moi; va prendre Mlle Cunégonde à Buenos Aires. Si le gouverneur fait quelques difficultés, donne-lui un million; s'il ne se rend pas, donne-lui en deux; tu n'as point tué d'inquisiteur, on ne se défiera point de toi. J'équiperai un autre vaisseau; j'irai t'attendre à Venise; c'est un pays libre où l'on n'a rien à craindre ni des Bulgares, ni des Abares, ni des Juifs, ni des inquisiteurs.» Cacambo applaudit à cette sage résolution. Il était au désespoir de se séparer d'un bon maître, devenu son ami intime; mais le plaisir de lui être utile l'emporta sur la douleur de le quitter. Ils s'embrassèrent en versant des larmes. Candide lui recommanda de ne point oublier la bonne vieille. Cacambo partit dès le jour même: c'était un très bon homme que ce Cacambo.

Candide resta encore quelque temps à Surinam, et attendit qu'un autre patron voulût le mener en Italie, lui et les deux moutons qui lui restaient. Il prit des domestiques, et acheta tout ce qui lui était nécessaire pour un long voyage; enfin monsieur Vanderdendur, maître d'un gros vaisseau, vint se présenter à lui. «Combien voulez-vous, demanda-t-il à cet homme, pour me mener en droiture à Venise, moi, mes gens, mon bagage, et les deux moutons que voilà?» Le patron s'accorda à dix mille piastres. Candide n'hésita pas.

«Oh! oh! dit à part soi le prudent Vanderdendur, cet étranger donne dix mille piastres tout d'un coup! il faut qu'il soit bien riche.» Puis, revenant un moment après, il signifia qu'il ne pouvait partir à moins de vingt mille. «Eh bien, vous les aurez», dit Candide.

«Ouais! se dit tout bas le marchand, cet homme donne vingt mille piastres aussi aisément que dix mille.» Il revint encore, et dit qu'il ne pouvait le conduire à Venise à moins de trente mille piastres. «Vous en aurez donc trente mille», répondit Candide. «Oh! oh! se dit encore le marchand hollandais, trente mille piastres ne coûtent rien à cet homme-ci; sans doute les deux moutons portent des trésors immenses; n'insistons pas davantage: faisons-nous d'abord payer les trente mille piastres, et puis nous verrons.» Candide vendit deux petits diamants, dont le moindre valait plus que tout l'argent que demandait le patron. Il le paya d'avance. Les deux moutons furent

Cunégonde is the governor's favorite mistress." Candide was thunderstruck; he wept for a long time; at last he drew Cacambo to one side. "Here's what you must do, my dear friend," he said to him. "We each have diamonds worth five or six million in our pockets; you're cleverer than I; go and get Miss Cunégonde from Buenos Aires. If the governor makes any difficulties, give him a million; if he still won't yield, give him two million; you haven't killed an inquisitor, no one will suspect you. I'll fit out another ship; I'll go to wait for you in Venice; it's a free country where there's nothing to fear from Bulgarians, Abares, Jews or inquisitors." Cacambo praised this wise decision. He was very sorry to have to part company with a good master who had become his intimate friend; but the pleasure of being of use to him prevailed over the sorrow of leaving him. Shedding tears, they embraced one another. Candide urged him not to forget the good old woman. Cacambo departed that same day: he was a very fine fellow, that Cacambo.

Candide remained a little while longer in Surinam, waiting for another captain who would take him to Italy, both him and the two sheep he had left. He hired some servants and bought everything he would need for a long voyage; finally, Mr. Vanderdendur, the master of a large ship, came to introduce himself to him. "How much do you want," Candide asked this man, "to take me straight to Venice, me, my servants, my baggage and those two sheep there?" The captain agreed to ten thousand piasters. Candide didn't hesitate to accept.

"Aha!" said the prudent Vanderdendur to himself, "this foreigner is prepared to give ten thousand piasters right away! he must be very wealthy." Then, returning a moment later, he made it clear that he couldn't go for less than twenty thousand. "Well, you'll have them," said Candide.

"Well now!" the merchant said to himself under his breath, "this fellow gives twenty thousand piasters as easily as ten thousand." He came back again and said that he could not take him to Venice for less than thirty thousand piasters. "Then you'll have thirty thousand," replied Candide. "Aha!" the Dutch merchant said to himself again, "thirty thousand piasters seem to cost this man here nothing; no doubt the two sheep are carrying immense treasures; let's not insist any further; let's first have him pay the thirty thousand piasters, and then we'll see." Candide sold two small diamonds, the lesser of which was worth more than all the money the captain was asking. He paid him in advance. The two sheep were taken on board. Can-

embarqués. Candide suivait dans un petit bateau pour joindre le vaisseau à la rade; le patron prend son temps, met à la voile, démarre; le vent le favorise. Candide, éperdu et stupéfait, le perd bientôt de vue. «Hélas! cria-t-il, voilà un tour digne de l'ancien monde.» Il retourne au rivage, abîmé dans la douleur; car enfin il avait perdu de quoi faire la fortune de vingt monarques.

Il se transporte chez le juge hollandais; et, comme il était un peu troublé, il frappe rudement à la porte; il entre, expose son aventure, et crie un peu plus haut qu'il ne convenait. Le juge commença par lui faire payer dix mille piastres pour le bruit qu'il avait fait. Ensuite il l'écouta patiemment, lui promit d'examiner son affaire sitôt que le marchand serait revenu, et se fit payer dix mille autres piastres pour les frais de l'audience.

Ce procédé acheva de désespérer Candide; il avait à la vérité essuyé des malheurs mille fois plus douloureux; mais le sang-froid du juge et celui du patron dont il était volé, alluma sa bile, et le plongea dans une noire mélancolie. La méchanceté des hommes se présentait à son esprit dans toute sa laideur; il ne se nourrissait que d'idées tristes. Enfin, un vaisseau français étant sur le point de partir pour Bordeaux, comme il n'avait plus de moutons chargés de diamants à embarquer, il loua une chambre du vaisseau à juste prix, et fit signifier dans la ville qu'il paierait le passage, la nourriture, et donnerait deux mille piastres à un honnête homme qui voudrait faire le voyage avec lui, à condition que cet homme serait le plus dégoûté de son état et le plus malheureux de la province.

Il se présenta une foule de prétendants qu'une flotte n'aurait pu contenir. Candide voulant choisir entre les plus apparents, il distingua une vingtaine de personnes qui lui paraissaient assez sociables, et qui toutes prétendaient mériter la préférence. Il les assembla dans son cabaret, et leur donna à souper, à condition que chacun ferait serment de raconter fidèlement son histoire, promettant de choisir celui qui lui paraîtrait le plus à plaindre et le plus mécontent de son état à plus juste titre, et de donner aux autres quelques gratifications.

La séance dura jusqu'à quatre heures du matin. Candide, en écoutant toutes leurs aventures, se ressouvenait de ce que lui avait dit la vieille en allant à Buenos Aires, et de la gageure qu'elle avait faite, qu'il n'y avait personne sur le vaisseau à qui il ne fût arrivé de très grands malheurs. Il songeait à Pangloss à chaque aventure qu'on lui

dide was following in a small boat to join the ship in the roadstead; the captain seized his opportunity, set sail and weighed anchor; the wind favored him. Candide, distraught and astounded, soon lost sight of him. "Alas!" he cried, "that's a trick worthy of the old world." He returned to shore, overwhelmed with sorrow; for, after all, he had lost enough to make the fortune of twenty monarchs.

He went to the house of the Dutch magistrate; and, as he was a little unsettled, he knocked loudly at the door; he went in, explained what had happened to him and shouted a little louder than was fitting. The magistrate began by making him pay ten thousand piasters for the noise he had made. Then he listened to him patiently, promised to examine his case as soon as the merchant returned, and made him pay another ten thousand piasters for the expenses of the hearing.

That proceeding put the finishing touch to Candide's despair; he had, to tell the truth, endured misfortunes a thousand times more painful; but the cold-bloodedness of the magistrate and of the captain who had robbed him roused his anger and plunged him into a black melancholy. The wickedness of men presented itself to his mind in all its ugliness; he entertained nothing but gloomy thoughts. Finally, a French ship being on the point of departing for Bordeaux, and since he had no more sheep laden with diamonds to take on board, he rented a cabin at a fair price, and had it announced in the town that he would pay for the passage and food and give two thousand piasters to an honest man who would make the voyage with him, provided that this man was the most disgusted with his condition and the most unfortunate in the province.

A crowd of applicants greater than could have been held by an entire fleet presented themselves. Candide, wishing to choose from among the most suitable ones, selected about twenty persons who appeared to him sociable enough and who all claimed to merit his preference. He assembled them at his inn and gave them supper on condition that each of them would swear to relate his story faithfully; he promised to choose the one who seemed to him the most deserving of pity and the most justly discontented with his condition, and to give the others some recompense.

The meeting lasted until four o'clock in the morning. Candide, listening to all their adventures, remembered what the old woman had told him on the way to Buenos Aires, and the wager she had made that there was no one on the ship who had not suffered very great misfortunes. He mused on Pangloss as each adventure was

contait. «Ce Pangloss, disait-il, serait bien embarrassé à démontrer son système. Je voudrais qu'il fût ici. Certainement, si tout va bien, c'est dans Eldorado, et non pas dans le reste de la terre.» Enfin il se détermina en faveur d'un pauvre savant qui avait travaillé dix ans pour les libraires d'Amsterdam. Il jugea qu'il n'y avait point de métier au monde dont on dût être plus dégoûté.

Ce savant, qui était d'ailleurs un bon homme, avait été volé par sa femme, battu par son fils, et abandonné de sa fille qui s'était fait enlever par un Portugais. Il venait d'être privé d'un petit emploi duquel il subsistait; et les prédicants de Surinam le persécutaient parce qu'ils le prenaient pour un socinien. Il faut avouer que les autres étaient pour le moins aussi malheureux que lui; mais Candide espérait que le savant le désennuierait dans le voyage. Tous ses autres rivaux trouvèrent que Candide leur faisait une grande injustice; mais il les apaisa en leur donnant à chacun cent piastres.

CHAPITRE XX

CE QUI ARRIVA SUR MER À CANDIDE ET À MARTIN

Le vieux savant, qui s'appelait Martin, s'embarqua donc pour Bordeaux avec Candide. L'un et l'autre avaient beaucoup vu et beaucoup souffert; et quand le vaisseau aurait dû faire voile de Surinam au Japon par le cap de Bonne-Espérance, ils auraient eu de quoi s'entretenir du mal moral et du mal physique pendant tout le voyage.

Cependant Candide avait un grand avantage sur Martin, c'est qu'il espérait toujours revoir Mlle Cunégonde, et que Martin n'avait rien à espérer; de plus, il avait de l'or et des diamants; et, quoiqu'il eût perdu cent gros moutons rouges chargés des plus grands trésors de la terre, quoiqu'il eût toujours sur le cœur la friponnerie du patron hollandais, cependant, quand il songeait à ce qui lui restait dans ses poches, et quand il parlait de Cunégonde, surtout à la fin du repas, il penchait alors pour le système de Pangloss.

«Mais vous, monsieur Martin, dit-il au savant, que pensez-vous

related to him. "That Pangloss," he said, "would be hard put to prove his system. I wish he were here. Certainly, if all's well anywhere, it's in Eldorado, and nowhere else in the world." Finally he decided in favor of a poor scholar who had worked for ten years for the booksellers in Amsterdam. He deemed that there was no profession in the world with which one could possibly be more disgusted.

This scholar, who was moreover a good man, had been robbed by his wife, beaten by his son and abandoned by his daughter who had eloped with a Portuguese. He had just been deprived of a small job on which he relied for his livelihood; and the preachers in Surinam were persecuting him because they took him for a Socinian. It must be admitted that the others were at least as unfortunate as he; but Candide hoped that the scholar would keep him from getting bored during the voyage. All the scholar's rivals thought that Candide was doing them a great injustice; but he appeased them by giving them each a hundred piasters.

Chapter XX

What happened to Candide and Martin at sea

So the old scholar, whose name was Martin, embarked for Bordeaux with Candide. They had both seen a great deal and suffered a great deal, and were the ship to have sailed from Surinam to Japan by way of the Cape of Good Hope, they would have had enough to talk to one another about on the subjects of moral evil and physical evil during the entire voyage.

However, Candide had one great advantage over Martin, that is, he still hoped to see Miss Cunégonde again, while Martin had nothing to hope for; moreover, he had some gold and diamonds; and, although he had lost a hundred large red sheep laden with the greatest treasures on earth, although he still had the Dutch captain's roguery on his mind, nevertheless, when he thought about what he had left in his pockets, and when he spoke of Cunégonde, especially at the end of a meal, then he inclined toward Pangloss's system.

"But you, Monsieur Martin," he said to the scholar, "what do you

de tout cela? Quelle est votre idée sur le mal moral et le mal physique?—Monsieur, répondit Martin, mes prêtres m'ont accusé d'être socinien; mais la vérité du fait est que je suis manichéen.—Vous vous moquez de moi, dit Candide, il n'y a plus de manichéens dans le monde.—Il y a moi, dit Martin; je ne sais qu'y faire, mais je ne peux penser autrement.—Il faut que vous ayez le diable au corps, dit Candide.—Il se mêle si fort des affaires de ce monde, dit Martin, qu'il pourrait bien être dans mon corps, comme partout ailleurs; mais je vous avoue qu'en jetant la vue sur ce globe, ou plutôt sur ce globule, je pense que Dieu l'a abandonné à quelque être malfaisant; j'en excepte toujours Eldorado. Je n'ai guère vu de ville qui ne désirât la ruine de la ville voisine, point de famille qui ne voulût exterminer quelque autre famille. Partout les faibles ont en exécration les puissants devant lesquels ils rampent, et les puissants les traitent comme des troupeaux dont on vend la laine et la chair. Un million d'assassins enrégimentés, courant d'un bout de l'Europe à l'autre, exerce le meurtre et le brigandage avec discipline pour gagner son pain, parce qu'il n'a pas de métier plus honnête; et dans les villes qui paraissent jouir de la paix et où les arts fleurissent, les hommes sont dévorés de plus d'envie, de soins et d'inquiétudes qu'une ville assiégée n'éprouve de fléaux. Les chagrins secrets sont encore plus cruels que les misères publiques. En un mot, j'en ai tant vu, et tant éprouvé, que je suis manichéen.

—Il y a pourtant du bon, répliquait Candide.—Cela peut être, disait Martin, mais je ne le connais pas.»

Au milieu de cette dispute, on entendit un bruit de canon. Le bruit redouble de moment en moment. Chacun prend sa lunette. On aperçoit deux vaisseaux qui combattaient à la distance d'environ trois milles; le vent les amena l'un et l'autre si près du vaisseau français qu'on eut le plaisir de voir le combat tout à son aise. Enfin l'un des deux vaisseaux lâcha à l'autre une bordée si bas et si juste qu'il le coula à fond. Candide et Martin aperçurent distinctement une centaine d'hommes sur le tillac du vaisseau qui s'enfonçait; ils levaient tous les mains au ciel et jetaient des clameurs effroyables; en un moment tout fut englouti.

«Eh bien, dit Martin, voilà comme les hommes se traitent les uns les autres.—Il est vrai, dit Candide, qu'il y a quelque chose de diabolique dans cette affaire.» En parlant ainsi, il aperçut je ne sais quoi d'un rouge éclatant qui nageait auprès de son vaisseau. On détacha la chaloupe pour voir ce que ce pouvait être: c'était un de ses moutons. Candide eut plus de joie de retrouver ce mouton qu'il

think of all this? What is your conception of moral evil and physical evil?" "Sir," replied Martin, "my priests accused me of being a Socinian; but the truth of the matter is that I'm a Manichaean." "You're making fun of me," said Candide, "there are no more Manichaeans in the world." "There's me," said Martin; "I don't know what to do about it, but I can't think differently." "You must be possessed by the devil," said Candide. "He meddles so much in the affairs of this world," said Martin, "that he could well be inside me, just as he's everywhere else; but I confess to you that in casting my eye over this globe, or rather over this globule, I think God has abandoned it to some maleficent being—always excepting Eldorado. I've hardly ever seen a town that didn't desire the ruin of some neighboring town, I've never seen a family that didn't want to exterminate some other family. Everywhere the weak abhor the strong before whom they grovel, and the strong treat them like flocks whose wool and flesh are to be sold. A million assassins formed into regiments, running from one end of Europe to the other, carry out murder and robbery in a disciplined fashion to earn their bread, because there's no more honest employment; and in towns that appear to enjoy peace, and where the arts flourish, men are consumed by more envy, cares and anxieties than the calamities suffered by a besieged town. Private afflictions are even more grievous than public miseries. In a word, I've seen so much and gone through so much that I've become a Manichaean."

"But there is some good," replied Candide. "That may be," said Martin, "but I'm not acquainted with it."

In the middle of this debate they heard a sound of gunfire. The sound increased from moment to moment. Everyone took up his telescope. At a distance of about three miles could be seen two ships fighting; the wind brought them both so close to the French ship that the passengers had the pleasure of watching the fight in comfort. Finally one of the two ships fired a broadside so low and so accurate at the other ship that it sank it. Candide and Martin perceived distinctly about a hundred men on the deck of the sinking ship; they were all raising their hands to heaven and were uttering dreadful cries; an instant later they had all been engulfed.

"Well," said Martin, "that's how human beings treat one another."
"It's true," said Candide, "that there's something diabolical in that business." As he was speaking these words, he noticed something bright red swimming close to his ship. The longboat was lowered to see what it could be: it was one of his sheep. Candide felt more joy

n'avait été affligé d'en perdre cent, tous chargés de gros diamants d'Eldorado.

Le capitaine français aperçut bientôt que le capitaine du vaisseau submergeant était espagnol, et que celui du vaisseau submergé était un pirate hollandais; c'était celui-là même qui avait volé Candide. Les richesses immenses dont ce scélérat s'était emparé furent ensevelies avec lui dans la mer, et il n'y eut qu'un mouton de sauvé. «Vous voyez, dit Candide à Martin, que le crime est puni quelquefois; ce coquin de patron hollandais a eu le sort qu'il méritait.—Oui, dit Martin; mais fallait-il que les passagers qui étaient sur son vaisseau périssent aussi? Dieu a puni ce fripon, le diable a noyé les autres.»

Cependant le vaisseau français et l'espagnol continuèrent leur route, et Candide continua ses conversations avec Martin. Ils disputèrent quinze jours de suite, et au bout de quinze jours ils étaient aussi avancés que le premier. Mais enfin ils parlaient, ils se communiquaient des idées, ils se consolaient. Candide caressait son mouton. «Puisque je t'ai retrouvé, dit-il, je pourrai bien retrouver Cunégonde.»

Chapitre XXI

Candide et Martin approchent des côtes de France et raisonnent

On aperçut enfin les côtes de France. «Avez-vous jamais été en France, monsieur Martin? dit Candide.—Oui, dit Martin, j'ai parcouru plusieurs provinces. Il y en a où la moitié des habitants est folle, quelques-unes où l'on est trop rusé, d'autres où l'on est communément assez doux et assez bête, d'autres où l'on fait le bel esprit; et, dans toutes, la principale occupation est l'amour, la seconde de médire, et la troisième de dire des sottises.—Mais, monsieur Martin, avez-vous vu Paris?—Oui, j'ai vu Paris; il tient de toutes ces espèces-là; c'est un chaos, c'est une presse dans laquelle tout le monde cherche le plaisir, et où presque personne ne le trouve, du moins à ce qu'il m'a paru. J'y ai séjourné peu; j'y fus volé, en arrivant, de

at recovering this sheep than he had felt sorrow at losing a hundred of them, all laden with large diamonds from Eldorado.

The French captain soon discerned that the captain of the victorious ship was a Spaniard, and that the captain of the sunken ship had been a Dutch pirate; it was the very same man who had robbed Candide. The immense riches that this villain had seized were buried with him in the ocean, and only one sheep was saved. "You see," said Candide to Martin, "that crime is sometimes punished; that rogue of a Dutch captain met the fate that he deserved." "Yes," said Martin; "but did the passengers who were on board his ship have to perish too? God punished that rogue, the devil drowned the others."

Meanwhile, the French ship and the Spanish one continued on their way, and Candide continued his conversations with Martin. They argued uninterruptedly for two weeks, and at the end of those two weeks they were no further in their discussion than on the first day. But, after all, they were talking, they were communicating ideas to one another and they were consoling one another. Candide made much of his sheep. "Since I've found you again," he said, "I'm sure I'll be able to find Cunégonde again."

Chapter XXI

Candide and Martin approach the French coast and continue to reason with one another

At last the French coast was sighted. "Have you ever been in France, Monsieur Martin?" said Candide. "Yes," said Martin, "I've traveled through several provinces. There are some where half the people are mad, a few where they're too cunning, others where they're commonly rather gentle and rather stupid, and others where they play the wit; and in all the provinces the principal occupation is lovemaking, the second, slander, and the third, talking nonsense." "But, Monsieur Martin, have you seen Paris?" "Yes, I've seen Paris; it contains all the above sorts; it's a chaos, it's a throng in which everyone is seeking pleasure, and where almost no one finds it, at least, so it seemed to me. I resided there for a while; on arriving

tout ce que j'avais, par des filous, à la foire Saint-Germain; on me prit moi-même pour un voleur, et je fus huit jours en prison; après quoi je me fis correcteur d'imprimerie pour gagner de quoi retourner à pied en Hollande. Je connus la canaille écrivante, la canaille cabalante, et la canaille convulsionnaire. On dit qu'il y a des gens fort polis dans cette ville-là; je le veux croire.

—Pour moi, je n'ai nulle curiosité de voir la France, dit Candide; vous devinez aisément que, quand on a passé un mois dans Eldorado, on ne se soucie plus de rien voir sur la terre que Mlle Cunégonde; je vais l'attendre à Venise; nous traverserons la France pour aller en Italie; ne m'accompagnerez-vous pas?—Très volontiers, dit Martin; on dit que Venise n'est bonne que pour les nobles Vénitiens, mais que cependant on y reçoit très bien les étrangers quand ils ont beaucoup d'argent; je n'en ai point, vous en avez, je vous suivrai partout.—A propos, dit Candide, pensez-vous que la terre ait été originairement une mer, comme on l'assure dans ce gros livre qui appartient au capitaine du vaisseau?—Je n'en crois rien du tout, dit Martin, non plus que toutes les rêveries qu'on nous débite depuis quelque temps.—Mais à quelle fin ce monde a-t-il donc été formé? dit Candide.—Pour nous faire enrager, répondit Martin.—N'êtes-vous pas bien étonné, continua Candide, de l'amour que ces deux filles du pays des Oreillons avaient pour ces deux singes, et dont je vous ai conté l'aventure?—Point du tout, dit Martin; je ne vois pas ce que cette passion a d'étrange; j'ai tant vu de choses extraordinaires qu'il n'y a plus rien d'extraordinaire.—Croyez-vous, dit Candide, que les hommes se soient toujours mutuellement massacrés comme ils le font aujourd'hui? qu'ils aient toujours été menteurs, fourbes, perfides, ingrats, brigands, faibles, volages, lâches, envieux, gourmands, ivrognes, avares, ambitieux, sanguinaires, calomniateurs, débauchés, fanatiques, hypocrites et sots?—Croyez-vous, dit Martin, que les éperviers aient toujours mangé des pigeons quand ils en ont trouvé?—Oui, sans doute, dit Candide.—Eh bien, dit Martin, si les éperviers ont toujours eu le même caractère, pourquoi voulez-vous que les hommes aient changé le leur?—Oh! dit Candide, il y a bien de la différence, car le libre arbitre . . .» En raisonnant ainsi, ils arrivèrent à Bordeaux.

there, I was robbed of all I had by some pickpockets at the Saint-Germain fair; I myself was arrested as a thief, and I spent a week in prison; after which I became a printer's proofreader in order to earn enough to return on foot to Holland. I got to know the writing rabble, the plotting rabble and the convulsionary[23] rabble. It's said that there are some very civil people in that city; I would like to believe it."

"As for me, I have no curiosity to see France," said Candide; "you'll easily understand that when one has spent a month in Eldorado one no longer cares to see anything on earth except Miss Cunégonde; I'm going to wait for her in Venice; we'll travel across France to get to Italy; won't you accompany me?" "Very gladly," said Martin; "they say that Venice is no good for anyone except the Venetian nobility, but that, nevertheless, foreigners are very well received there if they have a lot of money; I don't have any at all, you have some, I'll follow you anywhere." "By the way," said Candide, "do you think the earth was originally all ocean, as is affirmed in that large book belonging to our ship's captain?" "I don't believe it at all," said Martin, "no more than I believe all the other daydreams that people have been selling us for some time now." "But for what purpose, then, was this world created?" said Candide. "To drive us crazy," replied Martin. "Aren't you astonished," continued Candide, "at the love those two girls in the land of the Oreillons felt for those two monkeys, the adventure of which I related to you?" "Not at all," said Martin; "I don't see what's strange about that passion; I've seen so many extraordinary things that there's nothing extraordinary left." "Do you believe," said Candide, "that human beings have always slaughtered one another as they do today, that they've always been liars, knaves, traitors, ingrates, brigands, weaklings, fickle types, cowards, enviers, gluttons, drunkards, misers, self-seekers, blood seekers, calumniators, debauchees, fanatics, hypocrites and fools?" "Do you believe," said Martin, "that hawks have always eaten pigeons when they've found them?" "Yes, without a doubt," said Candide. "Well," said Martin, "if hawks have always had the same character, why would you imagine human beings have changed theirs?" "Oh!" said Candide, "there's a big difference, for free will . . ." Reasoning in this way, they reached Bordeaux.

[23] This refers to the Jansenists, a Christian sect founded by Cornelis Jansen (1585–1638) and active in France until the mid-eighteenth century. The sect's main tenets were predestination and asceticism; its members would often undergo "convulsions" of religious ecstasy.

Chapitre XXII

Ce qui arriva en France à Candide et à Martin

Candide ne s'arrêta dans Bordeaux qu'autant de temps qu'il en fallait pour vendre quelques cailloux du Dorado, et pour s'accommoder d'une bonne chaise à deux places; car il ne pouvait plus se passer de son philosophe Martin. Il fut seulement très fâché de se séparer de son mouton, qu'il laissa à l'Académie des sciences de Bordeaux, laquelle proposa pour le sujet du prix de cette année de trouver pourquoi la laine de ce mouton était rouge; et le prix fut adjugé à un savant du Nord qui démontra par A plus B, moins C, divisé par Z, que le mouton devait être rouge, et mourir de la clavelée.

Cependant tous les voyageurs que Candide rencontra dans les cabarets de la route lui disaient: «Nous allons à Paris.» Cet empressement général lui donna enfin l'envie de voir cette capitale; ce n'était pas beaucoup se détourner du chemin de Venise.

Il entra par le faubourg Saint-Marceau, et crut être dans le plus vilain village de la Westphalie.

A peine Candide fut-il dans son auberge qu'il fut attaqué d'une maladie légère causée par ses fatigues. Comme il avait au doigt un diamant énorme, et qu'on avait aperçu dans son équipage une cassette prodigieusement pesante, il eut aussitôt auprès de lui deux médecins qu'il n'avait pas mandés, quelques amis intimes qui ne le quittèrent pas, et deux dévotes qui faisaient chauffer ses bouillons. Martin disait: «Je me souviens d'avoir été malade aussi à Paris dans mon premier voyage; j'étais fort pauvre: aussi n'eus-je ni amis, ni dévotes, ni médecins, et je guéris.»

Cependant, à force de médecines et de saignées, la maladie de Candide devint sérieuse. Un habitué du quartier vint avec douceur lui demander un billet payable au porteur pour l'autre monde; Candide n'en voulut rien faire. Les dévotes l'assurèrent que c'était une

CHAPTER XXII

WHAT HAPPENED TO CANDIDE AND MARTIN IN FRANCE

Candide did not stop in Bordeaux any longer than was required to sell a few pebbles from Eldorado, and to fit himself out with a good two-seated carriage; for he could no longer do without his philosopher, Martin. He was very sorry, however, to have to part company with his sheep, which he left with the Bordeaux Academy of Science, which proposed as a prize theme for that year the discovery of why that sheep's wool was red; and the prize was awarded to a scholar from the North who demonstrated by A plus B, minus C, divided by Z,[24] that the sheep had to be red and would die of sheep pox.

Meanwhile, all the travelers Candide encountered at the inns along the road said to him, "We're going to Paris." This general eagerness finally aroused in him the desire to see that capital; it was not much of a detour from the road to Venice.

He entered through the Faubourg Saint-Marceau,[25] and thought he must be in the most shabby village in Westphalia.

Scarcely had Candide arrived at his inn when he was taken down with a slight illness caused by exhaustion. As he had an enormous diamond on his finger, and as a tremendously heavy money box had been noticed among his baggage, he immediately had at his bedside two physicians for whom he had not sent, several intimate friends who would not leave his side, and two pious ladies who warmed his broth. Martin said, "I remember that I too was ill in Paris on my first trip; I was very poor: so I had no friends, no pious ladies and no physicians, and I recovered."

However, by dint of the physicians and the phlebotomies, Candide's illness became serious. A non-beneficed priest of the neighborhood came to ask him politely for a note payable to bearer for the next world;[26] Candide wanted nothing to do with it. The pious

[24] A ridiculing of the attempt by the French astronomer and mathematician Maupertuis (1698–1759) to prove the existence of God.

[25] A poor and dirty suburb described by Jean-Jacques Rousseau in Book IV of his *Confessions*.

[26] A reference to the *billets de confession* that from 1746 were required to certify that someone on the point of death was not a Jansenist. Without such a *billet*, absolution would not be given and the body would not be buried in consecrated ground.

nouvelle mode; Candide répondit qu'il n'était point homme à la mode. Martin voulut jeter l'habitué par les fenêtres. Le clerc jura qu'on n'enterrerait point Candide. Martin jura qu'il enterrerait le clerc s'il continuait à les importuner. La querelle s'échauffa; Martin le prit par les épaules et le chassa rudement; ce qui causa un grand scandale, dont on fit un procès-verbal.

Candide guérit; et pendant sa convalescence il eut très bonne compagnie à souper chez lui. On jouait gros jeu. Candide était tout étonné que jamais les as ne lui vinssent; et Martin ne s'en étonnait pas.

Parmi ceux qui lui faisaient les honneurs de la ville, il y avait un petit abbé périgourdin, l'un de ces gens empressés, toujours alertes, toujours serviables, effrontés, caressants, accommodants, qui guettent les étrangers à leur passage, leur content l'histoire scandaleuse de la ville, et leur offrent des plaisirs à tout prix. Celui-ci mena d'abord Candide et Martin à la comédie. On y jouait une tragédie nouvelle. Candide se trouva placé auprès de quelques beaux esprits. Cela ne l'empêcha pas de pleurer à des scènes jouées parfaitement. Un des raisonneurs qui étaient à ses côtés lui dit dans un entracte: «Vous avez grand tort de pleurer: cette actrice est fort mauvaise; l'acteur qui joue avec elle est plus mauvais acteur encore; la pièce est encore plus mauvaise que les acteurs; l'auteur ne sait pas un mot d'arabe, et cependant la scène est en Arabie; et, de plus, c'est un homme qui ne croit pas aux idées innées: je vous apporterai demain vingt brochures contre lui.—Monsieur, combien avez-vous de pièces de théâtre en France?» dit Candide à l'abbé; lequel répondit: «Cinq ou six mille.—C'est beaucoup, dit Candide; combien y en a-t-il de bonnes?—Quinze ou seize, répliqua l'autre.—C'est beaucoup» dit Martin.

Candide fut très content d'une actrice qui faisait la reine Elisabeth dans une assez plate tragédie que l'on joue quelquefois. «Cette actrice, dit-il à Martin, me plaît beaucoup; elle a un faux air de Mlle Cunégonde; je serais bien aise de la saluer.» L'abbé périgourdin s'offrit à l'introduire chez elle. Candide, élevé en Allemagne, demanda quelle était l'étiquette, et comment on traitait en France les reines d'Angleterre. «Il faut distinguer, dit l'abbé; en province, on les mène au cabaret; à Paris, on les respecte quand elles sont belles,

ladies assured him that it was a new fashion; Candide replied that he was not at all a man of fashion. Martin wanted to throw the priest out the window. The cleric swore that Candide would not be buried. Martin swore that he would bury the cleric if he continued to pester them. The quarrel became heated; Martin grabbed him by the shoulders and drove him out roughly; that caused a great scandal, out of which a legal report was made.

Candide recovered; and during his convalescence he had very good company at supper. They gambled for high stakes. Candide was utterly amazed that the aces never came his way; but Martin was not amazed by it.

Among those who did him the honors of the city there was a little abbé from Périgord, one of those assiduous people, ever alert, ever obliging, shameless, fawning and accommodating, who lie in wait for foreigners, tell them the scandals of the city and offer them pleasures at any price. This particular one first took Candide and Martin to the theater. A new tragedy was being performed. Candide was seated near several wits. That did not prevent him from weeping at some perfectly performed scenes. One of the faultfinders who were on either side of him said to him during an interval, "You're very wrong to weep; that actress is extremely bad; the actor who is playing opposite her is an even worse performer; the play is even worse than the cast; the author doesn't know a word of Arabic, and yet the play is set in Arabia; and, furthermore, he's a man who doesn't believe in innate ideas; tomorrow I'll bring you twenty pamphlets written against him." "Sir, how many plays have been written in France?" said Candide to the abbé, who replied, "Five or six thousand." "That's a lot," said Candide; "how many good ones are there among them?" "Fifteen or sixteen," replied the other. "That's a lot," said Martin.

Candide was very pleased by an actress who was playing Queen Elizabeth in a rather dull tragedy that is sometimes performed.[27] "That actress pleases me very much," he said to Martin; "she looks something like Miss Cunégonde; I would like to pay my respects to her." The abbé from Périgord offered to introduce him at her home. Candide, having been brought up in Germany, asked what the proper etiquette was, and how Queens of England were treated in France. "One must distinguish," said the abbé; "in the provinces, they're taken to an inn; in Paris, they're respected when they're

[27] *Le Comte d'Essex* by Thomas Corneille (1625–1709).

et on les jette à la voirie quand elles sont mortes.—Des reines à la voirie! dit Candide.—Oui vraiment, dit Martin; monsieur l'abbé a raison: j'étais à Paris quand Mlle Monime passa, comme on dit, de cette vie à l'autre; on lui refusa ce que ces gens-ci appellent *les honneurs de la sépulture*, c'est-à-dire de pourrir avec tous les gueux du quartier dans un vilain cimetière; elle fut enterrée toute seule de sa bande au coin de la rue de Bourgogne; ce qui dut lui faire une peine extrême, car elle pensait très noblement.—Cela est bien impoli, dit Candide.—Que voulez-vous? dit Martin; ces gens-ci sont ainsi faits. Imaginez toutes les contradictions, toutes les incompatibilités possibles, vous les verrez dans le gouvernement, dans les tribunaux, dans les églises, dans les spectacles de cette drôle de nation.—Est-il vrai qu'on rit toujours à Paris? dit Candide.—Oui, dit l'abbé, mais c'est en enrageant; car on s'y plaint de tout avec de grands éclats de rire; même on y fait en riant les actions les plus détestables.

—Quel est, dit Candide, ce gros cochon qui me disait tant de mal de la pièce où j'ai tant pleuré et des acteurs qui m'ont fait tant de plaisir?—C'est un mal vivant, répondit l'abbé, qui gagne sa vie à dire du mal de toutes les pièces et de tous les livres; il hait quiconque réussit comme les eunuques haïssent les jouissants: c'est un de ces serpents de la littérature qui se nourrissent de fange et de venin; c'est un folliculaire.—Qu'appelez-vous folliculaire? dit Candide.—C'est, dit l'abbé, un faiseur de feuilles, un Fréron.»

C'est ainsi que Candide, Martin et le Périgourdin raisonnaient sur l'escalier, en voyant défiler le monde au sortir de la pièce. «Quoique je sois très empressé de revoir Mlle Cunégonde, dit Candide, je voudrais pourtant souper avec Mlle Clairon; car elle m'a paru admirable.»

L'abbé n'était pas homme à approcher de Mlle Clairon, qui ne voyait que bonne compagnie. «Elle est engagée pour ce soir, dit-il; mais j'aurai l'honneur de vous mener chez une dame de qualité, et

beautiful, and they're thrown onto the refuse dump when they're dead." "Queens on the refuse dump!" said Candide. "Yes, really," said Martin; "the abbé is right: I was in Paris when Miss Monime[28] passed, as they say, from this life to the next; she was refused what these people call 'the honors of burial,' that's to say, the honor of rotting with all the beggars of the district in a sordid cemetery; all alone of her troupe, she was buried at the corner of the Rue de Bourgogne; which must have hurt her greatly, for she had a very noble mind." "That's very uncivil," said Candide. "What do you expect?" said Martin; "these people are made that way. Imagine every contradiction, every possible inconsistency: you'll see them in the government, in the law courts, in the churches and in the playhouses of this queer nation." "Is it true that people are always laughing in Paris?" said Candide. "Yes," said the abbé, "but they laugh in frenzy; for they complain about everything here in great bursts of laughter; they even laugh while they are carrying out the most execrable deeds."

"Who's that fat swine," said Candide, "who was telling me so many bad things about the play at which I wept so much, and about the actors who gave me such pleasure?" "He's a wretched fellow," replied the abbé, "who earns his living by speaking ill of all plays and all books; he hates anyone who succeeds, just as eunuchs hate those who can enjoy sex: he's one of those snakes of literature who thrive on filth and venom; he's a hack." "What do you mean by a hack?" said Candide. "He's a newspaper scribbler, a Fréron,"[29] said the abbé.

Candide, Martin and the man from Périgord were debating in this way on the staircase as they watched the people filing out after the play. "Although I'm very eager to see Miss Cunégonde again," said Candide, "I'd still like to have supper with Miss Clairon;[30] for she seemed wonderful to me."

The abbé was not the man to approach Miss Clairon, who saw only good company. "She's engaged for the evening," he said; "but I shall have the honor of taking you to the home of a lady of quality,

[28] Adrienne Lecouvreur (1692–1730), a distinguished actress who performed the role of Monime in Racine's *Mithridate* at the Comédie Française. Not having renounced her profession before she died, she was refused burial in consecrated ground.
[29] Elie-Catherine Fréron (1719–1776), a French journalist, editor of *L'Année littéraire* [The Literary Year] and a severe critic of Voltaire.
[30] Claire Leris (1723–1803), a leading Parisian actress.

là vous connaîtrez Paris comme si vous y aviez été quatre ans.» Candide, qui était naturellement curieux, se laissa mener chez la dame, au fond du faubourg Saint-Honoré; on y était occupé d'un pharaon; douze tristes pontes tenaient chacun en main un petit livre de cartes, registre cornu de leurs infortunes. Un profond silence régnait, la pâleur était sur le front des pontes, l'inquiétude sur celui du banquier, et la dame du logis, assise auprès de ce banquier impitoyable, remarquait avec des yeux de lynx tous les parolis, tous les sept et le va de campagne, dont chaque joueur cornait ses cartes; elle les faisait décorner avec une attention sévère mais polie, et ne se fâchait point, de peur de perdre ses pratiques: la dame se faisait appeler la marquise de Parolignac. Sa fille âgée de quinze ans, était au nombre des pontes et avertissait d'un clin d'œil des friponneries de ces pauvres gens, qui tâchaient de réparer les cruautés du sort. L'abbé périgourdin, Candide et Martin entrèrent; personne ne se leva, ni les salua, ni les regarda; tous étaient profondément occupés de leurs cartes. «Madame la baronne de Thunder-ten-tronckh était plus civile», dit Candide.

Cependant l'abbé s'approcha de l'oreille de la marquise, qui se leva à moitié, honora Candide d'un sourire gracieux, et Martin d'un air de tête tout à fait noble; elle fit donner un siège et un jeu de cartes à Candide, qui perdit cinquante mille francs en deux tailles; après quoi on soupa très gaiement, et tout le monde était étonné que Candide ne fût pas ému de sa perte; les laquais disaient entre eux, dans leur langage de laquais: «Il faut que ce soit quelque milord anglais.»

Le souper fut comme la plupart des soupers de Paris: d'abord du silence, ensuite un bruit de paroles qu'on ne distingue point, puis des plaisanteries dont la plupart sont insipides, de fausses nouvelles, de mauvais raisonnements, un peu de politique et beaucoup de médisance: on parla même de livres nouveaux. «Avez-vous vu, dit l'abbé périgourdin, le roman du sieur Gauchat, docteur en théologie?—Oui, répondit un des convives, mais je n'ai pu l'achever. Nous avons une foule d'écrits impertinents, mais tous ensemble n'approchent pas de l'impertinence de Gauchat, docteur en théologie; je suis si rassasié de cette immensité de détestables livres qui nous

and there you'll get to know Paris as if you'd been here for four years."

Candide, who was curious by nature, allowed himself to be taken to the lady's house in the heart of the Faubourg Saint-Honoré; a game of faro was in progress there; twelve gloomy punters each held a little sheaf of cards, the dog-eared record of their misfortunes. A profound silence reigned, the punters' countenances were pale, the banker's was anxious, and the lady of the house, seated next to that merciless banker, observed with her lynx's eyes every paroli,[31] every underhand staking of winnings for which each player dog-eared his cards; with strict but polite attention, she made them unfold the corners, and did not become in the least annoyed, for fear of losing her customers: the lady went by the name of the Marquise de Parolignac. Her fifteen-year-old daughter was among the punters and with a wink informed her mother of the attempts to cheat practiced by those poor people who were trying to make up for the cruelties of chance. The abbé from Périgord, Candide and Martin walked in; no one stood up, greeted them or looked at them; they were all profoundly occupied with their cards. "Baroness Thunder-Ten-Tronckh was more civil," said Candide.

Meanwhile, the abbé whispered something in the marquise's ear; she half got up, honored Candide with a gracious smile, and Martin with a most dignified nod; she had a seat and a hand of cards given to Candide, who lost fifty thousand francs in two turns; after which they all had a very merry supper, and everyone was astonished that Candide was not affected by his loss; the lackeys said among themselves, in their lackey jargon, "He must be some English milord."

The supper was like most Parisian suppers: silence at first, then a noise of indistinguishable words, then witticisms, the majority of which are dull, false news, faulty lines of argument, a little politics and a great deal of backbiting; they even talked about new books. "Have you seen," said the abbé from Périgord, "the novel by a certain Gauchat,[32] Doctor of Theology?" "Yes," replied one of the guests, "but I couldn't finish it. We have a mass of impertinent writings, but all of them together don't come near the impertinence of Gauchat, Doctor of Theology; I'm so fed up with the vast number of execrable books with which we're inundated that I've begun punt-

[31] A doubling of the stake, here illegally.
[32] Gabriel Gauchat (1709–?1774), a critic of Voltaire.

inondent que je me suis mis à ponter au pharaon.—Et les *Mélanges* de l'archidiacre T. . ., qu'en dites-vous? dit l'abbé.—Ah! dit Mme de Parolignac, l'ennuyeux mortel! comme il vous dit curieusement tout ce que le monde sait! comme il discute pesamment ce qui ne vaut pas la peine d'être remarqué légèrement! comme il s'approprie sans esprit l'esprit des autres! comme il gâte ce qu'il pille! comme il me dégoûte! Mais il ne me dégoûtera plus: c'est assez d'avoir lu quelques pages de l'archidiacre.»

Il y avait à table un homme savant et de goût qui appuya ce que disait la marquise. On parla ensuite de tragédie; la dame demanda pourquoi il y avait des tragédies qu'on jouait quelquefois, et qu'on ne pouvait lire. L'homme de goût expliqua très bien comment une pièce pouvait avoir quelque intérêt et n'avoir presque aucun mérite; il prouva en peu de mots que ce n'était pas assez d'amener une ou deux de ces situations qu'on trouve dans tous les romans, et qui séduisent toujours les spectateurs, mais qu'il faut être neuf sans être bizarre, souvent sublime, et toujours naturel; connaître le cœur humain et le faire parler; être grand poète sans que jamais aucun personnage de la pièce paraisse poète; savoir parfaitement sa langue, la parler avec pureté, avec une harmonie continue, sans que jamais la rime coûte rien au sens. «Quiconque, ajouta-t-il, n'observe pas toutes ces règles peut faire une ou deux tragédies applaudies au théâtre, mais il ne sera jamais compté au rang des bons écrivains; il y a très peu de bonnes tragédies; les unes sont des idylles en dialogues bien écrits et bien rimés; les autres, des raisonnements politiques qui endorment, ou des amplifications qui rebutent; les autres, des rêves d'énergumène, en style barbare, des propos interrompus, de longues apostrophes aux dieux, parce qu'on ne sait point parler aux hommes, des maximes fausses, des lieux communs ampoulés.»

Candide écouta ce propos avec attention et conçut une grande idée du discoureur; et, comme la marquise avait eu soin de le placer à côté d'elle, il s'approcha de son oreille, et prit la liberté de lui demander qui était cet homme qui parlait si bien. «C'est un savant, dit la dame, qui ne ponte point, et que l'abbé m'amène quelquefois à souper; il se connaît parfaitement en tragédies et en livres, et il a fait une tragédie sifflée et un livre dont on n'a jamais vu hors de la

ing at faro." "And the *Miscellanea* of Archdeacon T . . . ,[33] what do you think of that?" said the abbé. "Oh!" said the Marquise de Parolignac, "the deadly bore! how meticulously he tells you everything everybody already knows! how ponderously he discusses that which isn't worth the trouble of being remarked upon in passing! how witlessly he appropriates other people's wit! how he spoils what he pilfers! how he disgusts me! But he'll disgust me no longer: it's enough to have read a few pages of the archdeacon."

There was at the table a man of learning and good taste who backed up what the marquise was saying. Then they talked of tragedy; the lady asked why there were tragedies that were sometimes performed but that were unreadable. The man of good taste explained very well how a play could have some interest and almost no merit; he proved in a few words that it was not enough to introduce one or two of those situations found in all novels, and that always win over the audience, but that one must be new without being bizarre, often sublime and always natural; understand the human heart and make it speak; be a great poet without any character in the play seeming to be a poet; have a perfect command of one's own language, speak it with purity, with continual harmony, without the rhyme ever detracting from the meaning. "Whoever," he added, "doesn't observe all these rules may create one or two tragedies that will be applauded in the theater, but he'll never be considered to rank among good writers; there are very few good tragedies; some tragedies are idylls in well-written and well-rhymed dialogue; others, political arguments that send you to sleep, or repulsive exaggerations; still others are fanatics' dreams, written in a barbarous style, interrupted speeches, long apostrophes to the gods—because the author has no idea how one should speak to human beings—false maxims and turgid commonplaces."

Candide listened attentively to these remarks and conceived a high opinion of the speaker; and, as the marquise had taken care to seat him next to her, he leaned over and took the liberty of asking her who this man was who spoke so well. "He's a scholar," said the lady, "who never plays cards and whom the abbé brings to have supper with me on occasion; he knows everything there is to know about tragedies and books, and he's written a tragedy that was hissed and a book that has never been seen outside his bookseller's shop

[33] Abbé Trublet (1697–1770), author of the *Essais de littérature* and a critic of Voltaire.

boutique de son libraire qu'un exemplaire qu'il m'a dédié.—Le grand homme! dit Candide; c'est un autre Pangloss.»

Alors, se tournant vers lui, il lui dit: «Monsieur vous pensez sans doute que tout est au mieux dans le monde physique et dans le moral, et que rien ne pouvait être autrement?—Moi, Monsieur, lui répondit le savant, je ne pense rien de tout cela: je trouve que tout va de travers chez nous; que personne ne sait ni quel est son rang, ni quelle est sa charge, ni ce qu'il fait, ni ce qu'il doit faire, et qu'excepté le souper, qui est assez gai et où il paraît assez d'union, tout le reste du temps se passe en querelles impertinentes: jansénistes contre molinistes, gens du parlement contre gens d'église, gens de lettres contre gens de lettres, courtisans contre courtisans, financiers contre le peuple, femmes contre maris, parents contre parents; c'est une guerre éternelle.»

Candide lui répliqua: «J'ai vu pis. Mais un sage, qui depuis a eu le malheur d'être pendu, m'apprit que tout cela est à merveille; ce sont des ombres à un beau tableau.—Votre pendu se moquait du monde, dit Martin! vos ombres sont des taches horribles.—Ce sont les hommes qui font les taches, dit Candide, et ils ne peuvent pas s'en dispenser.—Ce n'est donc pas leur faute», dit Martin. La plupart des pontes, qui n'entendaient rien à ce langage, buvaient; et Martin raisonna avec le savant, et Candide raconta une partie de ses aventures à la dame du logis.

Ayant soupé, la marquise mena Candide dans son cabinet et le fit asseoir sur un canapé. «Eh bien, lui dit-elle, vous aimez donc toujours éperdument Mlle Cunégonde de Thunder-ten-tronckh?—Oui, Madame», répondit Candide. La marquise lui répliqua avec un sourire tendre: «Vous me répondez comme un jeune homme de Westphalie; un Français m'aurait dit: «Il est vrai que j'ai «aimé Mlle Cunégonde; mais en vous voyant, Madame, je crains «de ne la plus aimer.»—Hélas! Madame, dit Candide, je répondrai comme vous voudrez.—Votre passion pour elle, dit la marquise, a commencé en ramassant son mouchoir; je veux que vous ramassiez ma jarretière.—De tout mon cœur», dit Candide; et il la ramassa. «Mais je veux que vous me la remettiez», dit la dame; et Candide la lui remit. «Voyez-vous, dit la dame, vous êtes étranger; je fais quelquefois languir mes amants de Paris quinze jours, mais je me rends à vous dès la première nuit, parce qu'il faut faire les honneurs de son pays à un jeune homme de Westphalie.» La belle, ayant aperçu deux énormes diamants aux deux mains de son jeune étran-

except for one copy that he inscribed to me." "What a great man!" said Candide; "he's another Pangloss."

Then, turning toward him, he said to him, "Sir, no doubt you think that everything is at its best in the physical and moral worlds, and that nothing could be otherwise?" "I, sir," replied the scholar, "I think nothing of the kind: I deem that everything goes awry with us; that no one knows his rank or his function, what he's doing or what he ought to be doing, and that, except during supper, which is a rather cheerful occasion when there appears to be a fair amount of harmony, the rest of the time is spent in impertinent quarrels: Jansenists against Molinists, men of parliament against churchmen, men of letters against men of letters, courtiers against courtiers, financiers against the people, wives against husbands, relatives against relatives; it's an eternal war."

Candide replied, "I've seen worse. But a wise man, who later had the misfortune to be hanged, taught me that all that is wonderful; those are shadows in a beautiful picture." "Your hanged man was joking!" said Martin; "your shadows are horrible stains." "It's people who cause the stains," said Candide, "and they can't avoid it." "Then it's not their fault," said Martin. The majority of the punters, who understood nothing of this kind of talk, were drinking; Martin debated with the scholar, and Candide related part of his adventures to the lady of the house.

After supper the marquise took Candide to her private room and invited him to sit down on a sofa. "So," she said to him, "you're still desperately in love with Miss Cunégonde of Thunder-Ten-Tronckh?" "Yes, Madam," answered Candide. The marquise replied with a tender smile, "You answer me like a young man from Westphalia; a Frenchman would have said to me, 'It's true that I did love Miss Cunégonde; but having beheld you, Madam, I fear that I love her no longer.'" "Alas! Madam," said Candide, "I'll answer as you wish." "Your passion for her," said the marquise, "began when you picked up her handkerchief; I want you to pick up my garter." "With all my heart," said Candide; and he picked it up. "But I want you to put it back on me," said the lady; and Candide put it back on her. "You see," said the lady, "you're a foreigner; sometimes I make my Parisian lovers languish for two weeks, but I'm yielding to you on the first night because one must do the honors of one's country to a young man from Westphalia." The beauty, having noticed two enormous diamonds on her young foreigner's hands, praised them

ger, les loua de si bonne foi que des doigts de Candide ils passèrent aux doigts de la marquise.

Candide, en s'en retournant avec son abbé périgourdin, sentit quelques remords d'avoir fait une infidélité à Mlle Cunégonde; monsieur l'abbé entra dans sa peine; il n'avait qu'une légère part aux cinquante mille livres perdues au jeu par Candide, et à la valeur des deux brillants, moitié donnés, moitié extorqués. Son dessein était de profiter, autant qu'il le pourrait, des avantages que la connaissance de Candide pouvait lui procurer. Il lui parla beaucoup de Cunégonde; et Candide lui dit qu'il demanderait bien pardon à cette belle de son infidélité, quand il la verrait à Venise.

Le Périgourdin redoublait de politesses et d'attentions, et prenait un intérêt tendre à tout ce que Candide disait, à tout ce qu'il faisait, à tout ce qu'il voulait faire.

«Vous avez donc, Monsieur, lui dit-il, un rendez-vous à Venise?—Oui, monsieur l'abbé, dit Candide; il faut absolument que j'aille trouver Mlle Cunégonde.» Alors, engagé par le plaisir de parler de ce qu'il aimait, il conta, selon son usage, une partie de ses aventures avec cette illustre Westphalienne.

«Je crois, dit l'abbé, que Mlle Cunégonde a bien de l'esprit, et qu'elle écrit des lettres charmantes?—Je n'en ai jamais reçu, dit Candide; car figurez-vous qu'ayant été chassé du château pour l'amour d'elle, je ne pus lui écrire; que bientôt après j'appris qu'elle était morte, qu'ensuite je la retrouvai, et que je la perdis, et que je lui ai envoyé à deux mille cinq cents lieues d'ici un exprès dont j'attends la réponse.»

L'abbé écoutait attentivement, et paraissait un peu rêveur. Il prit bientôt congé des deux étrangers après les avoir tendrement embrassés. Le lendemain Candide reçut à son réveil une lettre conçue en ces termes:

Monsieur, mon très cher amant, il y a huit jours que je suis malade en cette ville; j'apprends que vous y êtes. Je volerais dans vos bras si je pouvais remuer. J'ai su votre passage à Bordeaux; j'y ai laissé le fidèle Cacambo et la vieille, qui doivent bientôt me suivre. Le gouverneur de Buenos Aires a tout pris, mais il me reste votre cœur. Venez, votre présence me rendra la vie, ou me fera mourir de plaisir.

so sincerely that they passed from Candide's fingers to the marquise's fingers.

Candide, leaving with his abbé from Périgord, felt some remorse at having been unfaithful to Miss Cunégonde; the abbé sympathized with him; he had shared in only a small part of the fifty thousand pounds lost by Candide in the card game, and in the value of those two diamonds, half given, half extorted. His scheme was to profit as much as he could from the advantages that his acquaintance with Candide might obtain for him. He talked to him a great deal about Cunégonde; and Candide told him that he would ask forgiveness from that beautiful woman for his infidelity when he saw her in Venice.

The man from Périgord redoubled his civilities and attentions, and took an affectionate interest in everything Candide said, everything he did, everything he wanted to do.

"So, sir," he said to him, "you've arranged to meet up in Venice?" "Yes, Abbé," said Candide; "I absolutely must go to find Miss Cunégonde." Then, carried away by the pleasure of speaking about the object of his love, he related, as was his wont, a part of his adventures with that illustrious Westphalian woman.

"Am I right in thinking," said the abbé, "that Miss Cunégonde has a good deal of wit and that she writes charming letters?" "I've never received one," said Candide; "for you must realize that having been driven from the country residence for love of her, I couldn't write to her; that soon afterward I learned she was dead, that I then found her again, and that I lost her, and that I sent her, two thousand five hundred leagues from here, an express messenger and am awaiting the reply."

The abbé listened attentively and seemed to be musing on something. He soon took his leave of the two foreigners after having embraced them affectionately. The next day Candide received on waking a letter conceived in these terms:

> Sir, my dearest love, I have been ill in this city for a week now; I have just learned that you are here. I would fly to your arms were I able to move. I was informed that you had passed through at Bordeaux; I left the faithful Cacambo and the old woman there, and they should soon be following me here. The Governor of Buenos Aires took everything, but I still have your heart. Come to me, your presence will either return me to life or cause me to die of pleasure.

Cette lettre charmante, cette lettre inespérée, transporta Candide d'une joie inexprimable; et la maladie de sa chère Cunégonde l'accabla de douleur. Partagé entre ces deux sentiments, il prend son or et ses diamants, et se fait conduire avec Martin à l'hôtel où Mlle Cunégonde demeurait. Il entre en tremblant d'émotion, son cœur palpite, sa voix sanglote; il veut ouvrir les rideaux du lit, il veut faire apporter de la lumière. «Gardez-vous-en bien, lui dit la suivante, la lumière la tue»; et soudain elle referme le rideau. «Ma chère Cunégonde, dit Candide en pleurant, comment vous portez-vous? si vous ne pouvez me voir, parlez-moi du moins.—Elle ne peut parler», dit la suivante. La dame alors tire du lit une main potelée que Candide arrose longtemps de ses larmes, et qu'il remplit ensuite de diamants, en laissant un sac plein d'or sur le fauteuil.

Au milieu de ses transports arrive un exempt suivi de l'abbé périgourdin et d'une escouade. «Voilà donc, dit-il, ces deux étrangers suspects?» Il les fait incontinent saisir, et ordonne à ses braves de les traîner en prison. «Ce n'est pas ainsi qu'on traite les voyageurs dans le Dorado, dit Candide.—Je suis plus manichéen que jamais, dit Martin.—Mais, Monsieur, où nous menez-vous? dit Candide.—Dans un cul de basse-fosse», dit l'exempt.

Martin, ayant repris son sang-froid, jugea que la dame qui se prétendait Cunégonde était une friponne, monsieur l'abbé périgourdin un fripon qui avait abusé au plus vite de l'innocence de Candide, et l'exempt un autre fripon dont on pouvait aisément se débarrasser.

Plutôt que de s'exposer aux procédures de la justice, Candide, éclairé par son conseil, et d'ailleurs toujours impatient de revoir la véritable Cunégonde, propose à l'exempt trois petits diamants d'environ trois mille pistoles chacun. «Ah! Monsieur, lui dit l'homme au bâton d'ivoire, eussiez-vous commis tous les crimes imaginables, vous êtes le plus honnête homme du monde; trois diamants! chacun de trois mille pistoles! Monsieur! je me ferais tuer pour vous, au lieu de vous mener dans un cachot. On arrête tous les étrangers, mais laissez-moi faire; j'ai un frère à Dieppe en Normandie, je vais vous y mener; et si vous avez quelque diamant à lui donner, il aura soin de vous comme moi-même.

—Et pourquoi arrête-t-on tous les étrangers?» dit Candide. L'abbé périgourdin prit alors la parole et dit: «C'est parce qu'un gueux du

This charming letter, this unhoped-for letter, left Candide in the transports of an inexpressible joy; and his beloved Cunégonde's illness overwhelmed him with sorrow. Torn between these two feelings, he seized his gold and diamonds, and had himself conveyed with Martin to the hotel where Miss Cunégonde was staying. He entered, trembling with emotion, his heart was pounding, he was sobbing; he tried to draw back the curtains round the bed, he wished to have some light brought in. "Do nothing of the kind," the waiting maid said to him, "light would kill her"; and all of a sudden she closed the curtain. "My beloved Cunégonde," said Candide, weeping, "how are you feeling? if you can't see me, at least speak to me." "She can't speak," said the waiting maid. Then from the bed the lady stretched out a plump hand that Candide bathed with his tears for a long time, and that he then filled with diamonds, leaving a bag full of gold on the armchair.

In the midst of his transports a police officer arrived followed by the abbé from Périgord and a squad. "Are those the two suspicious foreigners, then?" he said. He had them seized on the spot, and ordered his heroes to drag them off to prison. "Travelers aren't treated this way in Eldorado," said Candide. "I'm more of a Manichaean than ever," said Martin. "But, sir, where are you taking us?" said Candide. "To the deepest dungeon," said the police officer.

Martin, having recovered his composure, deemed that the lady claiming to be Cunégonde was a cheat, the abbé from Périgord a rogue who had taken advantage as fast as possible of Candide's innocence, and the police officer another rogue of whom they could easily rid themselves.

Rather than expose himself to judicial proceedings, Candide, enlightened by Martin's advice, and, moreover, still impatient to see the real Cunégonde again, offered the police officer three small diamonds each worth about three thousand pistoles. "Ah! sir," said the man with the ivory truncheon, "had you committed every crime imaginable, you'd still be the most honest man in the world; three diamonds! each worth three thousand pistoles! Sir! I'd die for you rather than take you to a dungeon. All foreigners get arrested, but leave it to me; I have a brother in Dieppe, in Normandy, I'll take you there; and if you have a diamond to give to him, he'll take care of you, just like me."

"And why are all foreigners arrested?" said Candide. The abbé from Périgord then spoke up, saying, "It's because a beggar from the

pays d'Atrébatie a entendu dire des sottises: cela seul lui a fait commettre un parricide, non pas tel que celui de 1610 au mois de mai, mais tel que celui de 1594 au mois de décembre, et tel que plusieurs autres commis dans d'autres années et dans d'autres mois par d'autres gueux qui avaient entendu dire des sottises.»

L'expert alors expliqua de quoi il s'agissait. «Ah, les monstres! s'écria Candide; quoi! de telles horreurs chez un peuple qui danse et qui chante! Ne pourrai-je sortir au plus vite de ce pays où des singes agacent des tigres? J'ai vu des ours dans mon pays; je n'ai vu des hommes que dans le Dorado. Au nom de Dieu, monsieur l'exempt, menez-moi à Venise, où je dois attendre Mlle Cunégonde.—Je ne peux vous mener qu'en Basse-Normandie», dit le barigel. Aussitôt il lui fait ôter ses fers, dit qu'il s'est mépris, renvoie ses gens et emmène à Dieppe Candide et Martin, et les laisse entre les mains de son frère. Il y avait un petit vaisseau hollandais à la rade. Le Normand, à l'aide de trois autres diamants devenu le plus serviable des hommes, embarque Candide et ses gens dans le vaisseau qui allait faire voile pour Portsmouth en Angleterre. Ce n'était pas le chemin de Venise; mais Candide croyait être délivré de l'enfer, et il comptait bien reprendre la route de Venise à la première occasion.

Chapitre XXIII

Candide et Martin vont sur les côtes d'Angleterre; ce qu'ils y voient

«Ah, Pangloss! Pangloss! Ah, Martin! Martin! Ah, ma chère Cunégonde! qu'est-ce que ce monde-ci? disait Candide sur le vaisseau hollandais.—Quelque chose de bien fou et de bien abominable, répondait Martin.—Vous connaissez l'Angleterre; y est-on aussi fou qu'en France?—C'est une autre espèce de folie, dit Martin. Vous savez que ces deux nations sont en guerre pour quelques arpents de

province of Atrebatum[34] heard some stupidities: that alone caused him to commit parricide, not like the one in 1610, in the month of May, but like the one in 1594, in the month of December, and like several others committed in other years and in other months by other beggars who had heard stupidities." The expert then explained what it was all about. "Oh, the monsters!" exclaimed Candide; "what! such horrors among a people who dance and sing! Can I not depart at once from this country where monkeys bait tigers? I've seen bears in my own country; I've seen men only in Eldorado. In the name of God, Officer, take me to Venice, where I must await Miss Cunégonde." "I can only take you to Lower Normandy," said the chief constable. He immediately had his irons removed, said that he had made a mistake, dismissed his men and took Candide and Martin off to Dieppe, leaving them in the hands of his brother. There was a small Dutch ship in the roadstead. The Norman, having become with the help of three other diamonds the most obliging of men, embarked Candide and his men on the ship, which was about to set sail for Portsmouth in England. This was not the way to Venice; but Candide deemed himself to have been delivered from hell, and he counted on resuming his journey to Venice at the first opportunity.

Chapter XXIII

Candide and Martin travel to the English coast; what they see there

"Oh, Pangloss! Pangloss! Oh, Martin! Martin! Oh, my beloved Cunégonde! what is this world of ours?" Candide was saying on board the Dutch ship. "Something quite mad and quite abominable," replied Martin. "You know England; are people as mad there as in France?" "It's a different kind of madness," said Martin. "You are aware that these two nations are at war over a few acres of snow out

[34] The Latin name for the province of Artois, birthplace of Robert-François Damiens, who tried to assassinate Louis XV in 1757. The attempt by Jean Châtel to kill Henri IV in 1594 also failed, unlike that by François Ravaillac in 1610.

neige vers le Canada, et qu'elles dépensent pour cette belle guerre beaucoup plus que tout le Canada ne vaut. De vous dire précisément s'il y a plus de gens à lier dans un pays que dans un autre, c'est ce que mes faibles lumières ne me permettent pas. Je sais seulement qu'en général les gens que nous allons voir sont fort atrabilaires.»

En causant ainsi ils abordèrent à Portsmouth; une multitude de peuple couvrait le rivage, et regardait attentivement un assez gros homme qui était à genoux, les yeux bandés, sur le tillac d'un des vaisseaux de la flotte; quatre soldats, postés vis-à-vis de cet homme, lui tirèrent chacun trois balles dans le crâne le plus paisiblement du monde, et toute l'assemblée s'en retourna extrêmement satisfaite. «Qu'est-ce donc que tout ceci? dit Candide, et quel démon exerce partout son empire?» Il demanda qui était ce gros homme qu'on venait de tuer en cérémonie. «C'est un amiral, lui répondit-on.—Et pourquoi tuer cet amiral?—C'est, lui dit-on, parce qu'il n'a pas fait tuer assez de monde; il a livré un combat à un amiral français, et on a trouvé qu'il n'était pas assez près de lui.—Mais, dit Candide, l'amiral français était aussi loin de l'amiral anglais que celui-ci l'était de l'autre!—Cela est incontestable, lui répliqua-t-on; mais dans ce pays-ci il est bon de tuer de temps en temps un amiral pour encourager les autres.»

Candide fut si étourdi et si choqué de ce qu'il voyait, et de ce qu'il entendait, qu'il ne voulut pas seulement mettre pied à terre, et qu'il fit son marché avec le patron hollandais (dût-il le voler comme celui de Surinam) pour le conduire sans délai à Venise.

Le patron fut prêt au bout de deux jours. On côtoya la France; on passa à la vue de Lisbonne, et Candide frémit. On entra dans le détroit et dans la Méditerranée; enfin on aborda à Venise. «Dieu soit loué! dit Candide en embrassant Martin; c'est ici que je reverrai la belle Cunégonde. Je compte sur Cacambo comme sur moi-même. Tout est bien, tout va bien, tout va le mieux qu'il soit possible.»

Canada way, and that they're spending on that fine war a great deal more than all Canada is worth. As for telling you precisely whether there are more people who ought to be put away in one country than in another, that is something my feeble understanding does not allow me to do. I only know that in general the people we're going to see are extremely atrabilious."

Conversing in this way, they arrived at Portsmouth; a multitude of people were covering the shore and looking attentively at a rather stout man who was on his knees, blindfolded, on the deck of one of the ships of the fleet; four soldiers, stationed facing this man, each shot three bullets into his head in the most placid manner in the world, and the entire assembly went away extremely satisfied. "What's all this, then?" said Candide, "and what demon is it that holds sway everywhere?" He asked who that stout man was who had just been ceremoniously killed. "It was an admiral,"[35] was the reply. "And why kill that admiral?" He was told, "It's because he didn't kill enough people; he fought a battle with a French admiral, and it was deemed that he wasn't close enough to him." "But," said Candide, "the French admiral was just as far away from the English admiral as the latter was from the former!" "That's indisputable," he was answered; "but in this country it's good to kill an admiral from time to time to encourage the others."

Candide was so dazed and so shocked by what he saw and by what he heard that he did not even want to set foot on dry land, and made a bargain with the Dutch captain (even if he should rob him like the one from Surinam) to take him without delay to Venice.

The captain was ready two days later. They ran along the French coast; they passed within sight of Lisbon, and Candide shuddered. They sailed through the straits and into the Mediterranean; finally they landed at Venice. "God be praised!" said Candide, embracing Martin; "it's here that I'll see the beautiful Cunégonde again. I rely upon Cacambo as upon myself. All's well, all's going well, all's going the best it possibly could."

[35] Admiral John Byng (1704–1757), who was defeated off Minorca by the French fleet. Byng was executed by firing squad on 14 March 1757, after Voltaire had unsuccessfully intervened on his behalf.

Chapitre XXIV

De Paquette et de frère Giroflée

Dès qu'il fut à Venise, il fit chercher Cacambo dans tous les cabarets, dans tous les cafés, chez toutes les filles de joie, et ne le trouva point. Il envoyait tous les jours à la découverte de tous les vaisseaux et de toutes les barques: nulles nouvelles de Cacambo. «Quoi! disait-il à Martin, j'ai eu le temps de passer de Surinam à Bordeaux, d'aller de Bordeaux à Paris, de Paris à Dieppe, de Dieppe à Portsmouth, de côtoyer le Portugal et l'Espagne, de traverser toute la Méditerranée, de passer quelques mois à Venise, et la belle Cunégonde n'est point venue! Je n'ai rencontré au lieu d'elle qu'une drôlesse et un abbé périgourdin! Cunégonde est morte sans doute, je n'ai plus qu'à mourir. Ah! il valait mieux rester dans le paradis du Dorado que de revenir dans cette maudite Europe. Que vous avez raison, mon cher Martin! tout n'est qu'illusion et calamité.»

Il tomba dans une mélancolie noire, et ne prit aucune part à l'opéra *alla moda* ni aux autres divertissements du carnaval; pas une dame ne lui donna la moindre tentation. Martin lui dit: «Vous êtes bien simple, en vérité, de vous figurer qu'un valet métis, qui a cinq ou six millions dans ses poches, ira chercher votre maîtresse au bout du monde et vous l'amènera à Venise. Il la prendra pour lui s'il la trouve. S'il ne la trouve pas, il en prendra une autre: je vous conseille d'oublier votre valet Cacambo et votre maîtresse Cunégonde.» Martin n'était pas consolant. La mélancolie de Candide augmenta et Martin ne cessait de lui prouver qu'il y avait peu de vertu et peu de bonheur sur la terre, excepté peut-être dans Eldorado, où personne ne pouvait aller.

En disputant sur cette matière importante, et en attendant Cunégonde, Candide aperçut un jeune théatin dans la place Saint-Marc, qui tenait sous le bras une fille. Le théatin paraissait frais, potelé, vigoureux; ses yeux étaient brillants, son air assuré, sa mine haute, sa démarche fière. La fille était très jolie et chantait; elle regardait amoureusement son théatin, et de temps en temps lui pinçait ses grosses joues. «Vous m'avouerez du moins, dit Candide à Martin, que ces gens-ci sont heureux. Je n'ai trouvé jusqu'à présent dans

Chapter XXIV

Of Paquette and Brother Giroflée[36]

As soon as he was in Venice, he had a search made for Cacambo in all the inns, in all the cafés, in all the brothels, and found him nowhere. He sent someone every day to reconnoiter all the ships and all the barges: no news of Cacambo. "What!" he said to Martin, "I've had time to go from Surinam to Bordeaux, from Bordeaux to Paris, from Paris to Dieppe, from Dieppe to Portsmouth, to run along the coasts of Portugal and Spain, to cross the entire Mediterranean, to spend several months in Venice, and still the lovely Cunégonde hasn't come! Instead of her, I've met only a disreputable woman and an abbé from Périgord! Cunégonde is dead, without a doubt, and all that's left for me is to die too. Oh! it would have been better to remain in the paradise of Eldorado than to return to this accursed Europe. How right you are, my dear Martin! everything is merely illusion and calamity!"

He fell into a black melancholy, and refused to go to the opera *alla moda* or the other carnival entertainments; not a single lady tempted him in the least. Martin said to him, "You're really very naive to imagine that a half-breed valet who has five or six million in his pockets will go in search of your mistress at the end of the world and bring her to you in Venice. He'll take her for himself if he finds her. If he doesn't find her, he'll take another woman; I advise you to forget about your valet Cacambo and your mistress Cunégonde." Martin was not comforting. Candide's melancholy increased and Martin did not stop proving to him that there was little virtue and little happiness on earth, except perhaps in Eldorado, where no one could go.

While they were arguing this important matter and waiting for Cunégonde, Candide noticed a young Theatine monk in St. Mark's Square who was arm-in-arm with a girl. The Theatine appeared to be healthy, plump and robust; his eyes sparkled, his manner was assured, his bearing erect, his gait proud. The girl was very pretty and was singing; she gazed lovingly at her Theatine and from time to time pinched him on his chubby cheeks. "At least you'll admit to me," said Candide to Martin, "that these people are happy. So far

[36] *Giroflée* is the French word for gillyflower.

toute la terre habitable, excepté dans Eldorado, que des infortunés; mais, pour cette fille et ce théatin, je gage que ce sont des créatures très heureuses.—Je gage que non, dit Martin.—Il n'y a qu'à les prier à dîner, dit Candide, et vous verrez si je me trompe.»

Aussitôt il les aborde, il leur fait son compliment, et les invite à venir à son hôtellerie manger des macaronis, des perdrix de Lombardie, des œufs d'esturgeon, et à boire du vin de Montepulciano, du lacryma-christi, du chypre et du samos. La demoiselle rougit, le théatin accepta la partie, et la fille le suivit en regardant Candide avec des yeux de surprise et de confusion qui furent obscurcis de quelques larmes. A peine fut-elle entrée dans la chambre de Candide qu'elle lui dit: «Eh quoi! monsieur Candide ne reconnaît plus Paquette!» A ces mots, Candide, qui ne l'avait pas considérée jusquelà avec attention, parce qu'il n'était occupé que de Cunégonde, lui dit: «Hélas, ma pauvre enfant, c'est donc vous qui avez mis le docteur Pangloss dans le bel état où je l'ai vu?—Hélas! Monsieur, c'est moi-même, dit Paquette; je vois que vous êtes instruit de tout. J'ai su les malheurs épouvantables arrivés à toute la maison de madame la baronne et à la belle Cunégonde. Je vous jure que ma destinée n'a guère été moins triste. J'étais fort innocente quand vous m'avez vue. Un cordelier qui était mon confesseur me séduisit aisément. Les suites en furent affreuses; je fus obligée de sortir du château quelque temps après que monsieur le baron vous eut renvoyé à grands coups de pied dans le derrière. Si un fameux médecin n'avait pas pris pitié de moi, j'étais morte. Je fus quelque temps par reconnaissance la maîtresse de ce médecin. Sa femme, qui était jalouse à la rage, me battait tous les jours impitoyablement; c'était une furie. Ce médecin était le plus laid de tous les hommes, et moi la plus malheureuse de toutes les créatures d'être battue continuellement pour un homme que je n'aimais pas. Vous savez, Monsieur, combien il est dangereux pour une femme acariâtre d'être l'épouse d'un médecin. Celui-ci, outré des procédés de sa femme, lui donna un jour, pour la guérir d'un petit rhume, une médecine si efficace qu'elle en mourut en deux heures de temps dans des convulsions horribles. Les parents de madame intentèrent à monsieur un procès criminel; il prit la fuite, et moi je fus mise en prison. Mon innocence ne m'aurait pas sauvée si je n'avais été un peu jolie. Le juge m'élargit à condition qu'il succéderait au médecin. Je fus bientôt supplantée par une rivale, chassée sans récompense, et obligée de continuer ce métier abominable qui vous paraît si plaisant à vous autres hommes, et qui n'est pour nous qu'un abîme de misères. J'allai exercer la

I've found only unfortunates in all the habitable world, except in Eldorado; but, as for that girl and that Theatine, I'll wager that they're very happy creatures." "I'll wager they're not," said Martin. "We need only invite them to dinner," said Candide, "and you'll see whether I'm mistaken."

He immediately went up to them, paid them his respects and invited them to come to his inn to eat macaroni, Lombardy partridges and caviar, and to drink some wine from Montepulciano, Cyprus and Samos, and some Lachryma Christi. The young lady blushed, the Theatine accepted the invitation and the girl followed him, looking at Candide with eyes full of surprise and confusion and dimmed by a few tears. Scarcely had she entered Candide's room when she said to him, "What! does Monsieur Candide no longer recognize Paquette?" At these words, Candide, who until then had not examined her with any attention because he was occupied solely with Cunégonde, said to her, "Alas, my poor child, is it you, then, who put Doctor Pangloss in the fine state in which I saw him?" "Alas! sir, it is I," said Paquette; "I see that you're well informed about it all. I've been told about the terrible misfortunes visited upon the baroness's entire household, including the lovely Cunégonde. I swear to you that my fate has been scarcely less sad. I was extremely innocent when you knew me. A Franciscan who was my confessor easily seduced me. The consequences of that were frightful; I was obliged to leave the country residence a short time after the baron had sent you packing with great kicks in the backside. If a famous physician hadn't taken pity on me, I would have died. Out of gratitude I became that physician's mistress for a while. His wife, who was madly jealous, beat me pitilessly every day; she was a fury. This physician was the ugliest of men, and I the unhappiest of all creatures at being beaten continually for a man I didn't love. You know, sir, how dangerous it is for a peevish woman to be a physician's spouse. He, furious at his wife's behavior, gave her one day, to cure her of a minor cold, such an efficacious medicine that she died two hours later in horrible convulsions. The woman's family brought a criminal suit against the gentleman; he took flight, and I was put in prison. My innocence wouldn't have saved me if I hadn't been rather pretty. The judge set me at liberty on condition that he could take the physician's place. I was soon supplanted by a rival, thrown out without recompense and obliged to continue this abominable profession that seems so pleasant to you men, and that for us is only an abyss of miseries. I went to carry on my profession in Venice. Oh!

profession à Venise. Ah! Monsieur, si vous pouviez vous imaginer ce que c'est que d'être obligée de caresser indifféremment un vieux marchand, un avocat, un moine, un gondolier, un abbé; d'être exposée à toutes les insultes, à toutes les avanies; d'être souvent réduite à emprunter une jupe pour aller se la faire lever par un homme dégoûtant; d'être volée par l'un de ce qu'on a gagné avec l'autre; d'être rançonnée par les officiers de justice, et de n'avoir en perspective qu'une vieillesse affreuse, un hôpital et un fumier, vous concluriez que je suis une des plus malheureuses créatures du monde.»

Paquette ouvrait ainsi son cœur au bon Candide, dans un cabinet, en présence de Martin, qui disait à Candide: «Vous voyez que j'ai déjà gagné la moitié de la gageure.»

Frère Giroflée était resté dans la salle à manger, et buvait un coup en attendant le dîner. «Mais, dit Candide à Paquette, vous aviez l'air si gai, si content, quand je vous ai rencontrée; vous chantiez, vous caressiez le théatin avec une complaisance naturelle; vous m'avez paru aussi heureuse que vous prétendez être infortunée. —Ah! Monsieur, répondit Paquette, c'est encore là une des misères du métier. J'ai été hier volée et battue par un officier, et il faut aujourd'hui que je paraisse de bonne humeur pour plaire à un moine.»

Candide n'en voulut pas davantage; il avoua que Martin avait raison. On se mit à table avec Paquette et le théatin, le repas fut assez amusant, et sur la fin on se parla avec quelque confiance. «Mon père, dit Candide au moine, vous me paraissez jouir d'une destinée que tout le monde doit envier; la fleur de la santé brille sur votre visage, votre physionomie annonce le bonheur; vous avez une très jolie fille pour votre récréation, et vous paraissez très content de votre état de théatin.

—Ma foi, Monsieur, dit frère Giroflée, je voudrais que tous les théatins fussent au fond de la mer. J'ai été tenté cent fois de mettre le feu au couvent, et d'aller me faire Turc. Mes parents me forcèrent à l'âge de quinze ans d'endosser cette détestable robe, pour laisser plus de fortune à un maudit frère aîné que Dieu confonde! La jalousie, la discorde, la rage, habitent dans le couvent. Il est vrai que j'ai prêché quelques mauvais sermons qui m'ont valu un peu d'argent, dont le prieur me vole la moitié: le reste me sert à entretenir des filles; mais, quand je rentre le soir dans le monastère, je suis prêt de me casser la tête contre les murs du dortoir; et tous mes confrères sont dans le même cas.»

Martin se tournant vers Candide avec son sang-froid ordinaire: «Eh bien, lui dit-il, n'ai-je pas gagné la gageure tout entière?» Can-

sir, if you could imagine what it is to be obliged to caress alike an aged merchant, a lawyer, a monk, a gondolier or an abbé; to be exposed to every insult, every affront; to be often reduced to borrowing a skirt so as to go and have it pulled up by a disgusting man; to be robbed by one man of what one has earned with another; to be made to pay through the nose by officers of the law, and to have nothing to look forward to but a frightful old age, a poorhouse and a dunghill, you'd conclude that I'm one of the most unfortunate creatures in the world."

Paquette opened her heart in this way to the good Candide, in a private room, in the presence of Martin, who said to Candide, "You can see that I've already won half the wager."

Brother Giroflée had remained in the dining room, and was having a drink while awaiting dinner. "But," said Candide to Paquette, "you seemed so gay, so content, when I encountered you; you were singing, you were caressing the Theatine with natural affability; you seemed to me as happy as you claim to be unfortunate." "Oh! sir," replied Paquette, "that's another one of the miseries of the trade. Yesterday I was robbed and beaten by an officer, and today I must appear to be in a good mood to please a monk."

Candide wished to hear no more; he admitted that Martin was right. They sat down to table with Paquette and the Theatine; the meal was entertaining enough and by the end of it they were speaking fairly openly. "Father," said Candide to the monk, "you seem to me to enjoy a destiny that everyone would envy; the flower of health glows on your face, your appearance bespeaks happiness; you have a very pretty girl for your amusement, and you seem very content with your life as a Theatine."

"Upon my word, sir," said Brother Giroflée, "I would wish all Theatines at the bottom of the ocean. I've been tempted a hundred times to set fire to the monastery, and to go off and turn Turk. My parents compelled me at the age of fifteen to put on this loathsome habit, so that they might leave a larger fortune to an accursed elder brother, may God confound him! Jealousy, discord and anger inhabit the monastery. It's true that I've preached a few bad sermons that earned me a little money, half of which is stolen by the prior; the remainder serves me to keep girls; but when I return to the monastery each evening I'm ready to smash my head against the dormitory walls; and all my fellow monks are in the same state."

Martin, turning toward Candide with his usual composure, said to him, "Well, have I not won the entire wager?" Candide gave two

dide donna deux mille piastres à Paquette et mille piastres à frère Giroflée. «Je vous réponds, dit-il, qu'avec cela ils seront heureux.—Je n'en crois rien du tout, dit Martin; vous les rendrez peut-être avec ces piastres beaucoup plus malheureux encore.—Il en sera ce qui pourra, dit Candide; mais une chose me console, je vois qu'on retrouve souvent les gens qu'on ne croyait jamais retrouver; il se pourra bien faire qu'ayant rencontré mon mouton rouge et Paquette, je rencontre aussi Cunégonde.—Je souhaite, dit Martin, qu'elle fasse un jour votre bonheur; mais c'est de quoi je doute fort.—Vous êtes bien dur, dit Candide.—C'est que j'ai vécu, dit Martin.

—Mais regardez ces gondoliers, dit Candide; ne chantent-ils pas sans cesse?—Vous ne les voyez pas dans leur ménage, avec leurs femmes et leurs marmots d'enfants, dit Martin. Le doge a ses chagrins, les gondoliers ont les leurs. Il est vrai qu'à tout prendre le sort d'un gondolier est préférable à celui d'un doge; mais je crois la différence si médiocre que cela ne vaut pas la peine d'être examiné.

—On parle, dit Candide, du sénateur Pococuranté qui demeure dans ce beau palais sur la Brenta, et qui reçoit assez bien les étrangers. On prétend que c'est un homme qui n'a jamais eu de chagrin.—Je voudrais voir une espèce si rare», dit Martin. Candide aussitôt fit demander au seigneur Pococuranté la permission de venir le voir le lendemain.

Chapitre XXV

Visite chez le seigneur Pococuranté, noble Vénitien

Candide et Martin allèrent en gondole sur la Brenta et arrivèrent au palais du noble Pococuranté. Les jardins étaient bien entendus et ornés de belles statues de marbre; le palais, d'une belle architecture. Le maître du logis, homme de soixante ans, fort riche, reçut très poliment les deux curieux, mais avec très peu d'empressement, ce qui déconcerta Candide et ne déplut point à Martin.

D'abord deux filles jolies et proprement mises servirent du chocolat qu'elles firent très bien mousser. Candide ne put s'empêcher de

thousand piasters to Paquette and a thousand piasters to Brother Giroflée. "I guarantee you," he said, "that they'll be happy with that." "I don't think so in the least," said Martin; "with those piasters you'll perhaps make them much more unhappy." "That may be," said Candide; "but one thing comforts me: I see that one often finds again those people one believed one would never find again; it could well be that having come across my red sheep and Paquette, I'll also come across Cunégonde." "I hope," said Martin, "that one day she'll make you happy; but I very much doubt it." "You're very severe," said Candide. "It's because I've lived," said Martin.

"But look at those gondoliers," said Candide; "are they not always singing?" "You don't see them at home, with their wives and their brattish children," said Martin. "The doge has his afflictions, the gondoliers have theirs. It's true that, on the whole, the lot of a gondolier is preferable to that of a doge; but I think the difference so insignificant that it's not worth the trouble of being examined."

"People talk," said Candide, "of Senator Pococurante who lives in that beautiful palace on the Brenta, and who gives a rather good reception to foreigners. It's claimed that he's a man who has never suffered affliction." "I'd like to see such a rare species," said Martin. Candide immediately sent a request to Lord Pococurante for permission to come to see him on the following day.

CHAPTER XXV

VISIT TO LORD POCOCURANTE, VENETIAN NOBLEMAN

Candide and Martin traveled by gondola along the Brenta and reached the palace of the noble Pococurante. The gardens were well laid out and adorned with beautiful marble statues: the palace was a fine piece of architecture. The master of the house, an extremely wealthy man of sixty years of age, received the two inquisitive persons very politely, but with very little enthusiasm, which disconcerted Candide and did not displease Martin at all.

First, two pretty, well-dressed girls served chocolate that they had frothed up very nicely. Candide could not help praising them for

les louer sur leur beauté, sur leur bonne grâce et sur leur adresse. «Ce sont d'assez bonnes créatures, dit le sénateur Pococuranté; je les fais quelquefois coucher dans mon lit, car je suis bien las des dames de la ville, de leurs coquetteries, de leurs jalousies, de leurs querelles, de leurs humeurs, de leurs petitesses, de leur orgueil, de leur sottises, et des sonnets qu'il faut faire ou commander pour elles; mais, après tout, ces deux filles commencent fort à m'ennuyer.»

Candide, après le déjeuner, se promenant dans une longue galerie, fut surpris de la beauté des tableaux. Il demanda de quel maître étaient les deux premiers. «Ils sont de Raphaël, dit le sénateur; je les achetai fort cher par vanité il y a quelques années; on dit que c'est ce qu'il y a de plus beau en Italie, mais ils ne me plaisent point du tout: la couleur en est très rembrunie; les figures ne sont pas assez arrondies et ne sortent point assez; les draperies ne ressemblent en rien à une étoffe; en un mot, quoi qu'on en dise, je ne trouve point là une imitation vraie de la nature elle-même. Je n'aimerai un tableau que quand je croirai voir la nature elle-même: il n'y en a point de cette espèce. J'ai beaucoup de tableaux, mais je ne les regarde plus.»

Pococuranté, en attendant le dîner, se fit donner un concerto. Candide trouva la musique délicieuse. «Ce bruit, dit Pococuranté, peut amuser une demi-heure; mais, s'il dure plus longtemps, il fatigue tout le monde, quoique personne n'ose l'avouer. La musique aujourd'hui n'est plus que l'art d'exécuter des choses difficiles, et ce qui n'est que difficile ne plaît point à la longue.

«J'aimerais peut-être mieux l'opéra, si on n'avait pas trouvé le secret d'en faire un monstre qui me révolte. Ira voir qui voudra de mauvaises tragédies en musique, où les scènes ne sont faites que pour amener, très mal à propos, deux ou trois chansons ridicules qui font valoir le gosier d'une actrice; se pâmera de plaisir qui voudra, ou qui pourra, en voyant un châtré fredonner le rôle de César et de Caton et se promener d'un air gauche sur des planches; pour moi, il y a longtemps que j'ai renoncé à ces pauvretés, qui font aujourd'hui la gloire de l'Italie, et que des souverains paient si chèrement.» Candide disputa un peu, mais avec discrétion. Martin fut entièrement de l'avis du sénateur.

On se mit à table, et, après un excellent dîner, on entra dans la bibliothèque. Candide, en voyant un Homère magnifiquement relié, loua l'illustrissime sur son bon goût. «Voilà, dit-il, un livre qui faisait les délices du grand Pangloss, le meilleur philosophe de l'Allemagne.—Il ne fait pas les miennes, dit froidement Pococu-

their beauty, their grace and their dexterity. "They are pretty good creatures," said Senator Pococurante; "sometimes I take them to bed with me, for I'm thoroughly bored by the ladies of the city, with their coquetries, their jealousies, their quarrels, their moods, their meanness, their pride, their stupidities and the sonnets one has to write or commission for them; but, after all, these two girls are beginning to bore me greatly too."

Candide, after luncheon, while walking through a long gallery, was surprised by the beauty of the paintings. He asked the name of the master who had painted the first two. "They're by Raphael," said the senator; "I bought them out of vanity at a very high price a few years ago; they are said to be the most beautiful things in Italy, but they don't please me at all: the color has become very darkened; the figures aren't rounded enough and don't stand out enough; the draperies don't resemble fabric in the least; in a word, whatever anyone says, I don't find in them any genuine imitation of nature itself. I'll like a painting only when I believe I'm seeing nature itself: there are none of that kind. I have a great many paintings, but I no longer look at them."

Pococurante, while awaiting dinner, had a concerto performed. Candide found the music delightful. "That noise," said Pococurante, "may be amusing for half an hour; but if it lasts any longer it bores everyone, although no one dares to admit it. Music today is no longer anything but the art of executing difficult things, and that which is only difficult doesn't please for long.

"Perhaps I would prefer opera if they hadn't found the secret of turning it into a monstrosity that revolts me. Let anyone who wishes go to see bad tragedies set to music, in which the scenes exist only to introduce, very inappropriately, two or three ridiculous songs that are there to show off some actress's vocal cords; let anyone who wishes, or who is able, swoon with pleasure on seeing a castrato hum the role of Caesar or Cato, and strut awkwardly across the stage; as for me, it's a long time since I renounced those sorry things, which are today the glory of Italy and for which sovereigns pay such vast sums." Candide argued a little, but with discretion. Martin was entirely of the senator's opinion.

They sat down to table, and, after an excellent dinner, they went into the library. Candide, seeing a magnificently bound edition of Homer, praised the most illustrious lord on his good taste. "There's a book," he said, "that used to delight the great Pangloss, the best philosopher in Germany." "It doesn't delight me," said Pococurante

ranté; on me fit accroire autrefois que j'avais du plaisir en le lisant; mais cette répétition continuelle de combats qui se ressemblent tous, ces dieux qui agissent toujours pour ne rien faire de décisif, cette Hélène qui est le sujet de la guerre, et qui à peine est une actrice de la pièce, cette Troie qu'on assiège et qu'on ne prend point, tout cela me causait le plus mortel ennui. J'ai demandé quelquefois à des savants s'ils s'ennuyaient autant que moi à cette lecture. Tous les gens sincères m'ont avoué que le livre leur tombait des mains, mais qu'il fallait toujours l'avoir dans sa bibliothèque, comme un monument de l'antiquité, et comme ces médailles rouillées qui ne peuvent être de commerce.

—Votre Excellence ne pense pas ainsi de Virgile? dit Candide.—Je conviens, dit Pococuranté, que le second, le quatrième et le sixième livre de son *Enéide* sont excellents; mais pour son pieux Enée, et le fort Cloanthe, et l'ami Achates, et le petit Ascanius, et l'imbécile roi Latinus, et la bourgeoise Amata, et l'insipide Lavinia, je ne crois pas qu'il y ait rien de si froid et de plus désagréable. J'aime mieux le Tasse et les contes à dormir debout de l'Arioste.

—Oserais-je vous demander, Monsieur, dit Candide, si vous n'avez pas un grand plaisir à lire Horace?—Il y a des maximes, dit Pococuranté, dont un homme du monde peut faire son profit, et qui, étant resserrées dans des vers énergiques, se gravent plus aisément dans la mémoire. Mais je me soucie fort peu de son voyage à Brindes, et de sa description d'un mauvais dîner, et de la querelle des crocheteurs entre je ne sais quel Pupilus, dont les paroles, dit-il, *étaient pleines de pus*, et un autre dont les paroles *étaient du vinaigre*. Je n'ai lu qu'avec extrême dégoût ses vers grossiers contre des vieilles et contre des sorcières; et je ne vois pas quel mérite il peut y avoir à dire à son ami Mæcenas que, s'il est mis par lui au rang des poètes lyriques, il frappera les astres de son front sublime. Les sots admirent tout dans un auteur estimé. Je ne lis que pour moi; je n'aime que ce qui est à mon usage.» Candide, qui avait été élevé à ne jamais juger de rien par lui-même, était fort etonné de ce qu'il entendait; et Martin trouvait la façon de penser de Pococuranté assez raisonnable.

«Oh! voici un Cicéron, dit Candide; pour ce grand homme-là, je pense que vous ne vous lassez point de le lire.—Je ne le lis jamais, répondit le Vénitien. Que m'importe qu'il ait plaidé pour Rabirius ou pour Cluentius? J'ai bien assez des procès que je juge; je me serais

coldly; "formerly I was led to believe that I took pleasure in reading it; but that constant repetition of combats that are all alike, those gods who always act in such a way as to do nothing decisive, that Helen who is the cause of the war, and who scarcely plays a part in the drama, that Troy that is besieged and never taken, all that would cause me the most deadly boredom. I asked some scholars on a few occasions if they were as bored as I on reading it. All those who were sincere admitted to me that the book would fall from their hands, but that one must always have it in one's library, like a monument from antiquity, and like those rusty coins that can't be used as real currency."

"Your Excellency doesn't think that way of Virgil?" said Candide. "I acknowledge," said Pococurante, "that the second, the fourth and the sixth book of his *Aeneid* are excellent; but as for his pious Aeneas, and stalwart Cloanthes, and faithful Achates, and little Ascanius, and the imbecile King Latinus, and middle-class Amata and insipid Lavinia, I don't believe there's anything so lifeless and more disagreeable. I prefer Tasso, and Ariosto's cock-and-bull stories."

"Might I presume to ask you, sir," said Candide, "if you don't take great pleasure in reading Horace?" "There are some of his maxims," said Pococurante, "from which a man of the world could profit, and which, being condensed into lively verse, engrave themselves more readily in the memory. But I care very little for his journey to Brindisium, his description of a bad dinner, and the ruffians' quarrel between someone or other named Pupilus[37] whose words, he says, 'were full of pus,' and another whose words 'were vinegar.' I read only with extreme distaste his coarse verses against old women and against witches; and I don't see what merit there can be in telling his friend Maecenas that were he to be raised by him to the ranks of the lyric poets, he would strike the stars with his sublime brow. Fools admire everything in an esteemed author. I read only for myself; I like only that which is of use to me." Candide, who had been brought up never to judge anything by himself, was greatly astonished by what he was hearing; but Martin found Pococurante's way of thinking reasonable enough.

"Oh! here's a Cicero," said Candide; "now as for that great man, I imagine you never tire of reading him." "I never read him," replied the Venetian. "What do I care that he pleaded for Rabirius or for Cluentius? I have quite enough lawsuits with the ones I judge; I

[37] Pococurante's corruption of Rupilius, *Satires* 1.7.

mieux accommodé de ses œuvres philosophiques; mais, quand j'ai vu qu'il doutait de tout, j'ai conclu que j'en savais autant que lui, et que je n'avais besoin de personne pour être ignorant.

—Ah! voilà quatre-vingts volumes de recueils d'une académie des sciences, s'écria Martin; il se peut qu'il y ait là du bon.—Il y en aurait, dit Pococuranté, si un seul des auteurs de ces fatras avait inventé seulement l'art de faire des épingles; mais il n'y a dans tous ces livres que de vains systèmes et pas une seule chose utile.

—Que de pièces de théâtre je vois là! dit Candide; en italien, en espagnol, en français!—Oui, dit le sénateur, il y en a trois mille, et pas trois douzaines de bonnes. Pour ces recueils de sermons, qui tous ensemble ne valent pas une page de Sénèque, et tous ces gros volumes de théologie, vous pensez bien que je ne les ouvre jamais, ni moi ni personne.»

Martin aperçut des rayons chargés de livres anglais. «Je crois, dit-il, qu'un républicain doit se plaire à la plupart de ces ouvrages écrits si librement.—Oui, répondit Pococuranté, il est beau d'écrire ce qu'on pense; c'est le privilège de l'homme. Dans toute notre Italie, on n'écrit que ce qu'on ne pense pas; ceux qui habitent la patrie des Césars et des Antonins n'osent avoir une idée sans la permission d'un jacobin. Je serais content de la liberté qui inspire les génies anglais si la passion et l'esprit de parti ne corrompaient pas tout ce que cette précieuse liberté a d'estimable.»

Candide, apercevant un Milton, lui demanda s'il ne regardait pas cet auteur comme un grand homme. «Qui? dit Pococuranté, ce barbare qui fait un long commentaire du premier chapitre de la Genèse en dix livres de vers durs? ce grossier imitateur des Grecs, qui défigure la création, et qui, tandis que Moïse représente l'Etre éternel produisant le monde par la parole, fait prendre un grand compas par le Messiah dans une armoire du ciel pour tracer son ouvrage? Moi, j'estimerais celui qui a gâté l'enfer et le diable du Tasse; qui déguise Lucifer tantôt en crapaud, tantôt en pygmée; qui lui fait rebattre cent fois les mêmes discours; qui le fait disputer sur la théologie; qui, en imitant sérieusement l'invention comique des armes à feu de l'Arioste, fait tirer le canon dans le ciel par les diables? Ni moi, ni personne en Italie, n'a pu se plaire à toutes ces tristes extravagances. Le mariage du péché et de la mort et les couleuvres dont le péché accouche font vomir tout homme qui a le goût un peu délicat, et sa longue description d'un hôpital n'est bonne que

might have put up better with his philosophical works; but when I saw that he doubted everything, I concluded that I knew as much as he did, and that I needed no one's help to be ignorant."

"Ah! there are eighty volumes of collected papers from an academy of science," exclaimed Martin; "there may be something good in them." "There would be," said Pococurante, "if even one of the authors of that trash had invented only the art of making pins; but in all those books there are only empty systems and not one useful thing."

"What a lot of plays I see there!" said Candide; "in Italian, Spanish, French!" "Yes," said the senator, "there are three thousand, and not three dozen good ones. As for those collections of sermons, which all together aren't worth one page of Seneca, and all those large volumes of theology, you can be sure that I never open them, not I nor anyone else."

Martin noticed some shelves laden with English books. "I trust," he said, "that a republican must take pleasure in the majority of those books written with so much freedom." "Yes," replied Pococurante, "it's a fine thing to write what one thinks; it's the privilege of man. In all Italy people write only what they don't think; those who inhabit the native land of the Caesars and the Antonines don't dare to have an idea without the permission of a Dominican. I would be happy with the freedom that inspires the English geniuses if party feeling and party spirit didn't corrupt everything estimable in that precious freedom."

Candide, noticing a Milton, asked him if he did not consider that author a great man. "Who?" said Pococurante, "that barbarian who has created a long commentary on the first chapter of Genesis in ten books of harsh verse? that crude imitator of the Greeks who disfigures the Creation and who, while Moses presents the Eternal Being creating the world by the word, has the Messiah take up a huge pair of compasses from a closet in heaven to trace out his work? Would *I* esteem the man who spoiled the hell and the devil of Tasso; who disguises Lucifer sometimes as a toad, sometimes as a pygmy; who has him repeat the same speeches a hundred times; who has him argue about theology; who, while imitating in a serious manner the comic invention of firearms in Ariosto, has the devils fire cannon in heaven? Not I, nor anyone in Italy, has been able to take pleasure in all those sorry extravagances. The marriage of Sin and Death, and the snakes to which Sin gives birth, nauseate any man with a little delicacy of taste, and his long description of a hospital is only

pour un fossoyeur. Ce poème obscur, bizarre et dégoûtant, fut méprisé à sa naissance; je le traite aujourd'hui comme il fut traité dans sa patrie par les contemporains. Au reste, je dis ce que je pense, et je me soucie fort peu que les autres pensent comme moi.» Candide était affligé de ces discours; il respectait Homère, il aimait un peu Milton. «Hélas! dit-il tout bas à Martin, j'ai bien peur que cet homme-ci n'ait un souverain mépris pour nos poètes allemands.—Il n'y aurait pas grand mal à cela, dit Martin.—Oh, quel homme supérieur! disait encore Candide entre ses dents, quel grand génie que ce Pococuranté! rien ne peut lui plaire.»

Après avoir fait ainsi la revue de tous les livres, ils descendirent dans le jardin. Candide en loua toutes les beautés. «Je ne sais rien de si mauvais goût, dit le maître: nous n'avons ici que des colifichets; mais je vais dès demain en faire planter un d'un dessin plus noble.»

Quand les deux curieux eurent pris congé de Son Excellence: «Or çà, dit Candide à Martin, vous conviendrez que voilà le plus heureux de tous les hommes, car il est au-dessus de tout ce qu'il possède.—Ne voyez-vous pas, dit Martin, qu'il est dégoûté de tout ce qu'il possède? Platon a dit, il y a longtemps, que les meilleurs estomacs ne sont pas ceux qui rebutent tous les aliments—Mais, dit Candide, n'y a-t-il pas du plaisir à tout critiquer, à sentir des défauts où les autres hommes croient voir des beautés?—C'est-à-dire, reprit Martin, qu'il y a du plaisir à n'avoir pas de plaisir?—Oh bien! dit Candide, il n'y a donc d'heureux que moi, quand je reverrai Mlle Cunégonde.—C'est toujours bien fait d'espérer», dit Martin.

Cependant les jours, les semaines s'écoulaient; Cacambo ne revenait point, et Candide était si abîmé dans sa douleur qu'il ne fit pas même réflexion que Paquette et frère Giroflée n'étaient pas venus seulement le remercier.

of any good to a gravedigger. That obscure, bizarre and disgusting poem was scorned at its birth; I treat it today as it was treated in its own country by its contemporaries. Moreover, I say what I think, and I have very little concern that others should think as I do." Candide was distressed by these remarks; he respected Homer and he had some liking for Milton. "Alas!" he whispered to Martin, "I'm afraid this man may have utter contempt for our German poets." "There would be no great harm in that," said Martin. "Oh, what a superior man!" said Candide, again under his breath, "what a great genius this Pococurante is! nothing can please him."

Having thus examined all the books, they went downstairs to the garden. Candide praised all its beauties. "I know of nothing in such bad taste," said the master: "we have here nothing but trifles; but tomorrow I shall begin to have planted a garden of nobler design."

When the two inquisitive visitors had taken leave of His Excellency: "Well now," Candide said to Martin, "you'll agree that he is the most fortunate of all men, for he is superior to all he possesses." "Don't you see," said Martin, "that he is disgusted with all he possesses? Plato said a long time ago that the best stomachs aren't those that reject all nourishment." "But," said Candide, "isn't there pleasure in criticizing everything, in perceiving faults where other men think they see beauties?" "That is to say," rejoined Martin, "that there is pleasure in not having pleasure?" "Oh well," said Candide, "then no one is happy except me, when I see Miss Cunégonde again." "It's always good to hope," said Martin.

However, the days, the weeks passed; Cacambo did not return, and Candide was so overwhelmed with sorrow that he did not even reflect on the fact that Paquette and Brother Giroflée had not even come to thank him.

Chapitre XXVI

D'un souper que Candide et Martin firent avec six étrangers, et qui ils étaient

Un soir que Candide, suivi de Martin, allait se mettre à table avec les étrangers qui logeaient dans la même hôtellerie, un homme à visage couleur de suie l'aborda par-derrière, et, le prenant par le bras, lui dit: «Soyez prêt à partir avec nous, n'y manquez pas.» Il se retourne et voit Cacambo. Il n'y avait que la vue de Cunégonde qui pût l'étonner et lui plaire davantage. Il fut sur le point de devenir fou de joie. Il embrasse son cher ami. «Cunégonde est ici, sans doute, où est-elle? Mène-moi vers elle, que je meure de joie avec elle.—Cunégonde n'est point ici, dit Cacambo, elle est à Constantinople.—Ah, Ciel! à Constantinople! mais, fût-elle à la Chine, j'y vole, partons.—Nous partirons après souper, reprit Cacambo, je ne peux vous en dire davantage; je suis esclave, mon maître m'attend; il faut que j'aille le servir à table: ne dites mot; soupez et tenez-vous prêt.»

Candide, partagé entre la joie et la douleur, charmé d'avoir revu son agent fidèle, étonné de le voir esclave, plein de l'idée de retrouver sa maîtresse, le cœur agité, l'esprit bouleversé, se mit à table avec Martin, qui voyait de sang-froid toutes ces aventures, et avec six étrangers qui étaient venus passer le carnaval à Venise.

Cacambo, qui versait à boire à l'un de ces étrangers, s'approcha de l'oreille de son maître, sur la fin du repas, et lui dit: «Sire, Votre Majesté partira quand elle voudra, le vaisseau est prêt.» Ayant dit ces mots, il sortit. Les convives, étonnés, se regardaient sans proférer une seule parole, lorsqu'un autre domestique, s'approchant de son maître, lui dit: «Sire, la chaise de Votre Majesté est à Padoue, et la barque est prête.» Le maître fit un signe, et le domestique partit. Tous les convives se regardèrent encore, et la surprise commune redoubla. Un troisième valet, s'approchant aussi d'un troisième étranger, lui dit: «Sire, croyez-moi, Votre Majesté ne doit pas rester ici plus longtemps: je vais tout préparer»; et aussitôt il disparut.

Candide et Martin ne doutèrent pas alors que ce ne fût une mascarade du carnaval. Un quatrième domestique dit au quatrième maître: «Votre Majesté partira quand elle voudra», et sortit comme

CHAPTER XXVI

OF A SUPPER THAT CANDIDE AND MARTIN ATE
WITH SIX FOREIGNERS, AND WHO THEY WERE

One evening, when Candide, followed by Martin, was about to sit down to table with the foreigners who were staying at the same inn, a man with a face the color of soot came up to him from behind and, taking him by the arm, said to him, "Be ready to leave with us, without fail." He turned around and saw Cacambo. Only the sight of Cunégonde could have astonished and pleased him more. He was on the verge of becoming mad with joy. He embraced his dear friend. "Doubtless, Cunégonde is here, where is she? Take me to her that I may die with joy in her presence." "Cunégonde isn't here," said Cacambo, "she is in Constantinople." "Good Heavens! in Constantinople! but were she in China I would fly there, let's go!" "We'll leave after supper," rejoined Cacambo, "I can't tell you any more about it; I'm a slave, my master is waiting for me; I have to go to serve him at table; don't say a word; have supper and be ready."

Candide, torn between joy and grief, delighted to have seen again his faithful intermediary, astonished to see him a slave, full of the idea of finding his mistress again, his heart disquieted, his mind thrown into disorder, sat down to table with Martin—who looked on all these adventures with composure—and with six foreigners who had come to Venice for the carnival.

Cacambo, who was pouring drinks for one of these foreigners, leaned over to his master toward the end of the meal and said to him, "Sire, Your Majesty may leave when he wishes, the ship is ready." Having spoken these words, he went out. The guests, astonished, were gazing at one another without uttering a single word when another manservant, coming up to his master, said to him, "Sire, Your Majesty's carriage is in Padua, and the boat is ready." The master made a sign and the servant departed. All the guests gazed at one another once again, and the general surprise redoubled. A third valet, approaching a third foreigner, said to him, "Sire, believe me, Your Majesty shouldn't stay here any longer; I'll go to prepare everything"; and he immediately disappeared.

Candide and Martin did not doubt then that this was a carnival masquerade. A fourth manservant said to a fourth master, "Your Majesty may leave when he wishes," and went out like the others.

les autres. Le cinquième valet en dit autant au cinquième maître.

Mais le sixième valet parla différemment au sixième étranger, qui était auprès de Candide; il lui dit: «Ma foi, Sire, on ne veut plus faire crédit à Votre Majesté, ni à moi non plus; et nous pourrions bien être coffrés cette nuit, vous et moi: je vais pourvoir à mes affaires; adieu.»

Tous les domestiques ayant disparu, les six étrangers, Candide et Martin demeurèrent dans un profond silence. Enfin Candide le rompit. «Messieurs, dit-il, voilà une singulière plaisanterie: pourquoi êtes-vous tous rois? Pour moi je vous avoue que ni moi ni Martin nous ne le sommes.»

Le maître de Cacambo prit alors gravement la parole, et dit en italien: «Je ne suis point plaisant, je m'appelle Achmet III. J'ai été grand sultan plusieurs années; je détrônai mon frère; mon neveu m'a détrôné; on a coupé le cou à mes visirs; j'achève ma vie dans le vieux sérail; mon neveu le grand sultan Mahmoud me permet de voyager quelquefois pour ma santé, et je suis venu passer le carnaval à Venise.»

Un jeune homme qui était auprès d'Achmet parla après lui, et dit: «Je m'appelle Ivan; j'ai été empereur de toutes les Russies; j'ai été détrôné au berceau; mon père et ma mère ont été enfermés; on m'a élevé en prison; j'ai quelquefois la permission de voyager, accompagné de ceux qui me gardent, et je suis venu passer le carnaval à Venise.»

Le troisième dit: «Je suis Charles-Edouard, roi d'Angleterre; mon père m'a cédé ses droits au royaume; j'ai combattu pour les soutenir; on a arraché le cœur à huit cents de mes partisans, et on leur en a battu les joues. J'ai été mis en prison; je vais à Rome faire une visite au roi mon père, détrôné ainsi que moi et mon grand-père, et je suis venu passer le carnaval à Venise.»

Le quatrième prit alors la parole et dit: «Je suis roi des Polaques; le sort de la guerre m'a privé de mes Etats héréditaires; mon père a éprouvé les mêmes revers; je me résigne à la Providence comme le

The fifth valet said as much to the fifth master. But the sixth valet spoke differently to the sixth foreigner, who was seated next to Candide; he said to him, "On my word, Sire, no one will grant any more credit to Your Majesty, or to me either; and we could well be imprisoned this very night, both you and I: I'm going to attend to my affairs; farewell."

All the menservants having disappeared, the six foreigners, Candide and Martin remained in deep silence. At last Candide broke it. "Gentlemen," he said, "that's a singular joke: how come you're all kings? As for me, I confess to you that neither I nor Martin are kings."

Then Cacambo's master spoke up gravely, saying in Italian, "I'm not joking in the least; my name is Ahmed III.[38] I was Grand Sultan for many years; I dethroned my brother; my nephew dethroned me; my viziers were beheaded; I am ending my days in the old seraglio; my nephew, Grand Sultan Mahmud, permits me to travel sometimes for my health, and I've come to Venice for the carnival."

A young man who was seated next to Ahmed spoke after him, and said, "My name is Ivan;[39] I was Emperor of all the Russias; I was dethroned while still in the cradle; my father and mother were imprisoned; I was brought up in prison; I sometimes have permission to travel, accompanied by those who guard me, and I came to Venice for the carnival."

The third said, "My name is Charles Edward,[40] King of England; my father ceded to me his rights to the throne; I fought to maintain them; the hearts were torn from eight hundred of my supporters, and were thrown in their faces. I was put in prison; I'm going to Rome to pay a visit to the king, my father, dethroned like myself and my grandfather, and I came to Venice for the carnival."

The fourth then spoke up, saying, "I am King of the Poles;[41] the fortune of war deprived me of my hereditary states; my father suffered the same misfortune; I resign myself to Providence, like Sultan

[38] Ahmed III (1673–1736), Sultan of Turkey from 1703 to 1730. He was deposed during the uprising led by Patrona Halil, and died in captivity.

[39] Ivan VI Antonovich (1740–1764), reigned from October 1740 until December 1741, then imprisoned and finally assassinated.

[40] Bonnie Prince Charlie, the Young Pretender (1720–1788), leader of the Jacobite Rebellion of 1745–46, defeated on 16 April 1746 at Culloden. His grandfather was the exiled Roman Catholic King James II, and his father the exiled Old Pretender who affected the title King James III.

[41] Augustus III (1696–1763), Elector of Saxony and King of Poland, dethroned in 1756.

sultan Achmet, l'empereur Ivan et le roi Charles-Edouard, à qui
Dieu donne une longue vie, et je suis venu passer le carnaval à
Venise.»

Le cinquième dit: «Je suis aussi roi des Polaques; j'ai perdu mon
royaume deux fois; mais la Providence m'a donné un autre Etat,
dans lequel j'ai fait plus de bien que tous les rois des Sarmates en-
semble n'en ont jamais pu faire sur les bords de la Vistule; je me
résigne aussi à la Providence, et je suis venu passer le carnaval à
Venise.»

Il restait au sixième monarque à parler. «Messieurs, dit-il, je ne
suis pas si grand seigneur que vous; mais enfin j'ai été roi tout comme
un autre. Je suis Théodore; on m'a élu roi en Corse; on m'a appelé
Votre Majesté, et à présent à peine m'appelle-t-on *Monsieur*. J'ai fait
frapper de la monnaie, et je ne possède pas un denier; j'ai eu deux
secrétaires d'Etat, et j'ai à peine un valet; je me suis vu sur un trône,
et j'ai longtemps été à Londres en prison, sur la paille. J'ai bien peur
d'être traité de même ici, quoique je sois venu comme Vos Majestés
passer le carnaval à Venise.»

Les cinq autres rois écoutèrent ce discours avec une noble com-
passion. Chacun d'eux donna vingt sequins au roi Théodore pour
avoir des habits et des chemises; Candide lui fit présent d'un diamant
de deux mille sequins. «Quel est donc, disaient les cinq rois, ce
simple particulier qui est en état de donner cent fois autant que
chacun de nous, et qui le donne?»

Dans l'instant qu'on sortait de table, il arriva dans la même hôtelle-
rie quatre altesses sérénissimes qui avaient aussi perdu leurs Etats
par le sort de la guerre, et qui venaient passer le reste du carnaval à
Venise. Mais Candide ne prit pas seulement garde à ces nouveaux
venus. Il n'était occupé que d'aller trouver sa chère Cunégonde à
Constantinople.

Ahmed, Emperor Ivan and King Charles Edward, to whom may God grant long life, and I came to Venice for the carnival."

The fifth said, "I too am King of the Poles;[42] I lost my kingdom twice; but Providence granted me another state, in which I've done more good than all the Sarmatian kings together were ever able to do on the banks of the Vistula; I too resign myself to Providence, and I came to Venice for the carnival."

It remained for the sixth monarch to speak. "Gentlemen," he said, "I'm not as great a lord as any of you; but, after all, I was a king like any other. I am Theodore;[43] I was elected king in Corsica; I was addressed as 'Your Majesty,' and now I'm scarcely addressed as 'Sir.' I had money minted, and I don't possess a penny; I had two secretaries of state, and I scarcely have a valet; I saw myself on a throne, and for a long time I lay on straw in prison, in London. I'm afraid of being treated the same way here, although I came, like Your Majesties, to Venice for the carnival."

The five other kings listened to this speech with noble compassion. Each of them gave twenty sequins to King Theodore to pay for suits and shirts; Candide made him a gift of a diamond worth two thousand sequins. "Who, then," said the five kings, "is this private citizen who is in a position to give a hundred times as much as any of us, and who gives it?"

At the moment they were leaving the table, there arrived at the same inn four Serene Highnesses who had also lost their states through the fortune of war, and who were coming to Venice for the remainder of the carnival. But Candide did not even take any notice of these newcomers. He was occupied only with going to find his beloved Cunégonde in Constantinople.

[42] Stanislaw Leszczyński (1677–1766), father-in-law to Louis XV, driven into exile by Augustus III. He became Duke of Lorraine and a friend to Voltaire.

[43] Theodor, Baron von Neuhof (1694–1756). As Theodore I, he was nominal King of Corsica in 1736. He was imprisoned for debt in England.

Chapitre XXVII

Voyage de Candide à Constantinople

Le fidèle Cacambo avait déjà obtenu du patron turc qui allait reconduire le sultan Achmet à Constantinople qu'il recevrait Candide et Martin sur son bord. L'un et l'autre s'y rendirent après s'être prosternés devant Sa misérable Hautesse. Candide, chemin faisant, disait à Martin: «Voilà pourtant six rois détrônés, avec qui nous avons soupé, et encore dans ces six rois il y en a un à qui j'ai fait l'aumône. Peut-être y a-t-il beaucoup d'autres princes plus infortunés. Pour moi, je n'ai perdu que cent moutons, et je vole dans les bras de Cunégonde. Mon cher Martin, encore une fois, Pangloss avait raison: tout est bien.—Je le souhaite, dit Martin.—Mais, dit Candide, voilà une aventure bien peu vraisemblable que nous avons eue à Venise. On n'avait jamais vu ni ouï conter que six rois détrônés soupassent ensemble au cabaret.—Cela n'est pas plus extraordinaire, dit Martin, que la plupart des choses qui nous sont arrivées. Il est très commun que des rois soient détrônés; et à l'égard de l'honneur que nous avons eu de souper avec eux, c'est une bagatelle qui ne mérite pas notre attention.»

A peine Candide fut-il dans le vaisseau qu'il sauta au cou de son ancien valet, de son ami Cacambo. «Eh bien, lui dit-il, que fait Cunégonde? Est-elle toujours un prodige de beauté? M'aime-t-elle toujours? Comment se porte-t-elle? Tu lui as sans doute acheté un palais à Constantinople?

—Mon cher maître, répondit Cacambo, Cunégonde lave les écuelles sur le bord de la Propontide, chez un prince qui a très peu d'écuelles; elle est esclave dans la maison d'un ancien souverain nommé Ragotski, à qui le Grand Turc donne trois écus par jour dans son asile; mais ce qui est bien plus triste, c'est qu'elle a perdu sa beauté et qu'elle est devenue horriblement laide.—Ah! belle ou laide, dit Candide, je suis honnête homme, et mon devoir est de l'aimer toujours. Mais comment peut-elle être réduite à un état si abject avec les cinq ou six millions que tu avais apportés?—Bon, dit Cacambo, ne m'en a-t-il pas fallu donner deux millions au señor don Fernando d'Ibaraa, y Figueora, y Mascarenes, y Lampourdos, y Souza, gou-

Chapter XXVII

Candide's voyage to Constantinople

The faithful Cacambo had already obtained from the Turkish captain who was going to take Sultan Ahmed back to Constantinople consent for Candide and Martin to come aboard his ship. They both went there after having prostrated themselves before His Wretched Highness. On the way, Candide said to Martin, "We've had supper with six dethroned kings, and even among those six kings there was one to whom I gave alms. Perhaps there are a great many other princes even more unfortunate. As for me, I've only lost a hundred sheep, and I'm flying to Cunégonde's arms. My dear Martin, once again Pangloss was right: all's well." "I hope so," said Martin. "But," said Candide, "that was a very unlikely adventure we had in Venice. No one ever saw or heard of six dethroned kings having supper together at an inn." "It's no more extraordinary," said Martin, "than the majority of things that have happened to us. It's very common for kings to be dethroned; and as for the honor we've had of eating supper with them, it's a trifle that doesn't merit our attention."

Scarcely was Candide on board the ship when he flung his arms round the neck of his former valet, his friend Cacambo. "Well," he said to him, "what's Cunégonde up to? Is she still a paragon of beauty? Does she still love me? Is she well? No doubt you bought her a palace in Constantinople?"

"My dear master," replied Cacambo, "Cunégonde washes dishes on the shore of the Propontis, in the house of a prince who has very few dishes; she's a slave in the house of a former sovereign named Ragotski,[44] to whom the Grand Turk grants three crowns a day in his place of refuge; but what's considerably sadder is that she has lost her beauty and has become horribly ugly." "Ah! beautiful or ugly," said Candide, "I'm an honorable man, and my duty is to love her always. But how can she have been reduced to so abject a condition, with the five or six million that you brought her?" "All right," said Cacambo, "didn't I have to give two million to Señor Don Fernando de Ibaraa y Figueora y Mascarenes y Lampourdos y

[44] Ferenc Rákóczi II (1676–1735), elected Prince of Transylvania in 1704. His efforts to secure Transylvanian independence having failed, in 1717 he sought aid and then refuge in Constantinople. He lived out his remaining years in Turkey.

verneur de Buenos Aires, pour avoir la permission de reprendre mademoiselle Cunégonde? Et un pirate ne nous a-t-il pas bravement dépouillés de tout le reste? Ce pirate ne nous a-t-il pas menés au cap de Matapan, à Milo, à Nicarie, à Samos, à Petra, aux Dardanelles, à Marmora, à Scutari? Cunégonde et la vieille servent chez ce prince dont je vous ai parlé, et moi je suis esclave du sultan détrôné. —Que d'épouvantables calamités enchaînées les unes aux autres! dit Candide. Mais, après tout, j'ai encore quelques diamants; je délivrerai aisément Cunégonde. C'est bien dommage qu'elle soit devenue si laide.»

Ensuite, se tournant vers Martin: «Que pensez-vous, dit-il, qui soit le plus à plaindre, de l'empereur Achmet, de l'empereur Ivan, du roi Charles-Edouard, ou de moi?—Je n'en sais rien, dit Martin; il faudrait que je fusse dans vos cœurs pour le savoir.—Ah! dit Candide, si Pangloss était ici, il le saurait et nous l'apprendrait.—Je ne sais, dit Martin, avec quelles balances votre Pangloss aurait pu peser les infortunes des hommes et apprécier leurs douleurs. Tout ce que je présume, c'est qu'il y a des millions d'hommes sur la terre cent fois plus à plaindre que le roi Charles-Edouard, l'empereur Ivan et le sultan Achmet.—Cela pourrait bien être», dit Candide.

On arriva en peu de jours sur le canal de la mer Noire. Candide commença par racheter Cacambo fort cher, et, sans perdre de temps, il se jeta dans une galère, avec ses compagnons, pour aller sur le rivage de la Propontide chercher Cunégonde, quelque laide qu'elle pût être.

Il y avait dans la chiourme deux forçats qui ramaient fort mal, et à qui le levanti patron appliquait de temps en temps quelques coups de nerf de bœuf sur les épaules nues; Candide, par un mouvement naturel, les regarda plus attentivement que les autres galériens et s'approcha d'eux avec pitié. Quelques traits de leurs visages défigurés lui parurent avoir un peu de ressemblance avec Pangloss et avec ce malheureux jésuite, ce baron, ce frère de mademoiselle Cunégonde. Cette idée l'émut et l'attrista. Il les considéra encore plus attentivement. «En vérité, dit-il à Cacambo, si je n'avais pas vu pendre maître Pangloss, et si je n'avais pas eu le malheur de tuer le baron, je croirais que ce sont eux qui rament dans cette galère.»

Au nom du baron et de Pangloss les deux forçats poussèrent un grand cri, s'arrêtèrent sur leur banc et laissèrent tomber leurs rames. Le levanti patron accourait sur eux, et les coups de nerf de bœuf redoublaient. «Arrêtez, arrêtez, Seigneur, s'écria Candide, je vous donnerai tant d'argent que vous voudrez.—Quoi! c'est Candide! di-

it's Candide!" said the other. "Is it a dream?" said Candide; "am I
awake? am I really in this galley? Is that the baron I killed? Is that
Master Pangloss whom I saw hanged?"
"It's us, it's us!" they replied. "What! is that the great philosopher?"
said Martin. "Hey! Monsieur Levantine captain," said Candide,
"how much money do you want for the ransom of My Lord Thun-
der-Ten-Tronckh, one of the first barons of the Empire, and Master
Pangloss, the most profound metaphysician in Germany?" "Dog of
a Christian," replied the Levantine captain, "since those two dogs of
Christian convicts are barons and metaphysicians, which no doubt is
a great honor in their country, you'll have to give me fifty thousand
sequins for them." "You'll have them, sir; take me like lightning to
Constantinople, and you'll be paid on the spot. But no, take me to
Miss Cunégonde." The Levantine captain, at Candide's first offer,
had already steered the prow toward the city, and was making the
men row more quickly than a bird cleaves the air.
 Candide embraced the baron and Pangloss a hundred times. "And
how come I didn't kill you, my dear Baron? and my dear Pangloss,
how come you're alive after having been hanged? and why are you
both in the galleys in Turkey?" "Is it really true that my beloved sister
is in this country?" said the baron. "Yes," replied Cacambo. "So I see
my dear Candide again," exclaimed Pangloss. Candide introduced
Martin and Cacambo to them. They all embraced one another, they
all spoke at once. The galley was flying, they were already in the
harbor. A Jew was sent for, to whom Candide sold for fifty thousand
sequins a diamond worth a hundred thousand, and who swore to
him by Abraham that he could not give him any more for it. He
immediately paid the ransom for the baron and Pangloss. The latter
threw himself at his liberator's feet and bathed them in tears; the
other thanked him with a nod and promised to return him the money
at the first opportunity. "But is it really possible that my sister is in
Turkey?" he said. "Nothing is more possible," rejoined Cacambo,
"since she washes dishes at the house of a prince of Transylvania."
Two Jews were immediately sent for; Candide sold more diamonds;
and they all set out again in another galley to go to rescue Cu-
négonde.

Chapitre XXVIII

Ce qui arriva à Candide, à Cunégonde, à Pangloss, à Martin, etc.

«Pardon, encore une fois, dit Candide au baron; pardon, mon révérend père, de vous avoir donné un grand coup d'épée au travers du corps.—N'en parlons plus, dit le baron; je fus un peu trop vif, je l'avoue; mais, puisque vous voulez savoir par quel hasard vous m'avez vu aux galères, je vous dirai qu'après avoir été guéri de ma blessure par le frère apothicaire du collège, je fus attaqué et enlevé par un parti espagnol; on me mit en prison à Buenos Aires dans le temps que ma sœur venait d'en partir. Je demandai à retourner à Rome auprès du père général. Je fus nommé pour aller servir d'aumônier à Constantinople auprès de monsieur l'ambassadeur de France. Il n'y avait pas huit jours que j'étais entré en fonctions, quand je trouvai sur le soir un jeune icoglan très bien fait. Il faisait fort chaud: le jeune homme voulut se baigner; je pris cette occasion de me baigner aussi. Je ne savais pas que ce fût un crime capital pour un chrétien d'être trouvé tout nu avec un jeune musulman. Un cadi me fit donner cent coups de bâton sous la plante des pieds et me condamna aux galères. Je ne crois pas qu'on ait fait une plus horrible injustice. Mais je voudrais bien savoir pourquoi ma sœur est dans la cuisine d'un souverain de Transylvanie réfugié chez les Turcs.

—Mais vous, mon cher Pangloss, dit Candide, comment se peut-il que je vous revoie?—Il est vrai, dit Pangloss, que vous m'avez vu pendre; je devais naturellement être brûlé; mais vous vous souvenez qu'il plut à verse lorsqu'on allait me cuire: l'orage fut si violent qu'on désespéra d'allumer le feu; je fus pendu, parce qu'on ne put mieux faire: un chirurgien acheta mon corps, m'emporta chez lui, et me disséqua. Il me fit d'abord une incision cruciale depuis le nombril jusqu'à la clavicule. On ne pouvait pas avoir été plus mal pendu que je l'avais été. L'exécuteur des hautes œuvres de la sainte Inquisition, lequel était sous-diacre, brûlait à la vérité les gens à merveille, mais il n'était pas accoutumé à pendre: la corde était mouillée et glissa mal, elle fut nouée; enfin je respirais encore: l'incision cruciale me

Chapter XXVIII

What happened to Candide, Cunégonde, Pangloss, Martin, etc.

"Forgive me, once again," said Candide to the baron; "forgive me, Reverend Father, for having run you through with my sword." "Let's say no more about it," said the baron; "I was a little too hotheaded, I admit it; but since you wish to know by what chance you saw me in the galleys, I'll tell you that after having been healed of my wound by the brother apothecary of the college, I was attacked and carried off by a detachment of Spaniards; I was imprisoned in Buenos Aires just after my sister had departed. I asked to be allowed to return to Rome to the father general. I was appointed to go to serve as almoner to the French ambassador in Constantinople. I had not performed this duty for a week when one evening I came across a very handsome young ichoglan.[45] It was very hot: the young man wanted to bathe; I took this opportunity to bathe also. I didn't know that it was a capital offense for a Christian to be found stark naked with a young Muslim. A cadi had me given a hundred strokes on the soles of my feet and condemned me to the galleys. I don't believe a more horrible injustice has ever been committed. But I would very much like to know why my sister is working in the kitchen of a sovereign of Transylvania taking refuge among the Turks."

"But you, my dear Pangloss," said Candide, "how can it be that I see you again?" "It's true," said Pangloss, "that you saw me hanged; naturally I was supposed to have been burned; but you'll remember that it poured rain when they were about to cook me: the storm was so violent that they gave up all hope of lighting the fire; I was hanged for want of something better: a surgeon bought my corpse, took me home and dissected me. First he made a cross-shaped incision from my navel to my clavicle. No one could have been hanged more poorly than I had been. The executor of the lofty works of the Holy Inquisition, who was a subdeacon, burned people wonderfully well, to tell the truth, but he wasn't accustomed to hanging them: the rope was wet and didn't slide properly, it became knotted; in short, I was still breathing; the cross-shaped incision caused me to utter

[45] A page to the sultan.

fit jeter un si grand cri que mon chirurgien tomba à la renverse, et, croyant qu'il disséquait le diable, il s'enfuit en mourant de peur, et tomba encore sur l'escalier en fuyant. Sa femme accourut au bruit, d'un cabinet voisin; elle me vit sur la table étendu avec mon incision cruciale: elle eut encore plus de peur que son mari, s'enfuit et tomba sur lui. Quand ils furent un peu revenus à eux, j'entendis la chirurgienne qui disait au chirurgien: «Mon bon, de quoi vous avisez-vous «aussi de disséquer un hérétique? Ne savez-vous pas que le diable «est toujours dans le corps de ces gens-là? Je vais vite chercher un prêtre pour l'exorciser.» Je frémis à ce propos, et je ramassai le peu de forces qui me restaient, pour crier: «Ayez pitié de moi!» Enfin le barbier portugais s'enhardit; il recousit ma peau; sa femme même eut soin de moi; je fus sur pied au bout de quinze jours. Le barbier me trouva une condition, et me fit laquais d'un chevalier de Malte qui allait à Venise; mais mon maître n'ayant pas de quoi me payer, je me mis au service d'un marchand vénitien, et je le suivis à Constantinople.

«Un jour il me prit fantaisie d'entrer dans une mosquée; il n'y avait qu'un vieil iman et une jeune dévote très jolie qui disait ses patenôtres; sa gorge était toute découverte: elle avait entre ses deux tétons un beau bouquet de tulipes, de roses, d'anémones, de renoncules, d'hyacinthes et d'oreilles-d'ours; elle laissa tomber son bouquet; je le ramassai, et je le lui remis avec un empressement très respectueux. Je fus si longtemps à le lui remettre que l'iman se mit en colère, et, voyant que j'étais chrétien, il cria à l'aide. On me mena chez le cadi, qui me fit donner cent coups de latte sur la plante des pieds et m'envoya aux galères. Je fus enchaîné précisément dans la même galère et au même banc que M. le baron. Il y avait dans cette galère quatre jeunes gens de Marseille, cinq prêtres napolitains, et deux moines de Corfou, qui nous dirent que de pareilles aventures arrivaient tous les jours. M. le baron prétendait qu'il avait essuyé une plus grande injustice que moi; je prétendais, moi, qu'il était beaucoup plus permis de remettre un bouquet sur la gorge d'une femme que d'être tout nu avec un icoglan. Nous disputions sans cesse, et nous recevions vingt coups de nerf de bœuf par jour, lorsque l'enchaînement des événements de cet univers vous a conduit dans notre galère, et que vous nous avez rachetés.

—Eh bien, mon cher Pangloss, lui dit Candide, quand vous avez été pendu, disséqué, roué de coups, et que vous avez ramé aux galères, avez-vous toujours pensé que tout allait le mieux du

such a great cry that my surgeon fell on his back, and, thinking that he was dissecting the devil, he fled, dying of fear, and fell over again on the stairs while fleeing. At the noise, his wife came running from a nearby room; she saw me stretched out on the table with my cross-shaped incision: she was even more afraid than her husband; she fled and fell on top of him. When they had recovered a little, I heard the surgeon's wife say to the surgeon, 'My dear, what were you thinking of, dissecting a heretic? Don't you know that those people are always possessed by the devil? I'll go quickly to find a priest to exorcise him.' I shuddered at this remark, and I gathered the little strength I had left to cry out, 'Have pity on me!' Finally the Portuguese barber took courage; he sewed my skin back up; his wife even took care of me; I was back on my feet within two weeks. The barber found me a position as a lackey to a Knight of Malta who was going to Venice; but my master not having enough to pay me, I went into the service of a Venetian merchant, and I followed him to Constantinople.

"One day it took my fancy to enter a mosque; inside were only an aged imam and a very pretty young worshiper who was saying her prayers; her bosom was completely exposed: between her two breasts she had a beautiful bouquet of tulips, roses, anemones, buttercups, hyacinths and auriculas; she dropped her bouquet; I picked it up and put it back for her with very respectful alacrity. I was such a long time putting it back that the imam grew angry and, seeing that I was a Christian, he called for help. I was brought before the cadi, who had me given a hundred strokes with a cane on the soles of my feet and sent me off to the galleys. I was enchained in the very same galley and on the very same bench as the baron. In that galley there were four young men from Marseilles, five Neapolitan priests and two monks from Corfu who told us that similar things happened every day. The baron claimed that he had suffered a greater injustice than I; I claimed that it was a great deal more permissible to return a bouquet to a woman's bosom than to be stark naked with an icho-glan. We were still arguing ceaselessly, and were receiving twenty lashes a day, when the chain of events in this universe led you to our galley and you ransomed us."

"Well, my dear Pangloss," Candide said to him, "when you were hanged, dissected, beaten unmercifully and forced to row in the galleys, did you continue to think that everything was going for the

monde?—Je suis toujours de mon premier sentiment, répondit Pangloss, car enfin je suis philosophe: il ne me convient pas de me dédire, Leibnitz ne pouvant pas avoir tort, et l'harmonie préétablie étant d'ailleurs la plus belle chose du monde, aussi bien que le plein et la matière subtile.»

Chapitre XXIX

Comment Candide retrouva Cunégonde et la vieille

Pendant que Candide, le baron, Pangloss, Martin et Cacambo contaient leurs aventures, qu'ils raisonnaient sur les événements contingents ou non contingents de cet univers, qu'ils disputaient sur les effets et les causes, sur le mal moral et sur le mal physique, sur la liberté et la nécessité, sur les consolations que l'on peut éprouver lorsqu'on est aux galères en Turquie, ils abordèrent sur le rivage de la Propontide à la maison du prince de Transylvanie. Les premiers objets qui se présentèrent furent Cunégonde et la vieille, qui étendaient des serviettes sur des ficelles pour les faire sécher.

Le baron pâlit à cette vue. Le tendre amant Candide, en voyant sa belle Cunégonde rembrunie, les yeux éraillés, la gorge sèche, les joues ridées, les bras rouges et écaillés, recula de trois pas saisi d'horreur, et avança ensuite par bon procédé. Elle embrassa Candide et son frère; on embrassa la vieille: Candide les racheta toutes deux.

Il y avait une petite métairie dans le voisinage; la vieille proposa à Candide de s'en accommoder, en attendant que toute la troupe eût une meilleure destinée. Cunégonde ne savait pas qu'elle était enlaidie, personne ne l'en avait avertie: elle fit souvenir Candide de ses promesses avec un ton si absolu que le bon Candide n'osa pas la refuser. Il signifia donc au baron qu'il allait se marier avec sa sœur. «Je ne souffrirai jamais, dit le baron, une telle bassesse de sa part et une telle insolence de la vôtre; cette infamie ne me sera jamais reprochée: les enfants de ma sœur ne pourraient entrer dans les

very best?" "I am still of my former opinion," replied Pangloss, "for, after all, I'm a philosopher: it wouldn't be proper for me to retract, since Leibniz cannot be mistaken, and, moreover, since preestablished harmony is the most beautiful thing in the world, along with the plenum and subtle matter."

CHAPTER XXIX

HOW CANDIDE FOUND CUNÉGONDE AND THE OLD WOMAN AGAIN

While Candide, the baron, Pangloss, Martin and Cacambo were relating their adventures, reasoning on the contingent and noncontingent events of this universe, and arguing about effects and causes, moral evil and physical evil, freedom and necessity, and the consolations one can experience when in Turkish galleys, they landed on the shore of the Propontis, at the house of the Prince of Transylvania. The first things to present themselves were Cunégonde and the old woman, who were hanging towels out to dry on lines.

The baron turned pale at this sight. The tender lover Candide, seeing that his beautiful Cunégonde was now dark brown, her eyes bloodshot, her bosom withered, her cheeks wrinkled, her arms red and scaly, recoiled three paces, seized with horror, and then moved forward out of good manners. She embraced Candide and her brother; they embraced the old woman; Candide ransomed them both.

There was a small farm in the vicinity; the old woman proposed to Candide to occupy it, while awaiting a better destiny for the whole troop. Cunégonde did not know that she had become ugly, no one had informed her; she reminded Candide of his promises in such an imperious tone that the good Candide did not dare to refuse her. He therefore informed the baron that he was going to marry his sister. "I shall never tolerate," said the baron, "such baseness on her part and such insolence on yours; that disgrace shall never be held against me: my sister's children would not be able to enter the Chap-

chapitres d'Allemagne. Non, jamais ma sœur n'épousera qu'un
baron de l'Empire.» Cunégonde se jeta à ses pieds et les baigna de
larmes; il fut inflexible. «Maître fou, lui dit Candide, je t'ai réchappé
des galères, j'ai payé ta rançon, j'ai payé celle de ta sœur; elle lavait
ici des écuelles, elle est laide, j'ai la bonté d'en faire ma femme, et
tu prétends encore t'y opposer! Je te retuerais si j'en croyais ma
colère.—Tu peux me tuer encore, dit le baron, mais tu n'épouseras
pas ma sœur de mon vivant.»

CHAPITRE XXX

CONCLUSION

Candide, dans le fond de son cœur, n'avait aucune envie d'épouser
Cunégonde. Mais l'impertinence extrême du baron le déterminait à
conclure le mariage et Cunégonde le pressait si vivement qu'il ne
pouvait s'en dédire. Il consulta Pangloss, Martin et le fidèle Ca-
cambo. Pangloss fit un beau mémoire par lequel il prouvait que le
baron n'avait nul droit sur sa sœur, et qu'elle pouvait, selon toutes
les lois de l'Empire, épouser Candide de la main gauche. Martin
conclut à jeter le baron dans la mer. Cacambo décida qu'il fallait le
rendre au levanti patron et le remettre aux galères; après quoi on
l'enverrait à Rome au père général par le premier vaisseau. L'avis
fut trouvé fort bon; la vieille l'approuva; on n'en dit rien à sa sœur;
la chose fut exécutée pour quelque argent, et on eut le plaisir d'attra-
per un jésuite et de punir l'orgueil d'un baron allemand.
Il était tout naturel d'imaginer qu'après tant de désastres, Can-
dide, marié avec sa maîtresse et vivant avec le philosophe Pangloss,
le philosophe Martin, le prudent Cacambo et la vieille, ayant d'ail-
leurs rapporté tant de diamants de la patrie des anciens Incas, mène-

ters[46] in Germany. No, my sister shall never marry anyone but a baron of the Empire." Cunégonde threw herself at his feet and bathed them in tears; he was unbending. "Utter madman," Candide said to him, "I freed you from the galleys, I paid your ransom, I paid that of your sister; she was washing dishes here, she's ugly, I have the goodness to make her my wife, and you still presume to oppose it! I would kill you again were I to trust to my anger." "You may kill me again," said the baron, "but you'll never marry my sister while I'm alive."

Chapter XXX

Conclusion

At the bottom of his heart, Candide had no desire to marry Cunégonde. But the baron's extreme impertinence persuaded him to go through with the marriage, and Cunégonde urged him so vigorously that he could not go back on his word. He consulted Pangloss, Martin and the faithful Cacambo. Pangloss composed a fine dissertation in which he proved that the baron had no rights over his sister, and that she could, according to all the laws of the Empire, engage in a morganatic marriage with Candide. Martin concluded that they should throw the baron into the sea. Cacambo decided that they should return him to the Levantine captain and have him put back in the galleys; after which he could be sent back on the first available ship to the father general in Rome. This was found to be an extremely good idea; the old woman approved of it; nothing was said of it to the baron's sister; the scheme was carried out for a little money, and they had the pleasure of tricking a Jesuit and punishing the pride of a German baron.

It would be entirely natural to imagine that after so many disasters, Candide, married to his mistress and living with the philosopher Pangloss, the philosopher Martin, the prudent Cacambo and the old woman, and having, moreover, brought back so many diamonds

[46] Knightly assemblies.

rait la vie du monde la plus agréable; mais il fut tant friponné par les Juifs qu'il ne lui resta plus rien que sa petite métairie; sa femme, devenant tous les jours plus laide, devint acariâtre et insupportable; la vieille était infirme et fut encore de plus mauvaise humeur que Cunégonde. Cacambo, qui travaillait au jardin, et qui allait vendre des légumes à Constantinople, était excédé de travail et maudissait sa destinée. Pangloss était au désespoir de ne pas briller dans quelque université d'Allemagne. Pour Martin, il était fermement persuadé qu'on est également mal partout; il prenait les choses en patience. Candide, Martin et Pangloss disputaient quelquefois de métaphysique et de morale. On voyait souvent passer sous les fenêtres de la métairie des bateaux chargés d'effendis, de bachas, de cadis, qu'on envoyait en exil à Lemnos, à Mytilène, à Erzeroum. On voyait venir d'autres cadis, d'autres bachas, d'autres effendis, qui prenaient la place des expulsés et qui étaient expulsés à leur tour. On voyait des têtes proprement empaillées qu'on allait présenter à la Sublime Porte. Ces spectacles faisaient redoubler les dissertations; et quand on ne disputait pas, l'ennui était si excessif que la vieille osa un jour leur dire: «Je voudrais savoir lequel est le pire, ou d'être violée cent fois par des pirates nègres, d'avoir une fesse coupée, de passer par les baguettes chez les Bulgares, d'être fouetté et pendu dans un auto-da-fé, d'être disséqué, de ramer en galère, d'éprouver enfin toutes les misères par lesquelles nous avons tous passé, ou bien de rester ici à ne rien faire?—C'est une grande question», dit Candide.

Ce discours fit naître de nouvelles réflexions, et Martin surtout conclut que l'homme était né pour vivre dans les convulsions de l'inquiétude, ou dans la léthargie de l'ennui. Candide n'en convenait pas, mais il n'assurait rien. Pangloss avouait qu'il avait toujours horriblement souffert; mais ayant soutenu une fois que tout allait à merveille, il le soutenait toujours, et n'en croyait rien.

Une chose acheva de confirmer Martin dans ses détestables principes, de faire hésiter plus que jamais Candide, et d'embarrasser Pangloss. C'est qu'ils virent un jour aborder dans leur métairie Paquette et le frère Giroflée, qui étaient dans la plus extrême misère; ils avaient bien vite mangé leurs trois mille piastres, s'étaient quittés, s'étaient raccommodés, s'étaient brouillés, avaient été mis en prison, s'étaient enfuis, et enfin frère Giroflée s'était fait Turc. Paquette continuait son métier partout, et n'y gagnait plus rien. «Je l'avais

from the native land of the ancient Incas, would lead the most pleasant life in the world; but he was cheated so much by the Jews that all he had left was his small farm; his wife, growing uglier every day, became shrewish and insufferable; the old woman was infirm and of an even worse disposition than Cunégonde. Cacambo, who worked in the garden and who went to sell vegetables in Constantinople, was worn out by his labor and cursed his fate. Pangloss was in despair at not being able to shine in some German university. As for Martin, he was firmly persuaded that one is equally badly off everywhere; he took things with patience. Candide, Martin and Pangloss sometimes argued metaphysics and morals. They often saw passing beneath the farm windows boats laden with effendis, pashas and cadis who were being sent into exile on Lemnos, Mytilene and Erzurum. They saw other cadis, other pashas and other effendis coming to take the place of those who had been ousted and who were ousted in their turn. They saw neatly stuffed heads that were being taken to be presented at the Sublime Porte. These spectacles redoubled their discussions; and when they were not arguing, the boredom was so excessive that the old woman dared one day to say to them, "I would like to know which is worse: to be raped a hundred times by Negro pirates, to have one buttock cut off, to run the gauntlet among the Bulgarians, to be flogged and hanged at an auto-da-fé, to be dissected, to row in a galley, in short, to go through all the miseries that we've gone through, or to remain here doing nothing?" "That's a difficult question," said Candide.

That speech gave birth to new reflections, and Martin above all concluded that man was born to live either in the convulsions of anxiety or in the lethargy of boredom. Candide did not agree with this, but he did not assert anything to the contrary. Pangloss acknowledged that he had always suffered horribly; but, having once maintained that everything was going wonderfully, he continued to maintain it, though not believing it in the least.

One thing succeeded in confirming Martin in his detestable principles, in making Candide waver more than ever and in disconcerting Pangloss. It was that one day they saw Paquette and Brother Giroflée arrive at their farm in the most extreme poverty; they had quickly squandered their three thousand piasters, had broken up, had made up, had quarreled, had been put in prison, had escaped, and finally Brother Giroflée had turned Turk. Paquette continued to ply her trade everywhere, but no longer earned anything at it. "I

bien prévu, dit Martin à Candide, que vos présents seraient bientôt dissipés et ne les rendraient que plus misérables. Vous avez regorgé de millions de piastres, vous et Cacambo, et vous n'êtes pas plus heureux que frère Giroflée et Paquette.—Ah, ah! dit Pangloss à Paquette, le Ciel vous ramène donc ici parmi nous, ma pauvre enfant! Savez-vous bien que vous m'avez coûté le bout du nez, un œil et une oreille? Comme vous voilà faite! Eh! qu'est-ce que ce monde!» Cette nouvelle aventure les engagea à philosopher plus que jamais.

Il y avait dans le voisinage un derviche très fameux, qui passait pour le meilleur philosophe de la Turquie; ils allèrent le consulter; Pangloss porta la parole, et lui dit: «Maître, nous venons vous prier de nous dire pourquoi un aussi étrange animal que l'homme a été formé.

—De quoi te mêles-tu? dit le derviche, est-ce là ton affaire?—Mais, mon révérend père, dit Candide, il y a horriblement de mal sur la terre.—Qu'importe, dit le derviche, qu'il y ait du mal ou du bien? Quand Sa Hautesse envoie un vaisseau en Egypte, s'embarrasse-t-elle si les souris qui sont dans le vaisseau sont à leur aise ou non?—Que faut-il donc faire? dit Pangloss.—Te taire, dit le derviche.—Je me flattais, dit Pangloss, de raisonner un peu avec vous des effets et des causes, du meilleur des mondes possibles, de l'origine du mal, de la nature de l'âme et de l'harmonie préétablie.» Le derviche, à ces mots, leur ferma la porte au nez.

Pendant cette conversation, la nouvelle s'était répandue qu'on venait d'étrangler à Constantinople deux visirs du banc et le muphti, et qu'on avait empalé plusieurs de leurs amis. Cette catastrophe faisait partout un grand bruit pendant quelques heures. Pangloss, Candide et Martin, en retournant à la petite métairie, rencontrèrent un bon vieillard qui prenait le frais à sa porte sous un berceau d'orangers. Pangloss, qui était aussi curieux que raisonneur, lui demanda comment se nommait le muphti qu'on venait d'étrangler. «Je n'en sais rien, répondit le bonhomme, et je n'ai jamais su le nom d'aucun muphti ni d'aucun visir. J'ignore absolument l'aventure dont vous me parlez; je présume qu'en général ceux qui se mêlent des affaires publiques périssent quelquefois misérablement, et qu'ils le méritent; mais je ne m'informe jamais de ce qu'on fait à Constantinople; je me contente d'y envoyer vendre les fruits du jardin que je cultive.» Ayant dit ces mots, il fit entrer les étrangers dans sa maison: ses deux filles et ses deux fils leur présentèrent plusieurs sortes de sorbets

had foreseen," said Martin to Candide, "that your gifts would soon be frittered away and would only make them more unhappy. You were glutted with millions of piasters, you and Cacambo, and you're no happier than Brother Giroflée and Paquette." "Oh, oh!" said Pangloss to Paquette, "so Heaven has led you back to us, my poor child! Do you know that you cost me the tip of my nose, an eye and an ear? And look at you now! Oh! what a world is this!" This new adventure incited them to philosophize more than ever.

There lived in the neighborhood a very famous dervish who was deemed the finest philosopher in Turkey; they went to consult him; Pangloss spoke up, saying to him, "Master, we come to beg you to tell us why such a peculiar creature as man was created." "What are you meddling in?" said the dervish, "is that any business of yours?" "But, Reverend Father," said Candide, "there's a terrible amount of evil on earth." "What does it matter," said the dervish, "whether there is good or evil? When His Highness sends a ship to Egypt, is he troubled about whether the mice in the ship are comfortable or not?" "Then what should we do?" said Pangloss. "Keep quiet," said the dervish. "I felt sure," said Pangloss, "that I would reason with you a little on effects and causes, on the best of all possible worlds, on the origin of evil, on the nature of the soul and on preestablished harmony." At these words, the dervish slammed the door in their faces.

During this conversation, the news had spread that in Constantinople two viziers of the divan and the mufti had just been strangled, and that several of their friends had been impaled. This catastrophe caused a great commotion everywhere for a few hours. While returning to their small farm, Pangloss, Candide and Martin came across a good old man who was enjoying the cool air by his door beneath an arbor of orange trees. Pangloss, who was as inquisitive as he was inclined to reasoning, asked him the name of the mufti who had just been strangled. "I have no idea," replied the gentleman, "and I have never known the name of any mufti or any vizier. I'm completely ignorant of the incident you're talking to me about; I suppose that, in general, those who meddle in public affairs sometimes perish wretchedly, and that they deserve it; but I never inquire into what is going on in Constantinople; I content myself with sending there to be sold the fruits from the garden that I cultivate." Having spoken these words, he invited the strangers into his house; his two daughters and two sons offered them several kinds of sherbets that they

qu'ils faisaient eux-mêmes, du kaïmac piqué d'écorces de cédrat confit, des oranges, des citrons, des limons, des ananas, des pistaches, du café de Moka qui n'était point mêlé avec le mauvais café de Batavia et des îles. Après quoi les deux filles de ce bon musulman parfumèrent les barbes de Candide, de Pangloss et de Martin.

«Vous devez avoir, dit Candide au Turc, une vaste et magnifique terre?—Je n'ai que vingt arpents, répondit le Turc; je les cultive avec mes enfants; le travail éloigne de nous trois grands maux: l'ennui, le vice et le besoin.»

Candide, en retournant dans sa métairie, fit de profondes réflexions sur le discours du Turc. Il dit à Pangloss et à Martin: «Ce bon vieillard me paraît s'être fait un sort bien préférable à celui des six rois avec qui nous avons eu l'honneur de souper.—Les grandeurs, dit Pangloss, sont fort dangereuses, selon le rapport de tous les philosophes: car enfin Eglon, roi des Moabites, fut assassiné par Aod; Absalon fut pendu par les cheveux et percé de trois dards; le roi Nadab, fils de Jéroboam, fut tué par Baasa; le roi Ela, par Zambri; Ochosias, par Jéhu; Athalia, par Joïada; les rois Joachim, Jéchonias, Sédécias, furent esclaves. Vous savez comment périrent Crésus, Astyage, Darius, Denys de Syracuse, Pyrrhus, Persée, Annibal, Jugurtha, Arioviste, César, Pompée, Néron, Othon, Vitellius, Domitien, Richard II d'Angleterre, Edouard II, Henri VI, Richard III, Marie Stuart, Charles Iᵉʳ, les trois Henri de France, l'empereur Henri IV? Vous savez . . .—Je sais aussi, dit Candide, qu'il faut cultiver notre jardin.—Vous avez raison, dit Pangloss: car, quand l'homme fut mis dans le jardin d'Eden, il y fut mis *ut operaretur eum*, pour qu'il travaillât; ce qui prouve que l'homme n'est pas né pour le repos.—Travaillons sans raisonner, dit Martin; c'est le seul moyen de rendre la vie supportable.»

Toute la petite société entra dans ce louable dessein; chacun se mit à exercer ses talents. La petite terre rapporta beaucoup. Cunégonde était à la vérité bien laide; mais elle devint une excellente pâtissière; Paquette broda; la vieille eut soin du linge. Il n'y eut pas jusqu'à frère Giroflée qui ne rendît service; il fut un très bon menuisier, et même devint honnête homme; et Pangloss disait quelquefois à Candide: «Tous les événements sont enchaînés dans le meilleur des mondes possibles; car enfin, si vous n'aviez pas été chassé d'un

had made themselves, some *kaymak*[47] flavored with candied citron peel, oranges, lemons, limes, pineapples, pistachios and Mocha coffee that was not mixed with the bad coffee from Batavia and the West Indies. After which this good Muslim's two daughters perfumed the beards of Candide, Pangloss and Martin.

"You must have a vast, magnificent estate?" said Candide to the Turk. "I have only twenty acres," replied the Turk; "I cultivate them with my children; the work keeps us free of three great evils: boredom, vice and poverty."

On the way back to his farm, Candide made some profound reflections on the Turk's speech. He said to Pangloss and Martin, "That good old man seems to me to have created a way of life for himself quite preferable to that of those six kings with whom we had the honor of eating supper." "Greatness," said Pangloss, "is very dangerous, according to the statements of all the philosophers: for, after all, Eglon, King of the Moabites, was murdered by Ehud; Absalom was hung up by the hair and pierced with three darts; King Nadab, son of Jeroboam, was killed by Baasha; King Elah by Zimri; Ahaziah by Jehu; Athaliah by Jehoiada; the kings Jehoiakim, Jeconiah and Zedekiah became slaves. You know how Croesus, Astyages, Darius, Dionysius of Syracuse, Pyrrhus, Perseus, Hannibal, Jugurtha, Ariovistus, Caesar, Pompey, Nero, Otho, Vitellius, Domitian, Richard II of England, Edward II, Henry VI, Richard III, Mary Stuart, Charles I, the three Henrys of France and the Emperor Henry IV perished? You know . . ." "I also know," said Candide, "that we must cultivate our garden." "You're right," said Pangloss: "for, when man was placed in the Garden of Eden, he was placed there *ut operaretur eum*, to work; which proves that man was not born for repose." "Let's work without reasoning," said Martin; "it's the only way to make life bearable."

The entire little society entered into this praiseworthy scheme; each began to exercise his talents. The small estate yielded a great deal. Cunégonde was, to tell the truth, very ugly; but she became an excellent pastry cook; Paquette embroidered; the old woman took care of the laundry. Everyone did his part, even Brother Giroflée: he was a very good carpenter, and he even became an honest man; and sometimes Pangloss would say to Candide, "All events are connected in the best of all possible worlds; for, after all, if you hadn't

[47] A Turkish dish of sweetened clotted cream.

beau château à grands coups de pied dans le derrière pour l'amour de Mlle Cunégonde, si vous n'aviez pas été mis à l'Inquisition, si vous n'aviez pas couru l'Amérique à pied, si vous n'aviez pas donné un bon coup d'épée au baron, si vous n'aviez pas perdu tous vos moutons du bon pays d'Eldorado, vous ne mangeriez pas ici des cédrats confits et des pistaches.—Cela est bien dit, répondit Candide, mais il faut cultiver notre jardin.»

been driven off from a beautiful country residence with great kicks in the backside for the love of Miss Cunégonde, if you hadn't been brought before the Inquisition, if you hadn't traveled across America on foot, if you hadn't stabbed the baron, if you hadn't lost all your sheep from the good land of Eldorado, you wouldn't be here eating candied citrons and pistachios." "That's well said," replied Candide, "but we must cultivate our garden."

A CATALOG OF SELECTED
DOVER BOOKS
IN ALL FIELDS OF INTEREST

A CATALOG OF SELECTED
DOVER BOOKS
IN ALL FIELDS OF INTEREST

DRAWINGS OF REMBRANDT, edited by Seymour Slive. Updated Lippmann, Hofstede de Groot edition, with definitive scholarly apparatus. All portraits, biblical sketches, landscapes, nudes. Oriental figures, classical studies, together with selection of work by followers. 550 illustrations. Total of 630pp. 9⅛ × 12¼.
21485-0, 21486-9 Pa., Two-vol. set $29.90

GHOST AND HORROR STORIES OF AMBROSE BIERCE, Ambrose Bierce. 24 tales vividly imagined, strangely prophetic, and decades ahead of their time in technical skill: "The Damned Thing," "An Inhabitant of Carcosa," "The Eyes of the Panther," "Moxon's Master," and 20 more. 199pp. 5⅜ × 8½. 20767-6 Pa. $4.95

ETHICAL WRITINGS OF MAIMONIDES, Maimonides. Most significant ethical works of great medieval sage, newly translated for utmost precision, readability. Laws Concerning Character Traits, Eight Chapters, more. 192pp. 5⅜ × 8½.
24522-5 Pa. $4.50

THE EXPLORATION OF THE COLORADO RIVER AND ITS CANYONS, J. W. Powell. Full text of Powell's 1,000-mile expedition down the fabled Colorado in 1869. Superb account of terrain, geology, vegetation, Indians, famine, mutiny, treacherous rapids, mighty canyons, during exploration of last unknown part of continental U.S. 400pp. 5⅜ × 8½. 20094-9 Pa. $7.95

HISTORY OF PHILOSOPHY, Julián Marías. Clearest one-volume history on the market. Every major philosopher and dozens of others, to Existentialism and later. 505pp. 5⅜ × 8½. 21739-6 Pa. $9.95

ALL ABOUT LIGHTNING, Martin A. Uman. Highly readable nontechnical survey of nature and causes of lightning, thunderstorms, ball lightning, St. Elmo's Fire, much more. Illustrated. 192pp. 5⅜ × 8½. 25237-X Pa. $5.95

SAILING ALONE AROUND THE WORLD, Captain Joshua Slocum. First man to sail around the world, alone, in small boat. One of great feats of seamanship told in delightful manner. 67 illustrations. 294pp. 5⅜ × 8½. 20326-3 Pa. $4.95

LETTERS AND NOTES ON THE MANNERS, CUSTOMS AND CONDI-TIONS OF THE NORTH AMERICAN INDIANS, George Catlin. Classic account of life among Plains Indians: ceremonies, hunt, warfare, etc. 312 plates. 572pp. of text. 6⅛ × 9¼. 22118-0, 22119-9, Pa., Two-vol. set $17.90

ALASKA: The Harriman Expedition, 1899, John Burroughs, John Muir, et al. Informative, engrossing accounts of two-month, 9,000-mile expedition. Native peoples, wildlife, forests, geography, salmon industry, glaciers, more. Profusely illustrated. 240 black-and-white line drawings. 124 black-and-white photographs. 3 maps. Index. 576pp. 5⅜ × 8½. 25109-8 Pa. $11.95

CATALOG OF DOVER BOOKS

THE BOOK OF BEASTS: Being a Translation from a Latin Bestiary of the Twelfth Century, T. H. White. Wonderful catalog of real and fanciful beasts: manticore, griffin, phoenix, amphivius, jaculus, many more. White's witty erudite commentary on scientific, historical aspects enhances fascinating glimpse of medieval mind. Illustrated. 296pp. 5⅜ × 8¼. (Available in U.S. only) 24609-4 Pa. $6.95

FRANK LLOYD WRIGHT: Architecture and Nature with 160 Illustrations, Donald Hoffmann. Profusely illustrated study of influence of nature—especially prairie—on Wright's designs for Fallingwater, Robie House, Guggenheim Museum, other masterpieces. 96pp. 9¼ × 10¾. 25098-9 Pa. $8.95

FRANK LLOYD WRIGHT'S FALLINGWATER, Donald Hoffmann. Wright's famous waterfall house: planning and construction of organic idea. History of site, owners, Wright's personal involvement. Photographs of various stages of building. Preface by Edgar Kaufmann, Jr. 100 illustrations. 112pp. 9¼ × 10.

23671-4 Pa. $8.95

YEARS WITH FRANK LLOYD WRIGHT: Apprentice to Genius, Edgar Tafel. Insightful memoir by a former apprentice presents a revealing portrait of Wright the man, the inspired teacher, the greatest American architect. 372 black-and-white illustrations. Preface. Index. vi + 228pp. 8¼ × 11. 24801-1 Pa. $10.95

THE STORY OF KING ARTHUR AND HIS KNIGHTS, Howard Pyle. Enchanting version of King Arthur fable has delighted generations with imaginative narratives of exciting adventures and unforgettable illustrations by the author. 41 illustrations. xviii + 313pp. 6⅛ × 9¼. 21445-1 Pa. $6.95

THE GODS OF THE EGYPTIANS, E. A. Wallis Budge. Thorough coverage of numerous gods of ancient Egypt by foremost Egyptologist. Information on evolution of cults, rites and gods; the cult of Osiris; the Book of the Dead and its rites; the sacred animals and birds; Heaven and Hell; and more. 956pp. 6⅛ × 9¼.
22055-9, 22056-7 Pa., Two-vol. set $21.90

A THEOLOGICO-POLITICAL TREATISE, Benedict Spinoza. Also contains unfinished *Political Treatise*. Great classic on religious liberty, theory of government on common consent. R. Elwes translation. Total of 421pp. 5⅜ × 8½.
20249-6 Pa. $7.95

INCIDENTS OF TRAVEL IN CENTRAL AMERICA, CHIAPAS, AND YUCATAN, John L. Stephens. Almost single-handed discovery of Maya culture; exploration of ruined cities, monuments, temples; customs of Indians. 115 drawings. 892pp. 5⅜ × 8½. 22404-X, 22405-8 Pa., Two-vol. set $17.90

LOS CAPRICHOS, Francisco Goya. 80 plates of wild, grotesque monsters and caricatures. Prado manuscript included. 183pp. 6⅜ × 9⅜. 22384-1 Pa. $5.95

AUTOBIOGRAPHY: The Story of My Experiments with Truth, Mohandas K. Gandhi. Not hagiography, but Gandhi in his own words. Boyhood, legal studies, purification, the growth of the Satyagraha (nonviolent protest) movement. Critical, inspiring work of the man who freed India. 480pp. 5⅜ × 8½. (Available in U.S. only)
24593-4 Pa. $6.95

ILLUSTRATED DICTIONARY OF HISTORIC ARCHITECTURE, edited by Cyril M. Harris. Extraordinary compendium of clear, concise definitions for over 5,000 important architectural terms complemented by over 2,000 line drawings. Covers full spectrum of architecture from ancient ruins to 20th-century Modernism. Preface. 592pp. 7½ × 9⅜. 24444-X Pa. $15.95

THE NIGHT BEFORE CHRISTMAS, Clement C. Moore. Full text, and woodcuts from original 1848 book. Also critical, historical material. 19 illustrations. 40pp. 4⅝ × 6. 22797-9 Pa. $2.50

THE LESSON OF JAPANESE ARCHITECTURE: 165 Photographs, Jiro Harada. Memorable gallery of 165 photographs taken in the 1930s of exquisite Japanese homes of the well-to-do and historic buildings. 13 line diagrams. 192pp. 8⅞ × 11¼. 24778-3 Pa. $10.95

THE AUTOBIOGRAPHY OF CHARLES DARWIN AND SELECTED LETTERS, edited by Francis Darwin. The fascinating life of eccentric genius composed of an intimate memoir by Darwin (intended for his children); commentary by his son, Francis; hundreds of fragments from notebooks, journals, papers; and letters to and from Lyell, Hooker, Huxley, Wallace and Henslow. xi + 365pp. 5⅜ × 8. 20479-0 Pa. $6.95

WONDERS OF THE SKY: Observing Rainbows, Comets, Eclipses, the Stars and Other Phenomena, Fred Schaaf. Charming, easy-to-read poetic guide to all manner of celestial events visible to the naked eye. Mock suns, glories, Belt of Venus, more. Illustrated. 299pp. 5¼ × 8¼. 24402-4 Pa. $8.95

BURNHAM'S CELESTIAL HANDBOOK, Robert Burnham, Jr. Thorough guide to the stars beyond our solar system. Exhaustive treatment. Alphabetical by constellation: Andromeda to Cetus in Vol. 1; Chamaeleon to Orion in Vol. 2; and Pavo to Vulpecula in Vol. 3. Hundreds of illustrations. Index in Vol. 3. 2,000pp. 6⅛ × 9¼. 23567-X, 23568-8, 23673-0 Pa., Three-vol. set $41.85

STAR NAMES: Their Lore and Meaning, Richard Hinckley Allen. Fascinating history of names various cultures have given to constellations and literary and folkloristic uses that have been made of stars. Indexes to subjects. Arabic and Greek names. Biblical references. Bibliography. 563pp. 5⅜ × 8½. 21079-0 Pa. $8.95

THIRTY YEARS THAT SHOOK PHYSICS: The Story of Quantum Theory, George Gamow. Lucid, accessible introduction to influential theory of energy and matter. Careful explanations of Dirac's anti-particles, Bohr's model of the atom, much more. 12 plates. Numerous drawings. 240pp. 5⅜ × 8½. 24895-X Pa. $6.95

CHINESE DOMESTIC FURNITURE IN PHOTOGRAPHS AND MEASURED DRAWINGS, Gustav Ecke. A rare volume, now affordably priced for antique collectors, furniture buffs and art historians. Detailed review of styles ranging from early Shang to late Ming. Unabridged republication. 161 black-and-white drawings, photos. Total of 224pp. 8⅞ × 11¼. (Available in U.S. only) 25171-3 Pa. $14.95

VINCENT VAN GOGH: A Biography, Julius Meier-Graefe. Dynamic, penetrating study of artist's life, relationship with brother, Theo, painting techniques, travels, more. Readable, engrossing. 160pp. 5⅜ × 8½. (Available in U.S. only) 25253-1 Pa. $4.95

HOW TO WRITE, Gertrude Stein. Gertrude Stein claimed anyone could understand her unconventional writing—here are clues to help. Fascinating improvisations, language experiments, explanations illuminate Stein's craft and the art of writing. Total of 414pp. 4⅝ × 6⅜. 23144-5 Pa. $6.95

ADVENTURES AT SEA IN THE GREAT AGE OF SAIL: Five Firsthand Narratives, edited by Elliot Snow. Rare true accounts of exploration, whaling, shipwreck, fierce natives, trade, shipboard life, more. 33 illustrations. Introduction. 353pp. 5⅜ × 8½. 25177-2 Pa. $9.95

THE HERBAL OR GENERAL HISTORY OF PLANTS, John Gerard. Classic descriptions of about 2,850 plants—with over 2,700 illustrations—includes Latin and English names, physical descriptions, varieties, time and place of growth, more. 2,706 illustrations. xlv + 1,678pp. 8½ × 12¼. 23147-X Cloth. $75.00

DOROTHY AND THE WIZARD IN OZ, L. Frank Baum. Dorothy and the Wizard visit the center of the Earth, where people are vegetables, glass houses grow and Oz characters reappear. Classic sequel to *Wizard of Oz.* 256pp. 5⅜ × 8.
24714-7 Pa. $5.95

SONGS OF EXPERIENCE: Facsimile Reproduction with 26 Plates in Full Color, William Blake. This facsimile of Blake's original "Illuminated Book" reproduces 26 full-color plates from a rare 1826 edition. Includes "The Tyger," "London," "Holy Thursday," and other immortal poems. 26 color plates. Printed text of poems. 48pp. 5¼ × 7. 24636-1 Pa. $3.95

SONGS OF INNOCENCE, William Blake. The first and most popular of Blake's famous "Illuminated Books," in a facsimile edition reproducing all 31 brightly colored plates. Additional printed text of each poem. 64pp. 5¼ × 7.
22764-2 Pa. $3.95

PRECIOUS STONES, Max Bauer. Classic, thorough study of diamonds, rubies, emeralds, garnets, etc.: physical character, occurrence, properties, use, similar topics. 20 plates, 8 in color. 94 figures. 659pp. 6⅛ × 9¼.
21910-0, 21911-9 Pa., Two-vol. set $15.90

ENCYCLOPEDIA OF VICTORIAN NEEDLEWORK, S. F. A. Caulfeild and Blanche Saward. Full, precise descriptions of stitches, techniques for dozens of needlecrafts—most exhaustive reference of its kind. Over 800 figures. Total of 679pp. 8⅛ × 11. 22800-2, 22801-0 Pa., Two-vol. set $23.90

THE MARVELOUS LAND OF OZ, L. Frank Baum. Second Oz book, the Scarecrow and Tin Woodman are back with hero named Tip, Oz magic. 136 illustrations. 287pp. 5⅜ × 8½. 20692-0 Pa. $5.95

WILD FOWL DECOYS, Joel Barber. Basic book on the subject, by foremost authority and collector. Reveals history of decoy making and rigging, place in American culture, different kinds of decoys, how to make them, and how to use them. 140 plates. 156pp. 7⅞ × 10¾. 20011-6 Pa. $8.95

HISTORY OF LACE, Mrs. Bury Palliser. Definitive, profusely illustrated chronicle of lace from earliest times to late 19th century. Laces of Italy, Greece, England, France, Belgium, etc. Landmark of needlework scholarship. 266 illustrations. 672pp. 6¼ × 9¼. 24742-2 Pa. $16.95

ILLUSTRATED GUIDE TO SHAKER FURNITURE, Robert Meader. All furniture and appurtenances, with much on unknown local styles. 235 photos. 146pp. 9 × 12. 22819-3 Pa. $8.95

WHALE SHIPS AND WHALING: A Pictorial Survey, George Francis Dow. Over 200 vintage engravings, drawings, photographs of barks, brigs, cutters, other vessels. Also harpoons, lances, whaling guns, many other artifacts. Comprehensive text by foremost authority. 207 black-and-white illustrations. 288pp. 6 × 9.
24808-9 Pa. $9.95

THE BERTRAMS, Anthony Trollope. Powerful portrayal of blind self-will and thwarted ambition includes one of Trollope's most heartrending love stories. 497pp. 5⅜ × 8½. 25119-5 Pa. $9.95

ADVENTURES WITH A HAND LENS, Richard Headstrom. Clearly written guide to observing and studying flowers and grasses, fish scales, moth and insect wings, egg cases, buds, feathers, seeds, leaf scars, moss, molds, ferns, common crystals, etc.—all with an ordinary, inexpensive magnifying glass. 209 exact line drawings aid in your discoveries. 220pp. 5⅜ × 8½. 23330-8 Pa. $5.95

RODIN ON ART AND ARTISTS, Auguste Rodin. Great sculptor's candid, wide-ranging comments on meaning of art; great artists; relation of sculpture to poetry, painting, music; philosophy of life, more. 76 superb black-and-white illustrations of Rodin's sculpture, drawings and prints. 119pp. 8⅝ × 11¼. 24487-3 Pa. $7.95

FIFTY CLASSIC FRENCH FILMS, 1912–1982: A Pictorial Record, Anthony Slide. Memorable stills from Grand Illusion, Beauty and the Beast, Hiroshima, Mon Amour, many more. Credits, plot synopses, reviews, etc. 160pp. 8¼ × 11.
25256-6 Pa. $11.95

THE PRINCIPLES OF PSYCHOLOGY, William James. Famous long course complete, unabridged. Stream of thought, time perception, memory, experimental methods; great work decades ahead of its time. 94 figures. 1,391pp. 5⅜ × 8½.
20381-6, 20382-4 Pa., Two-vol. set $25.90

BODIES IN A BOOKSHOP, R. T. Campbell. Challenging mystery of blackmail and murder with ingenious plot and superbly drawn characters. In the best tradition of British suspense fiction. 192pp. 5⅜ × 8½. 24720-1 Pa. $4.95

CALLAS: Portrait of a Prima Donna, George Jellinek. Renowned commentator on the musical scene chronicles incredible career and life of the most controversial, fascinating, influential operatic personality of our time. 64 black-and-white photographs. 416pp. 5⅜ × 8¼. 25047-4 Pa. $8.95

GEOMETRY, RELATIVITY AND THE FOURTH DIMENSION, Rudolph Rucker. Exposition of fourth dimension, concepts of relativity as Flatland characters continue adventures. Popular, easily followed yet accurate, profound. 141 illustrations. 133pp. 5⅜ × 8½. 23400-2 Pa. $4.95

HOUSEHOLD STORIES BY THE BROTHERS GRIMM, with pictures by Walter Crane. 53 classic stories—Rumpelstiltskin, Rapunzel, Hansel and Gretel, the Fisherman and his Wife, Snow White, Tom Thumb, Sleeping Beauty, Cinderella, and so much more—lavishly illustrated with original 19th-century drawings. 114 illustrations. x + 269pp. 5⅜ × 8½. 21080-4 Pa. $4.95

SUNDIALS, Albert Waugh. Far and away the best, most thorough coverage of ideas, mathematics concerned, types, construction, adjusting anywhere. Over 100 illustrations. 230pp. 5⅜ × 8½. 22947-5 Pa. $5.95

PICTURE HISTORY OF THE NORMANDIE: With 190 Illustrations, Frank O. Braynard. Full story of legendary French ocean liner: Art Deco interiors, design innovations, furnishings, celebrities, maiden voyage, tragic fire, much more. Extensive text. 144pp. 8⅜ × 11¼. 25257-4 Pa. $10.95

THE FIRST AMERICAN COOKBOOK: A Facsimile of "American Cookery," 1796, Amelia Simmons. Facsimile of the first American-written cookbook published in the United States contains authentic recipes for colonial favorites—pumpkin pudding, winter squash pudding, spruce beer, Indian slapjacks, and more. Introductory Essay and Glossary of colonial cooking terms. 80pp. 5⅜ × 8½.
24710-4 Pa. $3.50

101 PUZZLES IN THOUGHT AND LOGIC, C. R. Wylie, Jr. Solve murders and robberies, find out which fishermen are liars, how a blind man could possibly identify a color—purely by your own reasoning! 107pp. 5⅜ × 8½. 20367-0 Pa. $2.95

ANCIENT EGYPTIAN MYTHS AND LEGENDS, Lewis Spence. Examines animism, totemism, fetishism, creation myths, deities, alchemy, art and magic, other topics. Over 50 illustrations. 432pp. 5⅜ × 8½. 26525-0 Pa. $8.95

ANTHROPOLOGY AND MODERN LIFE, Franz Boas. Great anthropologist's classic treatise on race and culture. Introduction by Ruth Bunzel. Only inexpensive paperback edition. 255pp. 5⅜ × 8½. 25245-0 Pa. $6.95

THE TALE OF PETER RABBIT, Beatrix Potter. The inimitable Peter's terrifying adventure in Mr. McGregor's garden, with all 27 wonderful, full-color Potter illustrations. 55pp. 4¼ × 5½. (Available in U.S. only) 22827-4 Pa. $1.75

THREE PROPHETIC SCIENCE FICTION NOVELS, H. G. Wells. *When the Sleeper Wakes, A Story of the Days to Come* and *The Time Machine* (full version). 335pp. 5⅜ × 8½. (Available in U.S. only) 20605-X Pa. $8.95

APICIUS COOKERY AND DINING IN IMPERIAL ROME, edited and translated by Joseph Dommers Vehling. Oldest known cookbook in existence offers readers a clear picture of what foods Romans ate, how they prepared them, etc. 49 illustrations. 301pp. 6¼ × 9¼. 23563-7 Pa. $7.95

SHAKESPEARE LEXICON AND QUOTATION DICTIONARY, Alexander Schmidt. Full definitions, locations, shades of meaning of every word in plays and poems. More than 50,000 exact quotations. 1,485pp. 6½ × 9¼.
22726-X, 22727-8 Pa., Two-vol. set $31.90

THE WORLD'S GREAT SPEECHES, edited by Lewis Copeland and Lawrence W. Lamm. Vast collection of 278 speeches from Greeks to 1970. Powerful and effective models; unique look at history. 842pp. 5⅜ × 8½. 20468-5 Pa. $12.95

CATALOG OF DOVER BOOKS

A CONCISE HISTORY OF PHOTOGRAPHY: Third Revised Edition, Helmut Gernsheim. Best one-volume history—camera obscura, photochemistry, daguerreotypes, evolution of cameras, film, more. Also artistic aspects—landscape, portraits, fine art, etc. 281 black-and-white photographs. 26 in color. 176pp. 8⅜ × 11¼.
25128-4 Pa. $14.95

THE DORÉ BIBLE ILLUSTRATIONS, Gustave Doré. 241 detailed plates from the Bible: the Creation scenes, Adam and Eve, Flood, Babylon, battle sequences, life of Jesus, etc. Each plate is accompanied by the verses from the King James version of the Bible. 241pp. 9 × 12.
23004-X Pa. $9.95

WANDERINGS IN WEST AFRICA, Richard F. Burton. Great Victorian scholar/adventurer's invaluable descriptions of African tribal rituals, fetishism, culture, art, much more. Fascinating 19th-century account. 624pp. 5⅜ × 8½. 26890-X Pa. $12.95

FLATLAND, E. A. Abbott. Intriguing and enormously popular science-fiction classic explores the complexities of trying to survive as a two-dimensional being in a three-dimensional world. Amusingly illustrated by the author. 16 illustrations. 103pp. 5⅜ × 8½.
20001-9 Pa. $2.50

THE HISTORY OF THE LEWIS AND CLARK EXPEDITION, Meriwether Lewis and William Clark, edited by Elliott Coues. Classic edition of Lewis and Clark's day-by-day journals that later became the basis for U.S. claims to Oregon and the West. Accurate and invaluable geographical, botanical, biological, meteorological and anthropological material. Total of 1,508pp. 5⅜ × 8½.
21268-8, 21269-6, 21270-X Pa., Three-vol. set $29.85

LANGUAGE, TRUTH AND LOGIC, Alfred J. Ayer. Famous, clear introduction to Vienna, Cambridge schools of Logical Positivism. Role of philosophy, elimination of metaphysics, nature of analysis, etc. 160pp. 5⅜ × 8½. (Available in U.S. and Canada only)
20010-8 Pa. $3.95

MATHEMATICS FOR THE NONMATHEMATICIAN, Morris Kline. Detailed, college-level treatment of mathematics in cultural and historical context, with numerous exercises. For liberal arts students. Preface. Recommended Reading Lists. Tables. Index. Numerous black-and-white figures. xvi + 641pp. 5⅜ × 8½.
24823-2 Pa. $11.95

HANDBOOK OF PICTORIAL SYMBOLS, Rudolph Modley. 3,250 signs and symbols, many systems in full; official or heavy commercial use. Arranged by subject. Most in Pictorial Archive series. 143pp. 8⅜ × 11. 23357-X Pa. $7.95

INCIDENTS OF TRAVEL IN YUCATAN, John L. Stephens. Classic (1843) exploration of jungles of Yucatan, looking for evidences of Maya civilization. Travel adventures, Mexican and Indian culture, etc. Total of 669pp. 5⅜ × 8½.
20926-1, 20927-X Pa., Two-vol. set $11.90

DEGAS: An Intimate Portrait, Ambroise Vollard. Charming, anecdotal memoir by famous art dealer of one of the greatest 19th-century French painters. 14 black-and-white illustrations. Introduction by Harold L. Van Doren. 96pp. 5⅜ × 8½.
25131-4 Pa. $4.95

PERSONAL NARRATIVE OF A PILGRIMAGE TO AL-MADINAH AND MECCAH, Richard F. Burton. Great travel classic by remarkably colorful personality. Burton, disguised as a Moroccan, visited sacred shrines of Islam, narrowly escaping death. 47 illustrations. 959pp. 5⅜ × 8½.
21217-3, 21218-1 Pa., Two-vol. set $19.90

PHRASE AND WORD ORIGINS, A. H. Holt. Entertaining, reliable, modern study of more than 1,200 colorful words, phrases, origins and histories. Much unexpected information. 254pp. 5⅜ × 8½.
20758-7 Pa. $5.95

THE RED THUMB MARK, R. Austin Freeman. In this first Dr. Thorndyke case, the great scientific detective draws fascinating conclusions from the nature of a single fingerprint. Exciting story, authentic science. 320pp. 5⅜ × 8½. (Available in U.S. only)
25210-8 Pa. $6.95

AN EGYPTIAN HIEROGLYPHIC DICTIONARY, E. A. Wallis Budge. Monumental work containing about 25,000 words or terms that occur in texts ranging from 3000 B.C. to 600 A.D. Each entry consists of a transliteration of the word, the word in hieroglyphs, and the meaning in English. 1,314pp. 6⅜ × 10.
23615-3, 23616-1 Pa., Two-vol. set $35.90

THE COMPLEAT STRATEGYST: Being a Primer on the Theory of Games of Strategy, J. D. Williams. Highly entertaining classic describes, with many illustrated examples, how to select best strategies in conflict situations. Prefaces. Appendices. xvi + 268pp. 5⅜ × 8½.
25101-2 Pa. $6.95

THE ROAD TO OZ, L. Frank Baum. Dorothy meets the Shaggy Man, little Button-Bright and the Rainbow's beautiful daughter in this delightful trip to the magical Land of Oz. 272pp. 5⅜ × 8.
25208-6 Pa. $5.95

POINT AND LINE TO PLANE, Wassily Kandinsky. Seminal exposition of role of point, line, other elements in nonobjective painting. Essential to understanding 20th-century art. 127 illustrations. 192pp. 6½ × 9¼.
23808-3 Pa. $5.95

LADY ANNA, Anthony Trollope. Moving chronicle of Countess Lovel's bitter struggle to win for herself and daughter Anna their rightful rank and fortune— perhaps at cost of sanity itself. 384pp. 5⅜ × 8½.
24669-8 Pa. $8.95

EGYPTIAN MAGIC, E. A. Wallis Budge. Sums up all that is known about magic in Ancient Egypt: the role of magic in controlling the gods, powerful amulets that warded off evil spirits, scarabs of immortality, use of wax images, formulas and spells, the secret name, much more. 253pp. 5⅜ × 8½.
22681-6 Pa. $4.50

THE DANCE OF SIVA, Ananda Coomaraswamy. Preeminent authority unfolds the vast metaphysic of India: the revelation of her art, conception of the universe, social organization, etc. 27 reproductions of art masterpieces. 192pp. 5⅜ × 8½.
24817-8 Pa. $6.95

CATALOG OF DOVER BOOKS

CHRISTMAS CUSTOMS AND TRADITIONS, Clement A. Miles. Origin, evolution, significance of religious, secular practices. Caroling, gifts, yule logs, much more. Full, scholarly yet fascinating; non-sectarian. 400pp. 5⅜ × 8½.
23354-5 Pa. $6.95

THE HUMAN FIGURE IN MOTION, Eadweard Muybridge. More than 4,500 stopped-action photos, in action series, showing undraped men, women, children jumping, lying down, throwing, sitting, wrestling, carrying, etc. 390pp. 7⅞ × 10⅝.
20204-6 Cloth. $24.95

THE MAN WHO WAS THURSDAY, Gilbert Keith Chesterton. Witty, fast-paced novel about a club of anarchists in turn-of-the-century London. Brilliant social, religious, philosophical speculations. 128pp. 5⅜ × 8½.
25121-7 Pa. $3.95

A CÉZANNE SKETCHBOOK: Figures, Portraits, Landscapes and Still Lifes, Paul Cézanne. Great artist experiments with tonal effects, light, mass, other qualities in over 100 drawings. A revealing view of developing master painter, precursor of Cubism. 102 black-and-white illustrations. 144pp. 8¾ × 6⅝.
24790-2 Pa. $6.95

AN ENCYCLOPEDIA OF BATTLES: Accounts of Over 1,560 Battles from 1479 B.C. to the Present, David Eggenberger. Presents essential details of every major battle in recorded history, from the first battle of Megiddo in 1479 B.C. to Grenada in 1984. List of Battle Maps. New Appendix covering the years 1967–1984. Index. 99 illustrations. 544pp. 6½ × 9¼.
24913-1 Pa. $14.95

AN ETYMOLOGICAL DICTIONARY OF MODERN ENGLISH, Ernest Weekley. Richest, fullest work, by foremost British lexicographer. Detailed word histories. Inexhaustible. Total of 856pp. 6½ × 9¼.
21873-2, 21874-0 Pa., Two-vol. set $19.90

WEBSTER'S AMERICAN MILITARY BIOGRAPHIES, edited by Robert McHenry. Over 1,000 figures who shaped 3 centuries of American military history. Detailed biographies of Nathan Hale, Douglas MacArthur, Mary Hallaren, others. Chronologies of engagements, more. Introduction. Addenda. 1,033 entries in alphabetical order. xi + 548pp. 6½ × 9¼. (Available in U.S. only)
24758-9 Pa. $13.95

LIFE IN ANCIENT EGYPT, Adolf Erman. Detailed older account, with much not in more recent books: domestic life, religion, magic, medicine, commerce, and whatever else needed for complete picture. Many illustrations. 597pp. 5⅜ × 8½.
22632-8 Pa. $8.95

HISTORIC COSTUME IN PICTURES, Braun & Schneider. Over 1,450 costumed figures shown, covering a wide variety of peoples: kings, emperors, nobles, priests, servants, soldiers, scholars, townsfolk, peasants, merchants, courtiers, cavaliers, and more. 256pp. 8⅜ × 11¼.
23150-X Pa. $9.95

THE NOTEBOOKS OF LEONARDO DA VINCI, edited by J. P. Richter. Extracts from manuscripts reveal great genius; on painting, sculpture, anatomy, sciences, geography, etc. Both Italian and English. 186 ms. pages reproduced, plus 500 additional drawings, including studies for *Last Supper*, *Sforza* monument, etc. 860pp. 7⅞ × 10¾. (Available in U.S. only) 22572-0, 22573-9 Pa., Two-vol. set $31.90

CATALOG OF DOVER BOOKS

THE ART NOUVEAU STYLE BOOK OF ALPHONSE MUCHA: All 72 Plates from "Documents Decoratifs" in Original Color, Alphonse Mucha. Rare copyright-free design portfolio by high priest of Art Nouveau. Jewelry, wallpaper, stained glass, furniture, figure studies, plant and animal motifs, etc. Only complete one-volume edition. 80pp. 9⅜ × 12¼. 24044-4 Pa. $10.95

ANIMALS: 1,419 Copyright-Free Illustrations of Mammals, Birds, Fish, Insects, Etc., edited by Jim Harter. Clear wood engravings present, in extremely lifelike poses, over 1,000 species of animals. One of the most extensive pictorial sourcebooks of its kind. Captions. Index. 284pp. 9 × 12. 23766-4 Pa. $10.95

OBELISTS FLY HIGH, C. Daly King. Masterpiece of American detective fiction, long out of print, involves murder on a 1935 transcontinental flight—"a very thrilling story"—NY Times. Unabridged and unaltered republication of the edition published by William Collins Sons & Co. Ltd., London, 1935. 288pp. 5⅜ × 8½. (Available in U.S. only) 25036-9 Pa. $5.95

VICTORIAN AND EDWARDIAN FASHION: A Photographic Survey, Alison Gernsheim. First fashion history completely illustrated by contemporary photographs. Full text plus 235 photos, 1840–1914, in which many celebrities appear. 240pp. 6½ × 9¼. 24205-6 Pa. $8.95

THE ART OF THE FRENCH ILLUSTRATED BOOK, 1700–1914, Gordon N. Ray. Over 630 superb book illustrations by Fragonard, Delacroix, Daumier, Doré, Grandville, Manet, Mucha, Steinlen, Toulouse-Lautrec and many others. Preface. Introduction. 633 halftones. Indices of artists, authors & titles, binders and provenances. Appendices. Bibliography. 608pp. 8⅜ × 11¼. 25086-5 Pa. $24.95

THE WONDERFUL WIZARD OF OZ, L. Frank Baum. Facsimile in full color of America's finest children's classic. 143 illustrations by W. W. Denslow. 267pp. 5⅜ × 8½. 20691-2 Pa. $7.95

FOLLOWING THE EQUATOR: A Journey Around the World, Mark Twain. Great writer's 1897 account of circumnavigating the globe by steamship. Ironic humor, keen observations, vivid and fascinating descriptions of exotic places. 197 illustrations. 720pp. 5⅜ × 8½. 26113-1 Pa. $15.95

THE FRIENDLY STARS, Martha Evans Martin & Donald Howard Menzel. Classic text marshalls the stars together in an engaging, nontechnical survey, presenting them as sources of beauty in night sky. 23 illustrations. Foreword. 2 star charts. Index. 147pp. 5⅜ × 8½. 21099-5 Pa. $3.95

FADS AND FALLACIES IN THE NAME OF SCIENCE, Martin Gardner. Fair, witty appraisal of cranks, quacks, and quackeries of science and pseudoscience: hollow earth, Velikovsky, orgone energy, Dianetics, flying saucers, Bridey Murphy, food and medical fads, etc. Revised, expanded In the Name of Science. "A very able and even-tempered presentation."—The New Yorker. 363pp. 5⅜ × 8. 20394-8 Pa. $6.95

ANCIENT EGYPT: Its Culture and History, J. E. Manchip White. From predynastics through Ptolemies: society, history, political structure, religion, daily life, literature, cultural heritage. 48 plates. 217pp. 5⅜ × 8½. 22548-8 Pa. $5.95

SIR HARRY HOTSPUR OF HUMBLETHWAITE, Anthony Trollope. Incisive, unconventional psychological study of a conflict between a wealthy baronet, his idealistic daughter, and their scapegrace cousin. The 1870 novel in its first inexpensive edition in years. 250pp. 5⅜ × 8½. 24953-0 Pa. $6.95

LASERS AND HOLOGRAPHY, Winston E. Kock. Sound introduction to burgeoning field, expanded (1981) for second edition. Wave patterns, coherence, lasers, diffraction, zone plates, properties of holograms, recent advances. 84 illustrations. 160pp. 5⅜ × 8¼. (Except in United Kingdom) 24041-X Pa. $3.95

INTRODUCTION TO ARTIFICIAL INTELLIGENCE: Second, Enlarged Edition, Philip C. Jackson, Jr. Comprehensive survey of artificial intelligence—the study of how machines (computers) can be made to act intelligently. Includes introductory and advanced material. Extensive notes updating the main text. 132 black-and-white illustrations. 512pp. 5⅜ × 8½. 24864-X Pa. $10.95

HISTORY OF INDIAN AND INDONESIAN ART, Ananda K. Coomaraswamy. Over 400 illustrations illuminate classic study of Indian art from earliest Harappa finds to early 20th century. Provides philosophical, religious and social insights. 304pp. 6⅜ × 9¾. 25005-9 Pa. $11.95

THE GOLEM, Gustav Meyrink. Most famous supernatural novel in modern European literature, set in Ghetto of Old Prague around 1890. Compelling story of mystical experiences, strange transformations, profound terror. 13 black-and-white illustrations. 224pp. 5⅜ × 8½. (Available in U.S. only) 25025-3 Pa. $6.95

PICTORIAL ENCYCLOPEDIA OF HISTORIC ARCHITECTURAL PLANS, DETAILS AND ELEMENTS: With 1,880 Line Drawings of Arches, Domes, Doorways, Facades, Gables, Windows, etc., John Theodore Haneman. Sourcebook of inspiration for architects, designers, others. Bibliography. Captions. 141pp. 9 × 12. 24605-1 Pa. $7.95

BENCHLEY LOST AND FOUND, Robert Benchley. Finest humor from early 30s, about pet peeves, child psychologists, post office and others. Mostly unavailable elsewhere. 73 illustrations by Peter Arno and others. 183pp. 5⅜ × 8½. 22410-4 Pa. $4.95

ERTÉ GRAPHICS, Erté. Collection of striking color graphics: *Seasons, Alphabet, Numerals, Aces* and *Precious Stones.* 50 plates, including 4 on covers. 48pp. 9⅜ × 12¼. 23580-7 Pa. $7.95

THE JOURNAL OF HENRY D. THOREAU, edited by Bradford Torrey, F. H. Allen. Complete reprinting of 14 volumes, 1837–61, over two million words; the sourcebooks for *Walden,* etc. Definitive. All original sketches, plus 75 photographs. 1,804pp. 8½ × 12¼. 20312-3, 20313-1 Cloth., Two-vol. set $130.00

CASTLES: Their Construction and History, Sidney Toy. Traces castle development from ancient roots. Nearly 200 photographs and drawings illustrate moats, keeps, baileys, many other features. Caernarvon, Dover Castles, Hadrian's Wall, Tower of London, dozens more. 256pp. 5⅜ × 8¼. 24898-4 Pa. $6.95

AMERICAN CLIPPER SHIPS: 1833–1858, Octavius T. Howe & Frederick C. Matthews. Fully-illustrated, encyclopedic review of 352 clipper ships from the period of America's greatest maritime supremacy. Introduction. 109 halftones. 5 black-and-white line illustrations. Index. Total of 928pp. 5⅜ × 8½.
25115-2, 25116-0 Pa., Two-vol. set $17.90

TOWARDS A NEW ARCHITECTURE, Le Corbusier. Pioneering manifesto by great architect, near legendary founder of "International School." Technical and aesthetic theories, views on industry, economics, relation of form to function, "mass-production spirit," much more. Profusely illustrated. Unabridged translation of 13th French edition. Introduction by Frederick Etchells. 320pp. 6⅛ × 9¼. (Available in U.S. only)
25023-7 Pa. $8.95

THE BOOK OF KELLS, edited by Blanche Cirker. Inexpensive collection of 32 full-color, full-page plates from the greatest illuminated manuscript of the Middle Ages, painstakingly reproduced from rare facsimile edition. Publisher's Note. Captions. 32pp. 9⅜ × 12¼.
24345-1 Pa. $5.95

BEST SCIENCE FICTION STORIES OF H. G. WELLS, H. G. Wells. Full novel *The Invisible Man*, plus 17 short stories: "The Crystal Egg," "Aepyornis Island," "The Strange Orchid," etc. 303pp. 5⅜ × 8½. (Available in U.S. only)
21531-8 Pa. $6.95

AMERICAN SAILING SHIPS: Their Plans and History, Charles G. Davis. Photos, construction details of schooners, frigates, clippers, other sailcraft of 18th to early 20th centuries—plus entertaining discourse on design, rigging, nautical lore, much more. 137 black-and-white illustrations. 240pp. 6⅛ × 9¼.
24658-2 Pa. $6.95

ENTERTAINING MATHEMATICAL PUZZLES, Martin Gardner. Selection of author's favorite conundrums involving arithmetic, money, speed, etc., with lively commentary. Complete solutions. 112pp. 5⅜ × 8½.
25211-6 Pa. $3.50

THE WILL TO BELIEVE, HUMAN IMMORTALITY, William James. Two books bound together. Effect of irrational on logical, and arguments for human immortality. 402pp. 5⅜ × 8½.
20291-7 Pa. $8.95

THE HAUNTED MONASTERY and THE CHINESE MAZE MURDERS, Robert Van Gulik. 2 full novels by Van Gulik continue adventures of Judge Dee and his companions. An evil Taoist monastery, seemingly supernatural events; overgrown topiary maze that hides strange crimes. Set in 7th-century China. 27 illustrations. 328pp. 5⅜ × 8½.
23502-5 Pa. $6.95

CELEBRATED CASES OF JUDGE DEE (DEE GOONG AN), translated by Robert Van Gulik. Authentic 18th-century Chinese detective novel; Dee and associates solve three interlocked cases. Led to Van Gulik's own stories with same characters. Extensive introduction. 9 illustrations. 237pp. 5⅜ × 8½.
23337-5 Pa. $5.95

Prices subject to change without notice.

Available at your book dealer or write for free catalog to Dept. GI, Dover Publications, Inc., 31 East 2nd St., Mineola, N.Y. 11501. Dover publishes more than 175 books each year on science, elementary and advanced mathematics, biology, music, art, literary history, social sciences and other areas.